For Cam

Chapter 1

Turning onto the highway that led into the town of Apex, Tiffany George saw an abandoned gray compact car. Her father's voice rang in her ears, *Don't drive by stalled cars on the highway. You never know who needs you.* Slowing to a stop, she grabbed her flashlight and tucked her cell phone into her pocket.

She expected to see an empty vehicle. Tiffany felt like an unprepared Girl Scout when the light illuminated dark eyes. A hand pushed through black hair. The man's discomfort was obvious. His shoulders braced against the seat.

"Can I help you?" she called through the window.

"I'm not sure." His jaw muscles tensed, while he shaded his eyes against the flashlight.

"I'm going to open the door." Her forearms and biceps bulged, and her sandals skidded on gravel but the driver door wouldn't budge.

"Locking system jammed." His speech was slurred.

"That doesn't happen. Have you been drinking?" She sniffed for alcohol.

"No. Pain."

"What kind of pain?" She watched him with first-responder alertness. "Heart attack?"

"No." He bent down toward the floor.

Growing up as her father's helper in the family plumbing business, Tiffany knew her way around vehicles.

The man's head slumped onto the headrest. "Okay, Mister, tell me what's happening."

"Muscle cramps in both legs." He sucked air through his teeth. "Need to get out of this sardine tin."

"Push on your knees," she said calmly.

"Thanks, Nurse Nancy. I've tried. I need out."

Tiffany rolled her eyes. "Release the hood latch."

She stomped across the highway. *Thanks, Dad. Just what an act of kindness needs, a jerk.* She parked her car bumper to bumper, broke a nail clipping booster cables onto both batteries, and started her car. Then she was back at the man's window. "Turn on the ignition."

He twisted the key, and his car sputtered.

Tiffany squeezed the handle, and the door latch gave way. He tipped sideways. The car engine stalled. She slid behind him and wedged her arms under his armpits. He leaned into her chest and using his upper body strength he shimmied until both legs were on the ground. Tiffany then squeezed out from between his back and the doorframe. While he kneaded his right leg, she knelt, lifted his pant leg, and massaged his left calf. "Is this helping?" His chest rose and fell in measured breaths. Her hands tingled while she continued her rhythmic push up his leg to his knee and pull down to the ankle. "Tell me what you need now." Her voice came from somewhere primal and dispersed into the darkness.

"Hand me my crutches from the back seat," he said, followed by a long exhale. "When I stand, the pain and cramping eases."

Wrapping her arms around her stomach, she quelled the sensual vibration in her abdomen caused by the intimacy of massaging a stranger's leg. "Did you say crutches?"

"Yes."

She retrieved elbow crutches from the backseat.

He stood and pressed both heels solidly into the ground. "There, that's got it."

"You're tall." Tipping her head, she searched his face for clues to his well-being. He was built like a linebacker but leaned on the crutches as if they were a permanent part of his life.

Black eyes stared down at her. "And you're a sprite out of place." He squinted toward the horizon. A tow truck's flashing yellow lights crested the hill. "Help has arrived," he said.

"What was I?" She put her hands on her hips.

He reached for her hand and drew her toward his chest, and his crutch banged against her leg. His breath skirted across her hair. "You are my liberator." He bent toward her mouth.

His lips were firm. Tiffany closed her eyes and breathed in his spicy aftershave, fabric softener, and perspiration.

A mosquito landed on her cheek. She leaned away from the enticing scents and waved away the pest. She nudged him. He dropped his arm. She moved toward her car. "Take care. Good luck wherever you're going."

"You too." He glanced toward the flashing lights on the highway. "Wait. I don't even know your name."

"That's true, and I don't know your name either." She brushed her hands on her shorts.

"I'm Will Cleaver."

"Good-bye, Will Cleaver. Nice kissing you." She was not getting involved with a stranger who was obviously needy. This brief respite of time was all about her.

Tiffany climbed into her car, closed her door, and drove into the night. She watched him in her rearview mirror, and he waved until she rounded the curve. His expensive pants would never be the same again. Nice butt, though. She put her finger to her lips. The kiss had been fun after eight-and-a-half hours on the road. Tiffany turned the music louder. She was going home for a rest. Thoughts about a man's butt, lips, and the feel of smooth skin and tiny hairs sliding along her palms trickled through her mind as she traveled along the straight blacktop highway toward her parents' home.

The empty driveway of her childhood home signaled a whole week of nothing to do, her reward for a year and a half of hard work at Winnipeg Art Academy studying the art of fresco and sculpting. The city that gave her a new life was a nine-hour drive away from her childhood home in Apex and past dreams.

Yawning and stretching, she jumped, startled when headlights on The George Family Plumbing van flashed. The garage door opened, and her father in cap, coveralls, and rubber boots was leaving the house after nine in the evening. That meant an emergency in their small town.

Tiffany whistled the signal they had used when they worked together.

He looked up, then he bent over, and she heard him choke out a chest-rumbling coughing fit.

She ran then slipped across the uneven cement. "Dad, are you okay?" With shaking hands, she positioned herself at his back ready to give him the Heimlich Maneuver if necessary.

Her mother stood in the open doorway to the house clinging to the edges of her bathrobe. "No, he's not okay. He's his typical stubborn self."

Tiffany put her arm around her father. "You're not choking?"

"No," he sputtered.

Tiffany led him to an overturned crate. "What's up?"

His face was gray. "Got a call from Willow Lodge." He gulped for air. "Need to turn off the water." He leaned his head against the wall. "The building could be in trouble."

"Mom, where are my boots?"

Her mom reached into the garage closet and brought out

lime-green plumber boots. "New hair style?" Her mother raised an eyebrow.

Tiffany held on to the boots. "Yes." This wasn't how she wanted her parents to see the new, modern her. "Are my coveralls in there too?" Tiffany's dreams of a quiet time in the swing on the deck dissipated with her father's continued coughing.

Her mother bunched up pink overalls and flung them toward Tiffany. Drawing the protective clothing over her black shorts and tank top was like putting on her old skin. "Don't go barefoot," her mother ordered.

"No choice." Her fuchsia-painted toenails rubbed against the wrinkled boot lining which used to fit like old slippers.

"Tiffy, I can't let you do this." Dad pushed against his knees and stood.

"You can't not let me do this, Dad. I'm here. I'll help." Tiffany selected the van keys from the holder.

He turned toward the passenger door. "You can't go alone. I know the security codes." He could have given her the code but they needed to get moving and convincing him would take time.

She tapped the fender of the van. "Hello, old girl." After adjusting the bucket seat to accommodate her height, she backed out of the driveway.

Her world had morphed from a highway drive, sipping cold coffee, an act of kindness and a nice kiss, right back into a life she thought she'd left behind. Another cough from her father blocked out every other sound and brought Tiffany back to the moment. Her dad settled into his seat. "You've caught your breath." She flipped the signal indicator, then turned onto Maple Avenue. "Your cold sounds serious." He pointed to red splatters on his sleeve. "Going into the city tomorrow for some tests." Wrapping his arms across his barrel chest, he breathed deeply. "Meds are kicking in."

"Okay, you and Mom take care of you, and I'll handle what needs to be repaired at the lodge." She watched him in her peripheral vision. "Tell me what we might find."

"If we're lucky, the hallways will be dry." With tug on his cap, he signaled he was ready for work.

She parked the truck. While she opened the rear double-panel doors her father ordered, "Bring the emergency bag with the torque wrench and clamps. I'll grab the . . ." He coughed.

"No you don't. Just lead the way. We'll assess the situation first."

Dad keyed in the security code. "This way."

Her tool belt hung loose on her hips. Florescent light from the hallway glared against her tired eyes. She knew the layout. But she hadn't been in the mechanical room for over a year. Things could have changed.

"Hello there!"

Her father raised his hand to a woman in a blue fluffy housecoat. "Fred, I'm so happy to see you," she said. "Donna told us you were sick but I didn't know who else to call." Her eyebrows rose. "Tiffany!"

"Hi, Lorraine." By morning, everyone would know Tiffany was back. "Tell us what's happening?"

"The alarm went off. I called your dad." Lorraine nodded toward him.

"You did the right thing," Tiffany said.

They opened the door to the mechanical room. Water covered the floor and a foot of the walls. Tiffany adjusted her tool belt and set the canvas bag on the top stair. She still hated sloshing through cold water. She found the main pipe, reached down into the water and shuddered from the cold. Clamping on the wrench and twisting with force, she closed the valve off. "Got it, Dad." She checked the furnace, air conditioner, and hot water tanks. "Because of the work we did when we installed the mechanics, everything of any importance is dry." Tiffany picked up the emergency tool bag and joined her dad in the hallway. "Not much more we can do until the water drains away."

"Thanks, partner." Her father chucked her on the shoulder. "If we'd known you were coming we could have planned a party."

She bumped his hip. "Oh, Dad."

"We've done everything we can right now, Lorraine." Tiffany yawned.

Lorraine yawned behind her hand. "Thanks for coming out."

The words "hello there" ploughed down the silent hallway as Tiffany's roadside linebacker advanced with a synchronized arm and leg crutch-walk.

"Lorraine, there isn't any water for a shower," he said.

Tiffany bit her cheek while she watched her father grab the railing on the wall. She stepped forward. "Tiffany George of George's Family Plumbing. There's a water break."

His gaze traveled up from her chest to the collar of her pink coveralls and then to the top of her head, where she was sure her spikes had tumbled like dominoes. Then down to the tips of her lime-green boots. "Nice boots, real nice boots."

"We've turned off the water." Tiffany tugged at the weight of the tool bag across her body.

"A sprite of many talents, I see." He gripped his walking aids.

"We can't all be just a pretty face." She could have bitten off her tongue.

He raised his eyebrows and his eyes sparkled. They weren't black after all, but a deep brown.

"You think I'm pretty?" He sounded amused.

She took a wide stance and began an assessment of him from the tip of his dusty loafers, gray trousers, a rumpled white shirt with the sleeves rolled up to the elbows exposing firm, and tanned arms. His whiskers shadowed across his firm jaw, his full lips held neutral, his straight nose and those dark watchful eyes had deep etched laugh lines around them. "You have a certain road weariness that I'd like to capture on paper." Reaching with her callused fingers, she touched his beard. She suddenly wished for pencils and sketchpad, followed by a desire for a little black dress and platform heels to give her height and throw her chest forward.

Lorraine coughed. "Tiffany?"

"Lorraine, I stopped on the highway and helped this man out of his car." She leaned back and stared at his nine o'clock shadow. "I've been in his space before."

"So you're an artist plumber?" he said, looking down at her.

"Artist, temporary plumber." Tiffany stepped out of his personal space. "Have you met my father, Fred George?"

"Yes, I've had the pleasure," the man said, giving a half-shrug. "Fred, you should go home, you're pale."

She saw her father putting his finger to his lips, asking this guy to stop talking. "You're right, Will." Fred George straightened his shoulders.

"The water bottle in the kitchen is empty," Lorraine said. "We'll need water for washing up and making coffee."

Her father pushed himself off the wall. "I'll handle this, Tiff."

"I got it," Tiffany and Will said in unison. Tiffany followed Will into the kitchen.

"The new bottle is in this cupboard." He pointed to the lower doors.

Tiffany bent her legs and hugged the full water bottle close to her chest and then set it on the counter. She expected admiration in his eyes that someone of her small stature could maneuver the weight. He wasn't even looking, he had placed his crutches in the corner and was leaning precariously against the water dispenser, hugging the empty bottle to his chest. Residual water dripped down his shirt and the front of his pants.

"One way to get cleaned up after sliding around on pavement," he said, setting the empty bottle aside.

Tiffany focused on the full container rather than the watermark all over the front of his pants. He stepped into her path when she swung the bottle. "Get out of my way, or I'll drop this." Tiffany's arms were on fire.

"I'm trying to help."

"You're not helping, believe me. Just move." Settling the bottle into the hole, she said. "Stay out of my way."

"You are a control freak," Will said, backing away toward a chair that he grasped.

Tiffany felt the heat of anger spread across her cheeks, although he hadn't said anything stupid like, *Sure, a little woman like you can do this?* or *Wow, those are some pipes on a little woman.*

Mr. Cleaver did worse. He mocked her. She clicked her tongue. "We're not on the playground, Mr. Cleaver."

He looked down at her feet. "If the boot fits."

Tiffany wanted her other life back right now. She wanted to spread plaster over a surface with wide sweeping arm movements and if Mr. Cleaver happened to be in the way, all the better.

"I hope Fred feels better soon. He has important work ahead of him," Will said breaking her moment of visualization.

She blew out a frustrated breath. What was her father up to now? Without a backward glance, Tiffany left the kitchen and called, "Hey, Dad. Ready to go?"

Then her father, Fred George, the best plumber in the area, walked slowly out of the building.

Will followed without a sound, allowing her to leave the building without further comments.

Watching her father hoist himself into the passenger seat without a word, she felt her shoulders slump under the weight of knowing that her planned rest had become complicated.

Chapter 2

Shifting the van into 'drive,' Tiffany glanced at her father. "How are you doing, Dad?"

"Better."

A soft flutter of her father's lips told her he had dropped off to sleep. He had to be okay. She had commitments. The van stuttered to a stop at the garage door.

When George stepped onto the cement, her mother reached for his hand. "Did you save the day?"

"Sure did." He turned toward Tiffany. "Thank you, little helper."

Tiffany blinked back tears. "You're welcome, daddy bear."

Mom reached for his arm. "Good thing Tiffany decided to come home. You didn't quit art school like you quit being an active partner in the business, did you?"

"No I didn't. I have a few days off." Tiffany kicked off her rubber boots and unzipped the coveralls.

"Since you've decided to come home, there's left over chicken salad on the second shelf of the refrigerator." Mother held the door open for them.

"I'm going straight to bed. I'm fasting for blood work tomorrow." Her dad almost bounced against the walls. "By the way, unusual hair."

Tiffany skimmed her fingers across her hair. A few wax-hardened strands held their form.

Her mom put her arm around her dad. Seeing her father's stooped back was a punch in her gut. Her parents were not invincible.

Tiffany opened the fridge. She grabbed one of her father's beers and the salad. Closet doors closing and the thump of feet across the floor were familiar sounds of her parents' bedtime ritual.

"He's settled." Her mother returned from the bedroom and turned on the tap, filling a tall glass of water. She set it down and covered her face with her hands.

"Mom." Tiffany slipped off her chair and wound her arms around her mother.

Mom shrugged out of Tiffany's embrace, and drank deeply from her glass of water. "I don't know why you came home without telling us, but it's a good thing you did. Your father won a bid on a big plumbing contract."

Tiffany peeled the label on the bottle. "Any chance Eric can come home?"

"Don't be silly." She frowned at Tiffany. "He has an important position. You know that mold affects his asthma, and in the plumbing business there are always moldy areas."

"Yes, Mom, but that was such a long time ago. What about his business experience? If Dad has a big job, the business experience is better than a plumber. We're a dime a dozen." Tiffany clasped her hands together.

"You'll have to stay as long as it takes. You're qualified and a partner whose tuition is being paid by the business." Mom's back was ramrod straight. "You've had your fun with this art business."

Tiffany's thoughts of her Winnipeg studio and the aquarium fresco contract for the new business center weighed on her mind as heavy as a bucket of dry plaster. "Mom, I have a week, and after that I have to go back." Tiffany pushed the salad around on her plate. She jumped up and scraped the soggy lettuce into the garbage.

"Tiffany, how can you be so selfish?" Her mom stood. "After Collin left you high and dry with your wedding invitations all stamped and ready to mail, Dad just felt sorry for you. He convinced me you needed a little escape." Her mother's eyes squinted and her lips thinned. "You have to be here now."

"No way," Tiffany said. "Eric receives benefits from the business too. It's his turn."

"It's time you grew up and gave up that sibling jealously," Mother said.

"I'm not jealous of Eric, I'm jealous of his asthma." Tiffany knew it was an immature answer but that was the best she could come up with on the spot after nine hours on the road, a broken nail, a kiss, and slogging through cold water. Even though her parents' world was collapsing, Tiffany wanted them to share her excitement about her artistic progress. It never seemed to be the time for her. Had it always been this way?

"Go to bed." Mother pushed her chair under the table.

Tiffany spilled the warm beer down the drain, turned off the lights. "Welcome home," she whispered, hugging herself. She wondered what her Dad was up to with that stranger, Will Cleaver. *I will not stay. I will not be guilted into staying.* She was thirty. She'd seen life. She'd been dumped and she had triumphed. She didn't have to be a plumber who dabbled in art. She could be an artist who worked as a plumber for a week. *Anything is doable for a week.*

At the lodge, Will scratched the stubble on his chin. "I need to go to a hotel for the night, Lorraine," Will muttered.

"Speak up, man." Lorraine held her hand to her ear.

"I'll need a ride into Regina," Will said louder.

"If you're going to live in this community, you will have to get used to roughing it." Lorraine crooked her finger at him.

He followed her.

"I always keep jugs of water, ever since the big scare

when the new century turned over and there was dire warnings." She entered her suite. "Wait here."

Will waited in the hall until Lorraine guided a three-gallon jug of water toward him on a makeshift trolley. "Use this and the water will be running in no time tomorrow."

He opened his door, and she steered the trolley into his kitchen. He lifted the jug of water onto the counter. "Thanks."

"Didn't you hire Lacy to be your driver?" Lorraine and her trolley trundled to the door.

"Yes, but my car was delivered to the depot tonight." Will blew out a breath of frustration. "Lacy was busy."

"I'm sure she has a friend who can drive both of you tomorrow, or get on the Internet, and have your car delivered." She pointed a finger at him. "Regina might be small in comparison to Toronto but I'm fairly certain they have everything you need." Lorraine tightened the belt on her robe. "I haven't seen you drive around town."

"I'm qualified to drive." Will shrugged. "I'm just not that good at it, and it's worse when I'm tired."

She pointed her finger at him again. "Get some sleep."

Will sank into the recliner chair. If he had packed his emergency case with extra medication, and a change of clothes, he would have asked the tow truck driver to take him into the city. He had taken a risk leaving at the end of his day. *Will Cleaver, you fool.* What was that old saying, 'pride comes before the fall?' He had wanted his SUV because Nikki, the woman who had discarded him like a bad plan, arrived tomorrow.

He couldn't have a hot shower, so a quick scrub of his essentials had to do. Then he settled into the center of his bed, and he wondered why women seemed to give him what he needed. He knew the answer but he didn't like it. Most women took one look at his crutches and swooped in to help, Nikki included, for a while.

He had wanted to assist Tiffany as any abled-bodied

man would, but he had been in her way and broken her momentum when she swung that heavy water bottle. She was a bundle of energy, who fit into him perfectly. When the compact car stopped on the side of the highway and the petite woman approached his car, he was sure he'd be in pain until the tow truck arrived. How wrong he had been. Tiffany had common sense and had used it. Her spiked hair seemed to be the only indication that she wanted personal space. Perhaps she was here to assist her father with the successful bid George's Family Plumbing had won for the planned residential community.

Will dozed then woke with a jerk from his recurring dream. He had been running again in his awkward stumble, with his arms windmilling but he ran. After the movie *Forrest Gump* came out, his friends had yelled, "Run, Will, Run." He hadn't run in a very long time. Adult men with a disability seldom ran, but in this dream he was running in a field of daisies toward a woman with black spiked hair. But then she turned and walked away from him. He scratched his chin and his fingertips rasped against his whiskers.

Now, he lay with his hands under his head. He recognized the sounds in Willow Lodge. The resident across the hall cried in her sleep and her wail crept under his door. The man next door flushed the toilet at least every hour. A motor cycle warmed up every morning at 4:45 a.m. as the oil refinery worker headed onto the highway. Even though he had been dropping in for a day or two over the past six months, it had only taken him a week to settle in as if he belonged. All had gone exceedingly well until this evening when he pushed his physical limits. He was sure he would have made it to Regina, except for the lack of battery current flowing along the right wires in that rental car, just as his brain's messages traveled confused and interrupted to his legs. But his cloud had a pink coverall lining. Even the burst pipe was only an inconvenience.

The next morning, Will eyed the sun as it slipped through the crack in the drapes. He leaned forward, eased his legs over the edge of the mattress, and snagged his boxers from a drawer. Will flexed his back. He'd have to join a gym. Exercise was the key to his mobility. He put on his designer blue jeans, white shirt, and midnight blue corduroy sports jacket. He had tossed his suit pants in the garbage last night. He was ready to face the day.

Will called his driver, Lacy. She'd been with him ever since he started to come to Apex from Toronto, sometimes for a day, sometimes for a week. Lacy had heard about the water break and his return with the tow truck.

"Dad's leaving for work in ten minutes so we can hitch a ride. If you're ready," Lacy said.

"I am ready, Lacy."

Chapter 3

Tiffany George, in her pajamas, polyester dressing gown, and holding onto a cup of coffee, strolled around the deck. The neighbor's black-and-white Persian cat, hunched with its ears pressed back, was ready to pounce if one unsuspecting bird dared to invade her space.

When the sun shone on Tiffany's face, she relaxed into meditative breathing against her trepidation of the next few days. Her parents were ready to dismiss her artistic career as if she hadn't left home, never struck out on her own, or won a prestigious seat in the art school that rewarded her raw talent. To them her community school plumbing certification was supposed to be her future. Eventually she would have become the majority owner and operator of the George Family Plumbing business. She would have married her fiancé, Collin, and raised a family in Apex. That was before Collin informed her she could keep her engagement ring but he wouldn't be adding the matching wedding band. Before he had found someone else. When she had been with Collin she assumed Apex would be enough, as if she might be content, as if it would be a big enough future without creating art. Nothing seemed safe, honorable or innocent after his betrayal. Dad had convinced her mother that Tiffany should leave for a while. Besides, business was slow and if it picked up they would look for an apprentice to help out.

Then Tiffany's world opened with her move to Winnipeg and her art. She wasn't too far from home but not too close either. The new welds, designs, and paint for different surface textures consumed her waking hours. She dreamt about murals. She embraced her art.

A breeze slipped between the folds of her dressing gown and a chill sliced through her core. Her new life had to be on hold for a few days, maybe a week. Tiffany ran her fingers through her short-cropped hair. Her stylist had cut off her blond ponytail, dyed the remainder black, and added gel. Tiffany's image had become a new work of art.

Outside, tires crunched along the streets and a motorcycle engine rumbled. Her mother tapped on the window and motioned for Tiffany to come inside. Clinging to her coffee cup, she returned to the kitchen. Her mother and father were dressed for the day. Her father was pale. "Tiffany, we're going to the hospital for the scheduled tests. I assume you can take care of everything here," her mother said, sweeping her arm as if indicating the whole town of Apex.

"Of course." Tiffany straightened her shoulders, kissed her father's cheek, and lightly wrapped her arm around her mother's shoulder. "Take care. I've got this under control."

"You can call Darryl anytime, he's up early," Dad said.

"Darryl's still in charge? Great." Tiffany followed them onto the driveway.

Her mother tucked her arm into her father's and directed him to the passenger seat of their Smart car. "You rest, I'll drive. Besides without anything in your system I don't want you passing out."

"Do I have to ride in this on the highway?" Fred George curled his lip. "The wind will push us off the bridge."

"You know parking is always an issue at the hospital. I can squeeze this baby in anywhere." The engine hummed.

Tiffany leaned into the window. "Text me when you can."

"Of course," her mother said while the car rolled backward.

"You've got a good memory. Rely on it," her dad called

through the open window, and then he started coughing again.

Back in the kitchen where she'd eaten breakfast almost all of her life, Tiffany nibbled at a piece of dry toast, digging deep for enthusiasm about the rest of her day. She placed the used coffee cups in the dishwasher. She showered, and dressed in her jeans, T-shirt, and finally, her coveralls. She snapped her baseball cap on her head. So much for the stylish urban woman.

While she drove toward the lodge, she wondered if a certain man with full lips and a firm butt might be around. She admired him, and thought that in some ways his external disability reflected her internal one. Right now, her mobility was hampered by her responsibilities. She waved at the locals sitting in the window at Cindy's coffee shop, before she stopped at Willow Lodge.

Darryl, Apex's foreman, opened his arms for her. "Morning, city gal, how's life?"

"Fabulous, exhausting, invigorating, scary." Tiffany walked into Darryl's arms.

"I hear you had some welcome home." Darryl lifted her off the ground.

"What could I do? Where were you by the way?" She squeezed his bicep.

Darryl blushed and set her back on the ground. "Never one to ask a question sideways, are you?"

"Not to someone I care about." She hooked her arm in his.

"And if I said, 'none of your business,' you'd do what?"

"If you really mean that," Tiffany said, "it's your life."

"Whoa, city life has gotten to you."

"Yes, I've learned to live with people and not know their names or their history," she said, removing her cap and twisting her hair at the roots.

"Tiffany, it's hard to take you seriously in that get up," Darryl said.

"Looks are always deceiving." Tiffany performed a little turn. "A purple coverall is the new serviceable navy."

"No time to talk fashion," Darryl said, keying in the code. "Time to work. These residents need water."

Tiffany scanned the hallways: no bob and thrust accompanied by the thump of two crutches. A group of the residents filed out of the kitchen with carafes and electric kettles filled with water for their morning coffee.

"When are we going to have water?" Mrs. Walker asked. The tall, distinguished woman with pure white chin-length hair continued, "I'm going to my son's for a holiday and I can't get on the airplane without a shower."

"As soon as we can," Darryl said. "The men are gathering the equipment as we speak. Tiffany's going to make sure the pipes are sound in the building."

"Tiffany, is that you?" Mrs. Walker shook her head and pursed her lips. "What have you done with your hair? Where's that blond ponytail?"

"Gone." Tiffany lifted her cap and bowed. "I had it styled."

"Oh dear. Black hair does not suit you. Tsk, Tsk. Just because you can, doesn't mean you should."

"Thank you for your opinion, Mrs. Walker." Tiffany waved to the residents and entered the mechanical room. After a quick inspection, she said, "We're good to go."

Darryl's phone beeped. He read a text. "The men are ready." He dialed a number. "Okay, turn it on, slowly . . . increase the pressure." The pipes rattled. Tiffany signalled Darryl with a thumbs-up. "Okay. That's got it," Darryl said, saluting against the brim of his baseball cap. "Call me if anything comes up. I'll post Jim on the hydrant for a few hours."

On their return from Regina, Lacy parked Will's SUV at Willow Lodge. A man in a safety vest stood beside the fire hydrant where an overland flexible pipe led into the lodge.

"Thank you, Lacy. I'll give you a call after I'm cleaned up and we'll make arrangements for the rest of the day." He wanted Lacy to realize the importance of communicating with him. "You have my number if anything comes up."

"Yes, Will." She held up her cell phone. "Your SUV is so much nicer to drive than the rentals you've had." Lacy turned and began walking home.

"Wait, Lacy. Take the car," Will called.

"That's okay. It isn't far." Lacy waved.

"Good morning," the man in the safety vest said, "water's on."

"Good news," Will said.

Once inside the lodge, he noticed the door to the mechanical room was open. He peered through the doorway. He should make himself known to Tiffany but he stood, transfixed, observing her dedication while she checked gauges and pipefittings. Her cap hid her spiked hairstyle. While she had massaged his legs and looked directly into his eyes without a hint of aversion, he felt as if he'd come home. She felt that right for him, custom-made, but there were big spaces to fill in between a Good Samaritan and a lover. Tiffany reached up and tested another fastener securing the furnace to the wall. He cleared his throat. He just wanted a sip of her personality before he continued with his day. "That is a good design."

"Yes, it is." She turned. "Mr. Cleaver, good morning."

"I've added them into all of the mechanical rooms I've designed since they've been patented."

She smiled at him. "Thank you. You're helping provide my freedom."

"Pardon?" Will leaned through the open doorway.

"George's Family Plumbing patented the design." Tiffany walked toward the open door.

He backed out of her way.

"You can have your shower now," she said with a smirk.

She remembered him. "I know my way around a bird bath when it's necessary."

She leaned toward him. Everything was delicate about her. "Nice shirt," she said.

"Thanks. Nice-looking coveralls, too." He inhaled deeply. "Just checking to see if your scent is lavender, too."

She held up her hands, protecting her space. "So what exactly are you doing living in a home for seniors? Why aren't you staying at the hotel?" She tipped her head to one side and fingered her strap on her toolkit that slid between her breasts.

"I like it here, and the hotel rooms are full of the construction crew for the new potash mine."

Tiffany moved toward the nearest chair. Perching on it, she asked, "How long have all the hotel rooms been filled?"

"Months now." How could someone not know about the changes in their hometown? "How far away have you been?"

"Distance? Nine hours by car, perhaps less if you don't stop and have a coffee, or check out the small towns along the way." She looked down at her calloused palms. "But in all other ways, halfway around the world."

He leaned on a chair next to her. "That's cryptic."

She checked the time on her phone. Will knew her attention slipped away from him, and he should be reviewing his notes for his meeting this afternoon. "Are you back home to work with your dad?"

"When I stopped on the road to help you out, I was on my way home for seven wonderful days of doing nothing." She sighed.

"Doesn't look as if you've started your wonderful nothing days." He didn't move. If she stayed, he would too.

"This happened," she said, tugging the toolkit strap restraining her body.

"Your father was sick last night." Will had the sudden

urge to wrap her in his arms but he heard residents shuffling and talking in the hallways.

"Yes." She gazed through the window that dominated the room. The framed view included the man standing guard beside the hydrant.

He matched her pace when she gathered her equipment and walked toward the door. At the end of the common area, it felt as if neither of them wanted to end this time before responsibilities separated them.

"I didn't thank you properly for coming to my aid last night," Will said.

She stopped and stepped in front of him. Then she lowered her toolkit on the floor. "I think you did." She put her hand on his jaw, and her palm reached around his neck. Standing on tiptoes, and with a little downward pressure on his neck, she was able to place her lips on his. He overcame his surprise and took her lips from playful to intimate. After he slowed the kiss and nibbled at the corners of her lips, he said, "Thank you for coming to my rescue."

"You're welcome." She closed her eyes, swaying toward him until their lips touched again. "My pleasure," she whispered.

Out of the corner of his eye, he saw the door open. He stepped away and shielded her from the intrusion.

A voice called down the hallway, "Oh, there you are, Tiffany. Can we get on with our day?"

"Yes, Lorraine, the water will be hot shortly." Tiffany picked up her toolkit. "Be seeing you. Can't miss each other in this community." She reached for the door. "Darryl will be wondering what happened to me."

Chapter 4

Tiffany watched Will use his powerful arms to propel himself toward the hallway. He turned and winked.

After the lodge doors swished closed behind her, she tipped her face toward the sun, savoring the remnants of the hypnotic moment when their lips met.

Initiating a kiss with this almost-stranger certainly nudged other neglected desires and longings. As if on cue, her body tingled from her vibrating cell phone. She glanced at the name. Her mother's text message said: *Admitting Dad to hospital for more tests. He's not fighting. Not a good sign. Hope you're doing your part.*

Old country tunes played on the van's radio. If Tiffany didn't change the channel, it meant that Dad would be back in the driver's seat again. She dipped her hand into her father's peppermint stash. When the cool mint hit the back of her throat and nose, the intense flavor reminded her of Dad crushing a candy between his molars, just after a cigarette, before he met a customer. Twisting the key, she white-knuckled the steering wheel and promised Dad's current illness would not drag her from her art and back to Apex.

Shifting the truck into 'reverse,' Tiffany thought, *There are times when backing up is necessary.*

She drove the few blocks to the town office. Darryl might be able to give her a closer time line for a repair to the water main.

She parked, jumped down from the seat, and then locked the door. With long strides across the parking lot, Tiffany tucked her T-shirt into her waistband and tightened her belt with the rhinestone-encrusted wrench belt buckle. It was her brother Eric's graduation gift to her when she had received her plumber certification. Right now she'd pawn her belt buckle just to have Eric here sharing what was coming down the pipe. But he was safely ensconced in his fifteenth floor office managing business in Calgary.

Tiffany pushed through the glass door and stepped into the municipal office with its cacophony of ringing phones, running copy machines, and booming voices.

"Hello there, Tiffany. Where is your old man?" came at her like a train roaring down the tracks.

"He isn't an old man. He's younger than you are, Aunt Rosie," Tiffany said.

The woman practically lifted Tiffany off the floor with her bear hug. "Nice to have my city girl home again."

"Thanks. You can put me down now. Congratulations on your re-election to town council." Tiffany returned the kiss and ducked out of the way of the dangling earrings.

"The voters know a good thing when they have it. I've always been straight up with them." Rosie used the pad of her thumb to remove the outline of lips on Tiffany's cheek.

Tiffany heard a throat clearing behind her.

"Nice tattoo peeking under the hem of your shirt. Is it a butterfly?"

Tiffany spun on her heels. Will Cleaver, all smirks and large hands, resting on the padded handles of his crutches. She turned, tugging on the hem of her shirt. His eyes widened. He let out a low whistle. "Look what else was under those coveralls. The front is almost as eye catching as the back. If you stood with the sun reflecting off those gems on your belt you could blind a fellow."

"My secret weapon for men gazing intently at that level."

"Then I'm glad I'm standing."

"Mr. Cleaver, I take it you've met my niece. She may be short but she carries a powerful punch." Tiffany's aunt was tall, slim and muscular from all the years of landscaping. "You still taking all those kick boxing classes and Kung Fu?"

"It's Karate, not Kung Fu," Tiffany said.

"I just watched the *Kung Fu Panda* movie. He's kinda short, like you."

"But not as slim," Will chimed in.

"As you are well aware, I have strength. I can move large objects." She placed her hands on her hips, a trick she learned in an improvisation class, which gave her body width, and took up space. She stared up at Will.

"Right, I always hope that when someone comes to the rescue he or she will either be strong or, if all else fails, bring whiskey like a St. Bernard in a snow storm."

"What's with you two?" Rosie turned her head from Will to Tiffany as if she were watching a ping-pong match. "Let me start from the beginning," she said. "Mr. Will Cleaver hails from Toronto. He represents the firm of Nosh, Nosh, and Crane. He's designed a barrier-free community for Apex. The goal is to have as many people as possible prospering from the new mine." Turning toward Will, she said, "Mr. Will Cleaver, Ms. Tiffany George, soon-to-be a renowned mixed-media artist."

Tiffany bowed. "With a contract."

"Tiffany, I'm so proud of you." Rosie wrapped Tiffany in a bear hug.

Tiffany turned her nose away from Aunt Rosie's bosom and her excessive use of Chanel No. 5.

"And when were you going to tell us about all this?" Rosie asked.

"Today. I just thought it would be under different circumstances." A cloud seemed to have drifted across the open window.

"Congratulations." Will's eyes sparkled. "Again you surprise me."

Just then, Tiffany found herself grabbed from behind. Instinctively, she aimed her elbow toward her attacker's nose.

"Stop," Darryl said.

"Do not come up behind a person." She turned and jabbed her finger into his chest.

He put his hands up, surrendering.

"At least give some indication that you're around, you jerk." She scrubbed her elbow. "I could have broken your nose."

"You were too busy extricating yourself from your proud auntie's arms." Darryl smirked at Tiffany.

"I just don't like to have my nose shoved into anyone's breasts. Sorry, Aunt Rosie."

"I apologize. I always forget how tall I am and how . . ." Rosie clamped her hand across her mouth but her eyes sparkled.

Tiffany frowned at her aunt.

She turned to Will. "We try to remember not to say s-h-o-r-t to her."

The phone rang, and Sylvia, the administrator, answered.

Will's eyes crinkled at the corners. "I design spaces to include vertical and girth challenges."

"I saw your truck, Tiffany. But since you're having a family visit, I'd better get back to the wrinkle ranch," Darryl said.

"The what?" Tiffany asked.

"The seniors' lodge," Darryl said.

"That's better," Tiffany said. "The words we use are important to show our respect."

"I agree wholeheartedly with that statement," Will said.

All eyes glanced at the man leaning on his crutches and then away. "Was there something else, Darryl?" Rosie glared at the Town Foreman.

Darryl straightened. "I came in to report that the men have located the break. The main line leading to the reservoir was cut." He pushed the brim of his hat up further on his head.

"Did you call the police?" Rosie asked.

Everyone turned when the door opened and two RCMP officers entered.

"Good morning, gentlemen. Let's go into the board room." Rosie pointed to the open door. Darryl and the RCMP followed Rosie into an inner room. Rosie turned. "Will, this is important to you as well. Please join us."

Sylvia, the Town Administrator, shook her head. "I just knew there would be problems. There are the new retirees who left the big city behind with hopes of finding their Shangri-La in Apex." She leaned across the desk. "With the construction, comes new traffic, new stop signs, and more bylaws, and it scares them. They recall the hassles of whatever larger urban center they came from."

"I like the idea of coming home to the familiar and the slower pace. So much is happening." Tiffany's cell phone vibrated in her pocket. "Got a call. Got to go." Tiffany waved to Sylvia. Turning on her heel, she slammed her hand against the glass door. When she was out of sight, she opened her cell, afraid to read the text from her mother, yet afraid not to. Tiffany skimmed the words as if dwelling on them would make them untrue. Her father was in intensive care. She must come, now.

Tiffany turned the radio playing country tunes loud while she drove the van back to her parents' house to pick up her car. *He will be fine. He will come back.* Reaching under the front seat of the van, she snagged her purse. She'd go as she was, bling belt buckle and all.

After starting her compact car, she sped along the highway. In the city every corner seemed to have a red light, purposefully delaying her arrival at the hospital.

A breeze on the way to the front doors held a chill. Disposable coffee cups rolled across the pavement, spun, and were then flattened by a handi-bus picking up patients in wheelchairs waiting outside the automatic doors.

The vibration in her pocket demanded attention again. The text wasn't from her mother or brother but her mentor, Owen. The demand to call him was in capital letters. Too bad. She wouldn't answer him right now.

She pressed the elevator button and the ride ended at the cardiac care unit.

Chapter 5

In the council chambers, Darryl explained to the RCMP that someone had deliberately cut straight through the line. Darryl shook his head. "Why would someone do this to the old folks? They're the most vulnerable."

Will said, "I live there, too."

"Have you had any other trouble?" the RCMP asked.

Rosie answered, "There are residents who do not want a planned subdivision in their backyard."

Will rolled out the blueprints of the neighborhood. "This design is composed of twenty multi-generational barrier–free households, accessible to persons with disabilities."

"Impressive," the older, hardened officer said.

"We'll need the names of those people," the younger officious officer said to Rosie, his pen poised above his notepad.

"You find Shirley Rassmussen and you'll find the troublemakers." Darryl rubbed the back of his neck. "You don't know how many things over the years she's spoiled."

"They can't hold a town hostage." Will sat up straight.

"Mark my words," Rosie said slowly, "watch your back, your front, and your sides."

"The residents who understand progress should step forward," Will said, with more confidence than he felt. He wanted this community to work.

"Family roots run deep. They can call in a lot of IOUs," Darryl said.

"Is there any proof?" the officer with the notebook asked.

The older officer moved his finger over the plans, around an enclosed swimming pool, then indicated the squares marked childcare facilities, woodworking building, craft place, library, and a small theatre. "Ambitious," he said, stepping back. "I have ideas about who might put a stick through your wheels."

"Everything is circumstantial. We need proof." The officer closed his notebook. "We'll be in touch."

Both officers left the building.

"I have to check on my men." Darryl slipped his phone from the case. "The RCMP should have stayed for the whole meeting. They'd get their evidence." Darryl looked back into the room. "Good luck."

Will's cell phone alarm rang. Time for a meeting with the council and district committee members. "Rosie, do you have any questions before the other members arrive?" Will took his position at the end of the chamber desk.

Rosie pursed her lips and shook her head. "I stand by my decisions since this whole discussion started. When can we put down our deposits on the apartment we would like to live in?" She pointed to a square on the plan. "Can I have this unit right here, next to the library?"

"Not over there by the pool?" Will pointed to the large wing.

"The library will be perfect. I may even be able to volunteer for some of the children's programs. I used to teach kindergarten, you know."

"No, I didn't," Will said.

Straightening, she said, "Sorry, Will, I forget that you are a newcomer. You seem to fit in so well."

"Thanks, Rosie, that's a compliment."

He heard Mayor Robert talking to Sylvia, the Town Administrator. Out of the window, he spotted people gathering in the parking lot. He was ready for this as an accomplished architect and a partner with the great firm of Nosh, Nosh, and Crane.

The council and district committee members chose their

chairs around the table with mumbled greetings to each other and to Will. The mayor called this meeting to order. The six members of council and six members of the planning committee looked up on cue from their papers. Sylvia's fingers were poised above her keyboard. "We're here today to finalize the plans for the new development. Have all the committee members and council had an opportunity to review Mr. Cleaver's notes he forwarded to you?"

The room reverberated with different assents, "yes, ah-huh, you bet, great job."

"When can we move in?" Rosie asked.

The door pushed open and half a dozen members of the community filed in and took the seats behind the railing. Shirley Rassmussen sat front and center. Leaning forward with her broad shoulders she appeared ready to block any forward movement of the plan. Over the months, Will had met with her on different occasions but she always said she wasn't convinced that a neighborhood that housed cripples, as she called them, was any good in the middle of an economic boom. "Why not just regular apartments for all those miners and their families and fill up our school and church again?" He had assured her that the families who moved into the homes would do just that.

Mr. Nosh, Senior, knew the benefits this boom would bring to Apex, while Mr. Nosh, Junior, had lived in the camps, and he knew the downside of camp life with only outlets of bars and gambling. There was always a hardship on family life. Although Nosh, Nosh, and Crane designs always created accessible buildings, Will's input was invaluable. He knew from experience what was required for differently abled men, women, and their families, alongside the other existing houses.

Will's mediation skills must convince Mrs. Rassmusen and her followers that their town would not become a town with an asylum or other institutions and never have a "home" as in the old days. He turned on the projector with the 3D plans. Will balanced with his stance wide, and then using his laser pointer, he described the features of the model. "We will build the structures and the families accompanied by support services will follow. Apex will be renowned as the first town in the western provinces providing these services in proximity to a mine. When proper housing is available, we encourage employees to put down roots. Rockwell's mission statement includes a commitment to training and employment opportunities, supporting business development, and achieving environment excellence."

Will pointed to the parcels of land where the planned neighborhood would be constructed. "The bicycle and walking trails will encourage exercise. We'll take advantage of the many hours of sunshine for solar power heating for the swimming pool and therapeutic tubs. Nosh, Nosh, and Crane are committed to bringing accessible living and employment for a totally integrated society."

Counsellor Tom stroked his beard. "We don't want to spoil the landscape view for the other residents."

"We have calculated the sight lines and there will be minimal disruption of personal views of the prairie and skyline."

Counsellor Roy flipped his pages. "Rockwell will increase our water system and sewage lagoon as part of their commitment to our community."

"Yes, we are anxious to begin development," Will said.

Betty Dumont gasped. "But this is our tourist time. Our local businesses rely on this season to carry them through. How much disruption will be caused for this important time?"

"We're counting on minimal."

"This all sounds too good to be true." A man from the gallery gripped the railing, glaring at Will.

Shirley's enthusiastic, "Yes!" from behind the rail confirmed that this man was part of the team.

Rosie spoke quietly. "How do you know that the miners will accept the differently abled?"

"In my experience and in our research we've found that those who work hard respect others who do the same. Everyone should have a chance. People with disabilities want to be productive members of the workforce."

"We're spinning our wheels here." Mayor Robert rapped his gavel. He went on to question the downside of progress. Other town mayors and administrators warned him about how the increased population brought a rise in the need for more social services, created pressures on the school, as well as traffic problems. The man's jowls wobbled. "We've been known as a sleepy, relaxing community where everyone knows everyone else's names. The place where we help out the less fortunate or kick rebel rousers out of town."

"Thank you, Mayor Robert, for voicing the dark side of developments." Will spoke about the studies that showed an increased drug use in camps due to boredom, excess money, fatigue, and loneliness. "Nosh, Nosh, and Crane are providing a sustained community alongside Rockwell Mines."

Mayor Robert tapped his gavel. "Thank you, ladies and gentlemen. The community information meeting will be held on Saturday."

Will kept his face calm even though he imagined his fist pumping the air. "Presenters from Rockwell, as well as my colleague, Nikki Cornwall, who is leading up the temporary residential camp, will be present to answer your questions."

"Tell them you have food and they'll be there," Rosie called.

"There will be food. I promise."

Will shook hands with the councillors and the committee members. He turned toward the group behind the rail, but they were leaving.

One man turned, looked at Will, and pointed as if he had a gun. "It isn't over yet."

Chapter 6

The large sign in the doorway instructed everyone to use the hand sanitizer before entering the ward. Tiffany pressed the plunger and the gel oozed into her palms. Then she elbowed her way through swinging double-doors.

The unit had an eerie quiet, even the beeps and hisses of various machines seemed subdued.

A nurse whispered, "Are you a family member?"

"Yes, my father is here. Mr. Fred George."

"Turn left. It's the third room. Don't be frightened. All of the machines are here to help us help him."

Tiffany hesitated. A pent-up breath exploded from her, and she inhaled three deep breaths before she stopped at the foot of her father's bed. Wired leads seemed to be coming from all parts of his body. The lights flickered and numbers changed. Her father's eyes were closed.

She moved quietly up to her mother and placed her hand on her shoulder. Her mother turned and indicated a chair.

Tiffany focused on the rhythmic dips and spikes on the monitor rather than on her father with tubes running into his arm and up his nostrils.

He gasped and coughed.

"Hey, Dad," Tiffany said.

"Tiffany." He sucked air in short breaths. "How's the water break?"

"Under control." She held up her cell phone. "Don't worry, Dad. I got it."

"Did anyone tell you?" Her dad gulped for air. "I won

the bid." His eyes opened wide. "I'll work with that Will fellow." His shoulders straightened on the pillow.

After a few deep breaths, she said, "Dad, you're full of surprises. From the bits and pieces I heard this morning, Shirley is fighting the change." Tiffany bit her lip. She'd talk about anything rather than what was happening to her father.

"I need to get out of here." Fred's eyes fluttered shut. He opened them and gasped. "First big opportunity and I'm as weak as a newborn calf."

Her mother patted Fred's hand. "One day at a time. Tiffany's back."

"So the art's not working out?" Her dad's eyebrows raised.

"The art's fine. I've been commissioned to paint a fresco for a business office tower and mall in Winnipeg." She held up her phone. "Would you like to see pictures of my design?"

"Oh." Dad curled the blanket in his fist. "Not now."

Her mother frowned at her. A nurse came with her clipboard and recorded numbers. "Mr. George. The lab is here. We need more samples."

Tiffany's phone buzzed in her pocket. She glanced at the caller ID. Apex's Town Office number. Tapping her mother on the arm, she pointed to her phone. Her mother nodded. Tiffany tilted her head toward the doors. If Darryl needed her now, would she stay or would she go and tell them to find another plumber?

In the hallway she answered the call. "George Family Plumbing."

She listened while Darryl told her that the aboveground water line would be in place until the administration got its priorities straight.

"Thank you, Darryl . . . No, Dad won't be back today, but I'll look after whatever you need for the next week . . . Yes, then I'm back to Winnipeg." Tiffany knew her back was against the wall.

She needed to phone her brother. Even if her parents didn't want to bother him, he had a right to know what was happening. Besides, there must be something he could do to help since he had a business degree. Tiffany quietly returned into her father's hospital room. "Mom, I'm going for a coffee. Want one?"

Mom nodded.

"Right back."

As the eldest and responsible daughter, she needed to step up and support her parents. Eric was always too small, too weak, too wheezy, especially when it came to taking out the garbage, mowing the lawn, shovelling the snow. When they were younger, Tiffany didn't mind when Eric didn't want to take her place next to Dad. She loved all the attention as Dad's little helper. Yet, Eric should know what was happening. They were building an adult relationship and she wasn't angry anymore after he left her behind in the George and Family business. But it wasn't totally his fault either. Tiffany's dream had included marrying Collin, living in Apex, and someday becoming the owner of the company.

Tiffany dialed her brother's phone number in Calgary, which went straight to voicemail. Great. "Eric, call me, it's important. It's about Dad. And you need to come home." She disconnected, then immediately redialed. "And don't call them. Text or phone me."

Will's attention was drawn back to the guest area in the council chamber when he heard, "So you gonna allow any pets in this compound of yours?" someone asked.

Will turned. "Absolutely. Your local community clubs raise money for service dogs who assist with hearing impairments, mobility issues, as well as blindness. And pets are all round good for anyone." Will felt his legs begin to quiver. He'd been standing too long. He sat on the chair behind him.

"They clean up after these dogs too?" the man in a brown cardigan asked.

"If you come around here, you'll see on the model that we have a corner marked for dogs. In fact, a dog groomer has asked to establish a business. And a veterinarian will provide for regular checkups for residents' pets," Will said, proud of his preplanning and the contacts he'd made.

"Ha! We can't get a doctor to move here and look after good folks and you talk about some fancy animals and low and behold they get a vet," the man in the cardigan said. "You got any plans there for us normal folks?"

"As a matter of fact," Will said, "a doctor and nurse practitioner are ready to open offices. A lab and X-ray unit are also interested."

"The meeting is over," Mayor Robert said. "Mr. Cleaver will be available to answer all of your questions on Saturday at the open house. This is going to be good for Apex and for all the folks who move here. We want people to come, stay, and help build up the community."

"We sure don't need a bunch of spastics. We'd rather be on the map for something good rather than something weird," a deep voice called from the back.

"That's enough, Carl. You can be charged with saying those kind of things now. It isn't yesterday when we didn't know any better. These are people with disabilities, and don't you forget it." Mayor Robert jabbed his index finger toward the man with his sleeves rolled up and fists bunched at his side.

"You can pretty it up all you want, but they are still cripples who walk around spastic, who are driving on our roads with those mobility scooters, and whose dog crap is going to stink up my neighbourhood." The tall man jammed his baseball cap on his head and stomped to the railing.

Will had heard it all before and worse, but that didn't mean that it hurt any less. No, he wasn't hurt, he was tired. His mother had always said sticks and stones. Now he was the one who was wielding the sticks and bricks by design. Will caught Mayor Robert's eye, and nodded.

The mayor said, "That's it, folks. Come to the open house on Saturday. This urban development will need team work."

Will clamped the mayor on the shoulder. "Good job."

"Just hang on a minute, Will," the mayor said quietly. "Sorry about all that water business at the lodge last night. I know the water is running again with an over ground line, but I want to get in touch with your people and Rockwell Mines. They may be willing to upgrade immediately, and then we can close up the hole."

"I'll contact them as soon as I get back to my apartment. But we'll have to check with the RCMP and make certain they've completed their investigation." Will rose unsteadily onto his feet, slipped his briefcase strap across his body, then positioned his crutches. His legs felt weak from standing too long.

"RCMP?" Mayor Robert asked.

"Sorry, Robert, I've got to go. My driver's here. Ask Rosie." Will pressed the handicap button and the door swung open. "I'll be in touch with Nosh, Nosh, and Crane. I'll email you." The breeze quick-jumped his fatigued body.

Lacy walked toward him with a driver's cap low on her forehead and her red hair in braids swung against each shoulder. "At your service, sir."

Will tossed her the keys. "Right on time."

"Where to, Mr. Cleaver?" she asked, holding the car door wide.

He sat his butt on the seat and then lifted each foot into the car.

After closing his door, she got in, started the car, and looked at him expectantly.

"Home, Lacy. Home."

A large truck towing a huge mobile home crossed the intersection. "Must be one of Rockwell's people. They've been preparing the section for mobile homes all week. Apex has been wanting to grow for as long as I can remember." She whistled. "That trailer is a beauty."

They both watched the truck and mansion on wheels maneuver the corner.

"Sure be nice if it was a family with three or four kids. I could do some childcare. I have my early childhood development certification." Lacy stared at the windows in the mobile home as if faces could appear at any moment. "There just hasn't been enough children born here." Lacy sighed.

A man on his bicycle stopped and watched the mobile home inch around the corner.

"Lacy, how easy it is to get down to the Canada Trail with my handcycle?"

"To be honest, Mr. Cleaver, it won't be that hard, but with the rain we had a couple of days ago it's still muddy in spots. I think if you just want a quick ride, the shoulder of the highway is still the best. Especially from where you live. That's easy-peasy."

"You're right about convenient but the other day when a truck swerved to miss a rabbit I got a good scare."

"Well there you go. He missed the rabbit and you're okay. We're good drivers unless of course someone is under the influence." She tipped her thumb to her lips indicating a bottle.

"I know what you mean. I'll ride around town. At least people are driving slower." Exercising built up his endurance.

"May be slower but you can't be sure about their eyesight," Lacy shot back. "It's going to be great having more young people here."

"So you're all for the development?"

"Absolutely." She parked between the yellow lines in the designated spot for his vehicle at the lodge.

"Thanks, Lacy. How are you getting home?" His seat belt recoiled.

"Walking." She handed Will the keys. "Call when you need me again. I'm usually a few minutes away."

Chapter 7

Will opened his apartment door. Home sweet home. After gulping half a bottle of water, he sat with his legs on the couch and opened his tablet.

He dealt with his emails, and then he challenged himself to change into his riding gear even though he'd rather stretch out on the sofa. He allowed his mother's words to run unheeded in his mind. *If you don't use it, you lose it.*

After locking the patio door, he unlocked his handcycle and clicked his crutches into the brackets. He lowered himself into the seat, cinched up his seat belt, tightened his helmet, then he disengaged the brake. He heard his neighbor. "Ride easy, Will."

He called back, "You bet."

His arms required little effort to move along the cement walkway until he bumped over the curb onto the paved road. Now he paid attention to the potholes. He applied the brakes at the four-way stop, glanced both ways, then cycled down Ash Avenue, past the abandoned brick high school with the team colors faded on the mural. This building had once projected confidence, assurance, and a promise of knowledge. He paused and scanned the exterior. With proper engineering techniques, heritage properties could be saved. The May pole, with its cement base, had been toppled. A rabbit paused, its ears erect, before leaping to the next patch of grass.

A compact car slowed beside him, and the window rolled down. "Hey, Mr. Cleaver, nice set of wheels."

He stopped pedalling. "Thank you, Tiffany George."

"You're welcome."

"Did you go to this high school?"

"Will Cleaver that building has been boarded up for a long time."

"Has anyone tried to repurpose it?"

"Not that I've heard. But I've missed huge chunks of news," Tiffany said, leaning out of her window. "I wouldn't be getting too romantic about Apex quite yet."

"We're planning for a long time into the future. How is your father?"

"All right." Tiffany's lips closed tight.

Will understood. He knew small towns were a bush fire where gossip was concerned.

"I hope you are free on Saturday and you'll come to the community hall meeting. I have the plans in my office or on my computer in my apartment, if you want to catch up on the development. You may know that the George's Family Plumbing won the tender to do the plumbing for the barrier-free development."

"Dad told me." Tiffany jabbed her fingers through her hair.

Just then, a Lexus 4x4 crept around Tiffany's car and made a U-turn. The door opened and a woman with long wavy hair bounced out of the car. "Will, Will, I just knew I'd find you. Where else but checking out the architecture." She leaned down gracefully and threw her arms around him and gave him a kiss on the lips.

Will disengaged himself from her embrace. "Nikki. When did you arrive?"

"Didn't you see my grand entrance?" She grabbed the hair from her neck and tousled it. "My beautiful temporary home away from home. I work hard and long, I need my amenities. Where are you staying, darling?"

"Nikki, I'd like to introduce you to Tiffany George.

Her company won the bid for the Nosh, Nosh, and Crane development."

"So happy to meet you. I love your hair."

Tiffany extended her hand through the open window. "Nice to meet you, Nikki."

"Yes." Nikki turned and focused on Will.

"I'm glad you're here, Nikki." Will leaned his head back, looking up at her. "There's a waterline break. Rockwell and Nosh designed for a larger pipe. The foreman and council hope we can install it now and then they won't have to disrupt service again."

"Will, I've just arrived." Nikki placed both hands on her hips. "I should know that there isn't any rest for anyone who works with you."

"Why don't I meet you at the town office? We can go over the logistics."

"Where is this establishment?" Nikki asked.

The weight of her hand on his shoulder reminded him of months ago when they used to be a couple. "End of the block, turn right. Has a bell tower with a real bell. You can't miss it. I'll be right behind you." Will surveyed the width of the road. He saw Tiffany's wave. He lifted his hand. "Just a sec, Tiffany."

"What exactly are you doing anyway?" Nikki asked with her head turned to one side.

"I'm getting to know the town. This is my new transportation. I don't need a driver and I can go further than using my sticks."

Nikki rubbed her palm along Will's bicep. "I can see that the repetitive pedal stroke would build up your muscles. But then I know all about those."

Will knew at the exact moment Tiffany shifted into 'drive' because the sound of the car engine changed. She called out the window, "I'll wait to hear from Darryl. I assume it won't take you two powerhouses long to make the right decision. See you both around."

He tucked away the pleasure he'd felt while they chatted on the road. Work needed to be done. Will pedalled the trike in a wide circle, following Nikki's taillights for about ten yards and then she was gone. Nikki, the woman he thought he'd spend his life with, until she decided that she no longer wanted a man of limited mobility for the long haul. Nikki was back in his life.

Will rode to the ramp, released the seatbelt and unfastened the straps across his legs. Gaining his balance, he concentrated on moving tall and strong into the town office. Inside, he found Nikki seated in the mayor's office with a cold glass of ice tea. Her office-length shorts were professional but showed off her toned and tanned legs. She was listening to Robert's tales about Apex. "And then the home team won the cup." Nikki applauded.

"Will, I'm going to just love working with Robert. Why don't we all go to your office and discuss the water line, I'm sure we can come to a consensus." Nikki was true to form. Will knew all the signs.

Will led the way, held a chair for Nikki before he opened the file with the diagrams in his computer and then projected them on the screen. With a pointer, he indicated the main line problem area. A construction engineer expert, Nikki took over, and all flirtation left her when she focused on the problem, listening to the arguments for and against replacing the old pipe with the new. She may not make the decision he hoped for him and the seniors in the lodge, but she'd make the one that needed to be made for the infrastructure as a whole.

"Will and Robert, I see your dilemma." She pointed. "But unless we begin the larger pipe from this section right here, it really is a waste of time. I recommend we do the normal fix for now, and then when we are in that phase we'll have to disrupt the old dears again."

"You'll be disrupting me too. That's where I'm living." Will stood tall.

"They put you up in a seniors' residence?"

"Nikki, no one put me anywhere. I live in an adapted apartment. And there are twelve other people up there who would not be happy that you're cavalier with their basic needs."

Will turned to see Tiffany standing in the doorway. "Sorry to be late but I changed my mind. I thought I should be in on the discussion about the seniors' lodge." Tiffany looked around. "Where is Darryl? Our foreman knows this system inside out, the repairs and the old clay pipes and the new PVC pipes."

"Tiffany, great idea. Sylvia, find Darryl," Mayor Robert ordered.

"What's the timeline on this development?" Tiffany frowned with concern.

"This is the site of the world's largest potash mine." And as she said "largest," Nikki lifted her shapely defined brows, and with flashing finger quotes continued, "We're bringing Apex into the twenty-first century. You see why I'm not worried about a few people in a seniors' home?"

"With that attitude you won't win very many friends." With her hands on her hips, Tiffany wasn't backing down from Nikki. "The seniors are my friends' grandparents and parents. They've been my teachers, Girl Scout leaders, and community hockey coaches. They're important."

"Tiffany, you've been away." Mayor Robert stepped forward and turned Tiffany toward the model. "This is our town after the urban development is completed." He put his finger on the cenotaph. "The new neighborhood is here on this land, with access to hiking paths, the park, and further along the street are the new family homes. And here's the new school and a new community hall." Mayor Robert spoke slowly, providing time for Tiffany to absorb all the changes that had been planned for Apex. "Then of course there will be infill. Some of the older places will be torn down and new buildings taking their place." Mayor Robert nodded. "Everything and everyone needs to adjust." He kept his arm securely around Tiffany's shoulder like a kindly uncle. "Nikki is the construction engineer. She's responsible for the infrastructure. She knows how large our lagoon and water supply will have to be."

Although Nikki was talking to Will, he watched Tiffany.

Mayor Robert gulped a deep breath. "I'm surprised your parents didn't mention anything. Or you haven't been watching our Facebook page or Twitter account."

"Facebook page? Twitter account?" Tiffany frowned. "It feels as if I left home and returned to a strange place." She stared at the three-dimensional model on the table in a makeshift office. "We can't stand still," Mayor Robert said. "I hear you haven't."

Tiffany's cell phone rang in her pocket.

She reached for it and pressed the silencing button as she checked the caller ID. "Hang on," she said into the phone. She turned to the mayor. "Thank you for briefing me." She hurried out of the office.

Will watched her leave.

Chapter 8

"Eric, thank you for calling me back." Tiffany swallowed the lump in her throat at the thought of her father.

"Hey sis, what's this all about?" Eric asked.

"Has Mom called you at all?" Tiffany tapped the steering wheel.

"No."

"Any chance you can come on home?"

"You're scaring me, Tiff. Just give me the facts."

"I came home last night for a week of relaxation and to bask in my success."

Tiffany stared out the windshield. "Dad is coughing up blood and is now in intensive care. He won a tender to do the plumbing for a new development in Apex. It is expected that I'll be here and I don't want to be. I want to get on with my life." She heard traffic and Eric's breathing.

"Slow down. Dad's in hospital. Which one?"

"The General."

"Okay, I'll get organized. Just hold yourself together. I'll find a way home as soon as I can."

"Eric, thanks."

"Why don't you go into Dad's office and look over the tender bid? We'll figure it out," Eric said with confidence.

Tiffany ended the telephone conversation and slumped against the seat of her car. She wasn't alone.

She jumped at a tap on the window, fumbled with the keys, started the car, and pressed the switch to lower the window.

"Tiffany, are you all right?" Will leaned against the back door.

"Yes, fine."

"If you need someone to talk to, I'm a good listener." He held up his crutches. "I can't leave very quickly."

"I'm sure if you needed a way to escape you would find one."

He leaned forward and with his dark-brown eyes seemed to note every movement of her face. "I'm a softy for a woman battling sadness."

"I'm okay." She looked up at him. "I do have a question. Why here, why now?"

"Why is the world round? Are you wanting a philosophical discussion?"

"Seriously. Why Apex? Why all of this attention to this sleepy community at this time?"

"Less than ten miles away is the newest and biggest potash mine in the Western Provinces." She felt the car shift when he leaned on the front fender. "Because Rockwell partnered with Nosh, Nosh, and Crane, a company with a vision for a sustainable community where skilled and unskilled laborers will come and stay, revitalizing a small community. If the families are close to work, even if they work long hours, the employees are more productive." Will's eyes had an inner light as if he'd just given his best speech.

"You mean there will be more than one restaurant in town, more than one beauty salon." Tiffany bit her lip to hold back a smile.

"Yes, and when persons with differing abilities are employed, therapists, nurse practitioners, doctors, and dentists will follow. There are plans for an intensive health care clinic."

Tiffany heard the pride and hope in his voice for the future and his part in it. "Where exactly is this mining development?" She had been more involved in her studies and her sculptures than she realized. Had her mom or dad mentioned anything? Had she just blocked them out?

"When you go out of town, head north for six miles then turn at the Saskatoon Berry Orchard corner and continue for four miles, until you see a large security gate. You'll have to register, but it is worth the trip. I could show you, if you want to take a drive." Even though he casually leaned against her vehicle, his excitement was palpable.

"Sure, why not?" Eric was coming home. She needed to know what they would be up against.

Will walked around the car and opened the passenger door, put one crutch next to the console, sat on the seat, then placed the other next to the door. He clicked the lock on the seatbelt. "Ready when you are."

"You don't drive often, do you?" she asked while she shoulder checked.

"You saw me behind the wheel." He slid the car seat back to give him more legroom. "You are right, I don't drive often."

"How come?" Tiffany glanced over at him. Most men she knew would never admit that they didn't get behind the wheel of a vehicle at every possible moment.

"When I'm tired, my leg reflexes aren't as quick as they should be. I'd rather leave the driving up to someone else and enjoy the view." He spread his hands as if offering her the blue sky on a platter.

"You have a driver?"

"Sure do. Lacy Turner came highly recommended."

Tiffany shook her head. "Little Lacy Turner. I taught her how to swim."

At the intersection of the highway and Elm Street Tiffany checked both ways before she proceeded.

"When we get to the mine site, you won't see much. The open house on Saturday is the final opportunity for people to try and grasp the scale of Rockwell and my company's commitment to the future of Apex and parts of the world."

"Here's the Saskatoon Berry Orchard." Tiffany smirked. "I don't suppose an Ontarian would consider this an orchard."

"I wondered why it was called that. I've had Saskatoon berry pie. Delicious."

"Toronto. Now Apex?" Tiffany pushed her jaw up with her left hand. He shrugged.

He asked her about homesteads visible from the highway. "Slow down. They know me. I've been here because I need to assess how we can be inclusive in the transportation to the work site." He waved to the security man who opened the gate.

"You don't mean that people in wheelchairs will be able to work here?"

"Why not?" His voice sounded tired. "Just because employees get around differently doesn't mean they aren't as capable."

"I'm sorry." She tapped him on his leg to get his attention. He turned toward her with his jaw set firmly, as if he wanted to say so much more but held it all clamped behind his lips. "It's just that I didn't think. I'm glad that Rockwell will be an inclusive employer."

He pushed his hand through his hair. "When I heard about the plan to build the community, I had to get on board. I want people to think and accept." He covered her hand with his and squeezed it. "Now drive on."

Tiffany turned her palm up and squeezed his hand.

"What are those?" She pointed to a cluster of machines.

"They're the drilling rigs for the caverns to supply the potash-rich brine to the plant for processing."

Tiffany surveyed the change in the landscape on the flat prairie with cranes swinging around steel where the skyline could be seen through the building skeletons. "That's a lot of investment for Rockwell."

"The quality of potash in this mine will make fertilizer accessible for more countries and sustain food production."

"Yes, okay, but what's it going to do for Apex? There are strangers in town already and you're expecting more." She closed her eyes and squished them tight, then opened them wide. "Look at all of the surveyors' stakes, and the heavy equipment. I remember when this was a canola field."

"This is why we need to move on the residential housing and why I need George's Plumbing." He tugged the seatbelt away from his chest. "Why haven't you heard about this? It's been in the news for months."

"Aunt Rosie told you, I'm an artist. I'm studying fine arts. I've been squeezing too many classes and labs into a short time."

"Perhaps one day you'll show me your portfolio." He touched her arm. "I'd like that." Tiffany felt the warmth from his tanned fingers on her sleeve, the well-trimmed nails and ring finger without any telltale jewelry or white mark where one might have been. "What about you?"

"Apex will be the showcase for the positive changes, rather than just the dark side of expansion. After the mine is built and a smaller labor force is required, Nosh, Nosh, and Crane's goal is that this town will be better off than it was before the resource development came." His words weren't particularly profound, nor were they boastful, but his confidence irritated her. This was her town, the place where she grew up. She'd just come home and it wasn't the same. "There has to be negative impacts. Where is the friendliness, the long term commitment to the community?" Her vocal cords were stretched taunt and issued shrill sounds like an untuned violin.

Instead of jerking his hand away, he stroked her arm. "You're right. Studies have shown when new money comes into a community some of residents leave. Small local stores can suffer. The barrier-free residential community and all the specialities that persons with disabilities require will be Apex's uniqueness."

"But the effects of mining on the environment is enormous." Tiffany didn't want to let this go. She felt like a bird with its beak on one end of a worm determined to nab the whole body from the wet ground.

"Rockwell has a solid reputation for obeying the rules that govern the way natural resources can be taken from the ground." His palm slid up and down her sleeve. She wanted to believe that everything would be all right even while watching earthmoving equipment dig, dump, and smooth, altering the landscape that had been part of Apex district possibly since the Ice Age.

"The employees work twelve-hour shifts away from family and friends for weeks at a time." She felt bereft when his hand lifted away from her arm and she heard his clothes rustle on the leather seat. "Because of research we understand how mental health problems develop when a mom or a dad can't say goodnight to their kids or share a hug with their partner." Will was silent for a minute. "Believe me, we've read the suicide statics. We don't want that here. That's why we're trying to stay ahead of the game. Nikki will prepare the housing for temporary workers, and I'm building the permanent future."

"I'm blown away by the impact this will have on Apex." Tiffany gripped Will's arm. "There won't be any chance of Rockwell cancelling or putting the project on hold?"

Will frowned. "There's always a chance. Resources depend on the world market price. Our homes and apartments are not dependent on the mine, but having potential jobs facilitates a faster completion."

Streaks of orange and red from the setting sun filled the sky. "I should get back."

"Sorry, I didn't mean to take up so much of your time."

"Not at all. I'm glad you've shown me this site. It adds context to past and future decisions." Tiffany drummed her thumbs on the steering wheel. *Eric has a level head. He'll help. I always think I have to fly solo and solve everything but I don't. This town is growing. This might be the time for George and Family Plumbing to form a partnership with another plumbing company.*

"Is there something you want to tell me about the tender?" Will broke through the noise of gravel ricocheting against the car body.

"No, no, there isn't, except I haven't read it. But I will. I was on my way to do that before this informative trip." Tiffany pressed her shoulder blades into the back of the seat. She didn't want to spoil anything for her dad yet. Right now, she hoped he would be well enough to follow through on his plans.

"Why don't you tell me about you and the George and Family Plumbing Company?"

"Not much to tell. Instead of going to the university when I completed high school, I decided to join my dad in the business he'd built up with his father. I went to the community college, accomplished my certification, and worked as a plumber for ten years and then, well, things changed and I left town for a couple of years, and now I came back for a holiday, and I'm right back in my rubber boots."

"Best looking boots I've seen on a plumber." Will chuckled.

"A woman in a stereotypical men's world has to find her way." She glanced at him. "What about you?"

"Much the same as you. Being a person with mobility issues in an abled world, I've had to find my own way. Would you mind dropping me at the town office? I'll pick up my cycle."

"No problem." She ran her tongue across her teeth and felt the grit from the dust created by the earthmovers. "Were you born with your less-than-perfect legs or did you have an accident?"

"Born," he answered matter-of-factly.

"Okay. Anything else you want to share about less than stellar mobility?" She lifted an eyebrow.

"No. After that I'm pretty much perfect." He shrugged and smiled.

"I'm glad," Tiffany said.

When she drove into the town office parking lot, the lights were off in the office and the parking spaces were empty. She touched his arm. "Everyone's gone."

"I have keys." He patted his pocket.

Tiffany watched him slip out of the car and position his crutches before he closed the door. Her throat worked against the familiar lump, because she sat there when he might have needed help. Shaking her head, she put the car into 'drive' after he opened the office door and turned on a light. He didn't need her.

Chapter 9

Was his answer important? Will wondered when he pedaled across the intersection. *Does it matter how or when someone becomes disabled? If I had known how to run, skip and jump, I may miss it but never having known I've adjusted to what I can do.* Hand-signaling left, he bumped over the intersection, then through his open gate. Setting his helmet on the cedar bench, he opened his seatbelt, and hoisted himself into a standing position. His neighbor was poking at the ground with her walking stick.

"Are you killing off one slug at a time, Mrs. Murphy?" Will's forward movement was slow but steady toward the small picket fence that separated small patches of grass in the Willow Lodge.

"Nasty invertebrate." Her head had a determined bend. "I'm counting the thirsty ones who drank my beer and drowned for their curiosity."

Will pushed his hand through his damp hair. "I could use a cold one right now."

"I have a few in my fridge. Come on over and join me." She looked at the sky. "It's past happy hour."

"If you don't mind body odor."

"Sweat's fine by me. It's the smell of urine that triggers my gag reflex." She placed her three-pronged cane on the stair and propelled her body up onto the deck. "We can sit on the patio. I'll get the libation."

Alternating crutch and foot placement between raised beds of new tomato plants, green-topped onions, corn stalks, winking pansies, and many-colored petunias required all of his concentration.

"Can you light the coils to keep those blood-sucking mosquitoes away? If it isn't one thing, it is another." Mrs. Murphy flung open the summer door and disappeared inside.

After maneuvering around pots of geraniums, Will lowered his butt onto a cushioned patio chair. He struck the match then held it until a curl of smoke rose. A hummingbird dipped into a red hibiscus. The door opened and Mrs. Murphy lifted her cane across the threshold, "Stay where you are. I have this under control." She reached into her apron pocket and brought out two bottles of beer and an opener. "I know these caps screw off, but I don't have the strength. Hope a bottle is good enough for you."

"Perfect. I'll have to find an apron like that. I'm always looking for ways of carrying stuff while maneuvering these sticks." He popped the cap off both bottles and set his neighbor's within her reach. She held it up. He clinked against her bottle, and they both drank deeply. He wiped his lips with the back of his hand. "Thank you."

"It's wonderful to share a drink with a neighbor. Poor old Joe, his ruined guts can't take any kind of booze." Squinting toward her garden, she said, "Those slimy plant-destroyers shouldn't be the only ones that share my beer."

"I'll return the favor. I'm trying to get to know my neighbors. Have you always lived in Apex, Mrs. Murphy?"

"No. Let me think. When did Noah dock the ark? If we listen to the first families in the area you'd think they came off that boat and straight onto the pier two by two." She closed her eyes. "Guess it was a few years after that."

"You attended school in Apex?"

"Yes, we were bussed from the Five Nations Reserve into The Village, as it was then."

"Any difficulties with the locals?"

"I can't say there was. I know the elders and my great-grandparents used to say that without their help the settlers would have never survived the first winter. Some of the people who came to this land were not prepared to live on the prairie. They accepted our help back then." She swallowed deeply. "They let us serve in the army and die, but when I was ready to marry I had to pretend to be some sort of European exotic creature. But my kids are half-white anyway. My daughter married into one of the first settler families so between my roots and her in laws, her kids are the first generation who can claim to be real residents." Mrs. Murphy looked at her beer bottle. "Loose lips."

"Believe me, your stories are safe with me." Will tipped the last of the cold beer into his mouth. "That hit the spot."

"Thanks again." Will gripped the arms and lifted his butt out of the chair. I'll provide the beverages next time."

"I'd like that." She raised her bottle in a salute to Will.

Looking around, he added, "You've created an oasis in your tiny outdoor space." The long dusk provided light for him to return to his apartment's flat, grassed area.

"Gardening keeps me in shape," Mrs. Murphy called. "You should try it sometime."

After his shower and he was dressed in clean jeans and T-shirt, he heard a knock followed by call from the patio door. "Woo-who, Will, are you there?" Will opened the drape across the patio door. Nikki was framed in the overhead light with her hand on her hip. Her white teeth flashed.

"Hey. What can I do for you?"

"You can invite me in and offer me something cold to drink." Nikki tipped her head to the side.

He stepped back into the apartment.

"Oh you have come down in the world. What's with the hounds' tooth sofa and the recliner? And the old-style TV?"

Will took in his surroundings. They were clean and comfortable. "Works for me."

"Be serious. You can't live here. It's uninspiring." She moved toward the scale model of the adaptive living complex. She leaned down and studied the detail of the miniature mobility scooters, the angle of the ramps. "You are a stubborn man. You could have been part of the Rockwell team. We are going to make a huge name for ourselves."

"I'm sorry you feel that way. Nosh, Nosh, and Crane value my expertise." Will moved toward the model like a protective parent.

"They should never have given you the prize. It's gone to your head."

He watched her hold up the crystal tower he'd received for innovation in workspaces. "You brought this with you," she said, her nostrils flaring.

It was after receiving his recognition that she cooled toward their relationship. They had been on different aspects of the design team, and his part had won. "I realized that to create change I focus on the specific needs of persons with disabilities. That's what I'm doing here."

She chuckled low in her throat while she moved with slow grace toward him. "Let's not argue, Will. I want us to be together again. We're a great team. I've missed you."

He shifted to a solid stance. "You should have thought of that before you decided to play on someone else's team. Where is what's-his-name now?"

She ran her finger along the edge of the slide in the model playground. "He doesn't matter. It's you, me, the mine, and our community plan." Looking into his eyes, her voice low and husky, she said, "Will, we can be together again in this back woods. There won't be too many distractions. You have to admit we work well together. Mr. Crane is adamant that the designed accessible housing development will be the example for all other potash companies around the world. Fame will come our way."

He felt her breath on his neck. Her fingers massaged his ear lobe. He leaned against her and felt her breasts press against his side. There were good memories. He hadn't been able to believe his luck when Nikki flirted with him, and then agreed to go out with him, and then she stayed over more than she went home. It had been months since he'd held Nikki, and his skin desired the memory of her touch and warmth. He laid his head against her and allowed her to run her hands over his body.

"Help me. Somebody help me," a frail female voice cried, as if from faraway.

Will pushed away from their embrace and slammed the patio door open wide. "Nikki, go quickly. You're faster than I am. Find out who is calling for help." Will reached for his crutches. "Nikki, now." Will gave her a firm push on the small of her back. "I'll be right behind you."

Nikki's long legs made quick work of crossing the patio and small yard.

"What do you see?" Will called from the deck.

"There is someone on the side of the road. Two dogs seem to be standing guard." Nikki slowly edged toward a bundle of clothing, and someone crying out in pain. "Nice doggies."

Will positioned his body for his fast swing-through gait. He dropped one hand, allowing the brown, male, Labrador Retriever to smell his palm. "We're here to help."

Nikki knelt beside a woman in a blue cardigan, jeans, and white runners lying in the yellow pool of streetlight.

"This is Pat." Nikki looked up at Will. "She's in a great deal of pain."

"Where does it hurt?" Will asked.

The strawberry-blond had a sheen of perspiration on her forehead, while her hand hovered over her right hip. "Here."

Will dialed 9-1-1 on his cellphone. "The First Responders will be here shortly."

Tiffany turned her back on the dusk, fortifying herself with a deep breath before entering her father's office. She had spent many hours in this room talking over detailed plumbing jobs. The florescent lights flickered and buzzed. The blue prints laid out in Dad's office were straight lines, with beautiful scripted numbers. Beauty aside, *What was he thinking?* This was a complex job. She paged through correspondence granting permission to hire foreign workers, the copies of advertisements he had placed in national and international newspapers. Was his brain affected by whatever else was going on? As if people were going to leave their homes and resettle in Apex, Saskatchewan. Tiffany couldn't deny the tingling excitement she felt while her fingertips followed the lines drawn through the various apartments and corridors. Her artistic mind followed the curves in the rooms, the spacious living area, the lowered cupboards, and the attention to details. The strengthened concrete between floors and notes for transporting the differently abled into their beds or baths told her that every detail seemed to be covered.

Tiffany automatically answered the annoying cellphone ring. Her mother again. She should bring some essentials when she came for her visit. Her father's electric razor. His favorite robe. Her mother's snuggly blanket for comfort when she curled up in a chair in Dad's room. Tiffany wrote furiously on a scrap of paper.

Another phone down the hall rang with the First Responders' distinct tone. "Sorry, Mom, got to run, the emergency phone is ringing." Tiffany leapt at the phone, instinct and habit focusing her attention. "George here."

"Personnel needed at Fir Street East. Woman injured."

"Responder Tiffany George on her way."

She ran to the closet to fetch her First Responder vest.

Tiffany's socks, steel-toed shoes, the carrier bag with barrier gloves, mask, and immediate first- aid supplies were in the closet. The captain would bring the oxygen, backboard, and automated external defibrillator. The grandfather clock ticked. The summer door slammed behind her, then she pounded across the driveway and jumped into her car. Reversing out of the drive, she sped with caution and was the second on the scene. Captain Ralph's crouched body blocked the patient's identity while he set up the oxygen. But the presence of the two chocolate labs, Tony and Cleo could mean that Tiffany knew who was injured. She placed her first-aid kit next to the woman then whispered. "Aunt Pat."

Will's friend Nikki stood on the sidelines with a phone pressed to her ear. Will held Aunt Pat's hand.

Tiffany knelt and the dogs, Tony and Cleo, crawled over and lay next to her. She slid her hand over their muzzles. "Everything's okay. We'll keep your mommy safe."

Aunt Pat opened her eyes. She gave a weak smile, then closed her eyes again and breathed deeply. Her aunt's right leg lay twisted. The general consensus was that it was broken.

Tiffany held on to her aunt's wrist and counted the heartbeats that registered through her body.

Will kept his eyes on Pat's face. His fingers laced through hers, and Tiffany saw Pat's knuckles turning white as she gripped his hand.

"We won't move her," Ralph said.

"The ambulance just turned onto Highway Thirty-nine," Nikki called.

"Hang in there, Pat." Ralph felt Pat's forehead. "The ambulance will be here in ten minutes."

Tiffany monitored Pat's pulse and occasionally witnessed a spasm of pain rip through her body. But it wasn't Tiffany's strength she searched for, it was Will's. What did he have that caused people to believe he held the key to understanding pain?

They heard the siren wail before they saw the ambulance. Tiffany led Tony and Cleo to the pathway, allowing the paramedics space to evaluate and move Pat. Ralph gave a brief description of the observations and actions they had taken. Will slid on his backside. Ralph gave him an arm then passed him his crutches.

Aunt Pat motioned for Will and then Tiffany to come over to the stretcher before they wheeled her into the back of the vehicle. "I'll never be able to thank you enough, sir."

Will merely dipped his head in acknowledgement.

"Tiffany," Pat said, "get this man's address and I'll be in touch. Take care of Tony and Cleo."

Tiffany bent and kissed her aunt's cheek. "You can count on me."

"What hospital is your dad in?"

"The Regina General."

"That's where I want to go."

The ambulance driver with a graying mustache, closed the back doors on the ambulance, rolled off his latex gloves and bagged them before climbing into the driver's seat. The siren wailed on the way out of town.

Ralph's safety vest gaped across his belly as he tidied his equipment. "Good to have you here." He nodded at Tiffany. "I see you haven't lost any of your skills."

"Thanks." The dogs leaned against Tiffany's thighs.

"You're coming to the fire hall for a debriefing." Ralph zipped up the equipment bag.

"As soon as I put these two in their yard."

Will shook Ralph's hand. "Good job. I wondered about emergency response time. Do you need my or Nikki's statement for your debriefing?"

"I have your statement about your first observations. Very astute, Will."

Tiffany gripped the leads and led the dogs over to where Nikki sat on a patio chair at Willow Lodge. "Thank you for helping my aunt."

"You're welcome," Nikki said.

Tiffany and the dogs returned to the street.

"You seem to turn up everywhere, Tiffany," Will said.

"In a small community, we're always ready." She held the dogs' leads. "Thanks for being available for Aunt Pat, she's special to me. I noticed that Nikki was the communication link."

"You don't miss much."

"I miss many things."

Will's crutch slipped on the gravel. The startled dogs strained against the leads.

Nikki ran toward them. "Take those dogs away before they hurt someone."

"Nikki, I'm fine. The dogs are upset." Will lowered his hand again toward the female dog. "Cleo is an appropriate name for Tony's partner."

"Tony, Cleo, in the car," Tiffany said.

"If you need help with them, I'll do what I can," Will said.

"Thank you." Tiffany drove away.

Chapter 10

Twelve inches separated Will's solid pine patio chair from Nikki's. "It's late for Mrs. Murphy to be out. She would have heard the siren. I hope she's okay."

"This is how it's going to be, isn't it?" Nikki reached for him. "You're in the middle of this community and these folks have needs, and you're going to keep track of them."

"Yes. So what are you getting at?"

"Where's the time for *us* in this equation?"

"Nikki, you gave up on us."

"I made a mistake. I know your talents." She put her hand on his thigh.

Will moved her hand away. "We'll work together, show each other respect. I'll help you, and I'll expect that you'll help me, but that's as far as I can go."

"It's that woman with her dyed-black hair, isn't it? I saw you looking at her."

"Nikki, it isn't anyone. I've got work to do. The days fly by."

"See you around, Will." Nikki straightened the crease in her designer jeans and brushed dust off her knees. She turned when a door in the next unit opened. "Looks like your neighbor is home."

"What's all the hubbub?" Mrs. Murphy leaned around the patio wall.

"Good luck with that work." Nikki strode away without a backward glance.

Will stood. "Why don't you pop over, and I'll fill you in."

He knew what it felt like to have the world speed by and always have to catch up.

Will went inside his apartment and opened the door for Mrs. Murphy.

"Come on in. Have a seat."

Mrs. Murphy walked with careful steps. Her cane provided stability.

"You haven't done anything to this place."

"I didn't bring much. I'm living minimally," Will said.

"You'd better not bring too many people in here or they'll be organizing a Good Will drive for you."

"Tell them I'm fine. My furniture is in Toronto until the new apartments are ready." Will swiped at beads of perspiration forming on his forehead while he imagined more mismatched furniture filling up the space he needed to move around.

"You believe the neighborhood will go ahead." Mrs. Murphy leaned toward the model.

"Of course. It's necessary. Companies are bringing temporary workers from other countries when we have available employees right here. All we have to do is to make sure they have a safe place to live as well as the necessary qualifications. But let me tell you about Pat."

"Oh, was it dear Pat? My, oh, my." Mrs. Murphy searched for a safe place to sit.

"Take this chair, Mrs. Murphy. I'll bring in a kitchen chair." Will patted the back of the recliner. "Would you like a glass of ice water?"

She slid her backside deep into the recliner.

Will placed the glass on a trolley then scanned his meager possessions. His work was important, not what he lived with or where. He had a bed, a bath, kitchen facilities, a TV, and Internet service. There wasn't much more he needed.

"Nikki and I heard a call and then the dogs were barking. When we looked out, we saw the dogs and heard someone calling for help. Nikki reached Pat first. It appears as if she's broken a hip."

"Those dogs won't like to be without Pat."

"Tiffany answered the First Responder call. She seems to know what to do."

"Oh yes, Tiffany. I forgot she came back into town."

"She seems to be an integral part of the community." Will wanted to know so much more about Tiffany.

"Grew up fine. Always a cooperative girl, and since she left Apex, according to Pat, Tiffany is a talented woman. She'll take care of Tony and Cleo, and the business, worry about her father, and now Pat, too. Her life in the city will have to sink to the bottom of her pile again. Poor girl."

Will found himself on the edge of his seat. He wanted to hear all about Tiffany. But he knew small communities. If he showed too much interest, they'd either warn her away, or begin to make wedding plans for the two of them. The first seemed the most likely, and the second possibility didn't frighten him as much as it should have.

"Where does Pat live? Perhaps I can help out. Take the dogs for a run. Feed them?"

"Over on Maple Avenue. Tiffany will set up a schedule to care for the dogs." She sipped her water as if it were champagne.

Mrs. Murphy didn't once suggest he shouldn't participate. His heart swelled.

As if she read the satisfaction on his face, she added the qualifier, "You know that some of the locals are going to wonder how you are going to look after two rambunctious dogs when you can't walk properly."

"I'll show them that I'm an Alpha dog."

"Lead dog. That I'll pay to see." She drank deeply from her glass and looked hard at Will. "Thanks for being there for Pat. I don't know what would have happened. She could have been run over by some of those new half-ton trucks that are all over town. I usually keep an eye on our street but I was at my granddaughter's." She fluffed her curled auburn hair.

Will leaned forward. "You changed your hair color. Looks striking, Mrs. Murphy."

"Thank you. I think it's time you called me Dorothy." She patted her curls again. "Any man who notices the little things deserves first-name basis."

Both of them turned toward the patio doors at the sound of a rumble of mufflers and then watched a Rockwell Mining Company truck speed by.

Dorothy pushed out of the chair then glanced toward the model of the new apartment complex and training center and then turned toward the map on the wall indicating the mining site. "I miss knowing who is in town. Before, we knew everyone's truck or car. We knew who we could count on. Now there are strangers all over town. It's hard to get used to."

"It's hard for me to understand knowing everyone in your area. I grew up in the city with strangers everywhere."

"That's sad," Dorothy said. "All I've been hearing on the news is potash this and potash that. With all these new mining sites supposed to be developed, do you think this one will really go ahead?"

"I hope so. The mine provides the impetus but this development can stand alone."

"If your neighborhood,"—Dorothy took a deep breath—"was ready now, there might be a job for one of your friends. They're looking for a new cook at the hotel restaurant. They can't keep staff because the young people go to the oil fields and now the mines for the money and then they buy trucks."

"How do you know this?" Will had his phone ready to tap in the details.

"New sign at the post office this morning." She shrugged her shoulders. "You are new in town. If you want to know any births, deaths, or anything in-between, it is on a bulletin board outside the post office."

Will shook his head. "I thought these things would be on the town's home page."

"That is our home page," Dorothy said.

"Of course it is," Will said. "I just may have someone in mind that would be able to cook in a restaurant."

"While you're at it, find a plumber and plumber's assistant because Tiffany can't stay here and take over Fred's business. Just because it has been in the family forever doesn't mean it's her responsibility." Dorothy pointed a finger at him.

"I think that Fred might have something to say about that."

Dorothy harrumphed. "Don't ask why Tiffany shouldn't stay, I don't gossip. And it was a couple of years ago and I hear she's done well in the city."

"I know she's studying fine art and she told Rosie she has a commission." His antennae was up. She may provide more details. He fidgeted with the cap on his bottle of water.

"There you go. She's got to go back and be the new Tiffany. I'd better be getting back now."

She stopped at the map on the wall showing the mine site. "Right here is where I had my first kiss. Guess everything has to change."

"That it does. Potash is concentrations of potassium found in salt beds from an ancient but shallow inland sea."

"So not the tears that flowed over the years?" Her face crumpled and her blue eyes watered. "All that was such a long time ago."

"Who can know for certain?" Will said.

"In this life we don't get away without tears. At least the mined potash should help food shortages and perhaps stop some tears of hunger."

Will was stunned by her philosophical answer.

"Don't forget about that cook, though. I enjoy going to the hotel for meals and we need some new blood in that kitchen." Dorothy elegantly maneuvered her three-pronged cane to the door.

After she left, Will opened his contact information in his cell phone and scrolled down to his childhood friend, Paula Day.

He typed a text message. *You still looking for a chef position? Would applying to be a cook in a hotel restaurant work? Hugs. Will.*

The next morning, coffee cup in hand, Will scanned the design for the portable houses, hockey rink, cafeteria, and the gym at the mine site. Even though the politicians and businessmen quickly promoted the virtues of a boom town they often ignored the many trade-offs. He wanted a place for people to come and grow their businesses. *To grow themselves and to find love. Now where did that come from? What is it about this place that has me thinking about love? About something permanent?* Will changed into his riding gear. *There isn't anything a ride along the trail won't fix.* With his helmet in place, he closed and locked the patio doors. Each time he prepared to ride, the positioning of his crutches, his legs, his rhythmic movement on the pedals became easier.

He rode on the brand new pavement courtesy of Rockwell Mining. The road wound past the post office. He stopped and craned his neck toward the bulletin board searching for the poster about the chef/cook job at the hotel.

"Can I help you?" asked a woman with a baby strapped into a baby carrier. She looked at him suspiciously. "Are you here with the mining people or are you looking for part-time work?"

"No, not part of the mining directly. I have a friend who is a chef and might be interested in coming to Apex. I was told there is a poster advertising a position at the restaurant."

She removed the tacks and handed the poster to him. He snapped a photo of it. When Paula got back to him, he could send her the information. "An apartment in the hotel comes with the position. Fantastic."

"I'm hoping enough people move to Apex and a new school will be built."

"I know a school has been discussed as part of the new neighborhood. We want permanent residents settling in Apex."

"You go, man. I hope they get it right. But now we have to worry about strangers." She clutched her daughter to her chest.

"There is that too. Thanks for your help."

"That's why we live in Apex. We help people," she said in a singsong voice to sooth her baby. "Cool bike. Going somewhere special?"

"Just down the trail." He positioned his hands on the pedals.

"Watch out for cougars."

"Really?"

"Yes, that's the talk around the coffee shops this morning."

"I'll have to whistle while I wheel." He saluted against his helmet and pedaled toward the entrance to the trail.

Chapter 11

After the First Responders de-briefing, Tiffany ran around the old high school track with Tony and Cleo. The lights from the street gave an eerie feeling to the open space. She smelled burning wood from an outdoor fire pit. The dogs obeyed Tiffany's commands and were anxious to return to their house. They sniffed in every room for their mistress. "She's not here." Tiffany ran her hand down their backs. "She'll be back. Don't worry." They leaned against her for comfort. Tiffany called Pat's neighbour who agreed to check on the dogs early in the morning. After a final kiss from Tony and Cleo, she locked Pat's door, made sure the gate was secure, and then climbed back into her car, drove back home, and quickly gathered her father's shaving kit, the dressing gown, and her mother's comfy blanket.

During the drive back into the city, Tiffany rolled down her window and turned the radio up. She could not fall asleep at the wheel. Life was suddenly very complicated. While she was on the highway, her phone rang. She stopped on the shoulder and listened to her mother's voice message. "Visiting hours are over. Just drop the things at Beth's back door. She's at the hospital visiting with Dad and me and then we're going for something to eat."

Tiffany yawned, found Beth's address in her contact list, and activated her GPS. If Dad were worse, Mom wouldn't be leaving the hospital.

On the way home, the clock turned over to a new day. When Tiffany drove past the place where she first met Will Cleaver, she wished again for a reason to stop, massage a muscled leg, and have warm lips pressed against hers in appreciation. Putting her fingertips to her lips, she recalled the kiss in Willow Lodge and his hand on her thigh this afternoon. His brown eyes sparkling with confidence in his abilities. His passion for Apex. Will had been her bright light since she'd arrived home.

The next morning after she checked on her father's condition and still hadn't heard from her brother, Tiffany drove to Aunt Pat's. Tony and Cleo bounded up to the fence and barked their greeting as soon as she closed her car door. "Who wants to go for a run along the trail?"

The dogs yipped and yelped when Tiffany clipped their leads onto their collars. They ran along the tree-lined streets. She remembered picking Saskatoon berries with her gran beside the big rock she had thought of as a dinosaur back. She squeezed her shoulder blades recalling the wasp sting that had burned for weeks, and when her foot skidded on a pebble, slimy Paul's grade three face came to mind while he pelted her with stones and called her every horrible name in his puny mind, and she had run away.

She had done what others often do after the day that Collin had driven into the driveway and parked behind the plumbing van. That afternoon her thoughts had been full of color swatches for bridesmaid dresses when he held her by the shoulders, and spoke slowly as if he were speaking to someone who was a welding torch without a flint lighter. "Tiffany, I'm only saying this once. I'm not going to marry you. Keep the ring, but I'm not putting on the matching wedding band. We're done." She had stared at the hair growing out of his nose, the large pores on his cheeks, his eyes that were too close together. He went on and on about how he didn't want his wife to be a plumber or a business owner. He wanted his wife to pay attention to him and to have babies. She had thrown a left punch to his gut and then she had run.

But now it was different, she watched Cleo and Tony's tails disappear in and out of the brush on the side of the trail. While surveying the surroundings, over a dip in the road she recognized Will's handcycle. The dogs turned toward the tires crunching on gravel. Tony let out a warning bark while Cleo's ears went down.

"Come," Tiffany commanded. An alert Tony and Cleo returned to her side. "Sit." She stepped into the long grass. Wrapping the leads tight around her palms, she watched the top of Will's sleek black helmet rather than look at his open face, his deep brown eyes, and his inviting lips. He came closer and gradually rolled the big wheels to a stop.

"Going my way?" Will's hands rested on the brake levers.

"No, looks as if I'm going where you came from." She pointed behind him.

"Any cougars down the part of the path you were on?"

"You're not afraid of a prowling eight-foot, one hundred and thirty pound wild pussy cat, are you?" She swayed.

"No, just concerned for its safety. I wouldn't want to frighten it with my speed and prowess. The advertisement said these bikes are swift and silent."

"They may be silent on pavement but Tony and Cleo heard you."

The dogs' tails wagged and they whimpered for their leads to be loosened.

"How is Pat doing?" Will asked.

"The nursing unit receptionist told me she is having all the preliminary tests for a hip replacement. She'll be needing help with these two for a while."

"When you set up a group to care for them, I'd like my name added."

"Thank you. There will be a private Facebook page and a clipboard near the door to sign the dogs in and out." She ruffled Cleo's coat then reached into her pocket and handed the dogs a treat.

"Could you lengthen their leads so they become more familiar with my scent? Then they won't try to defend their territory against me, especially when I have my walking sticks."

"Tony, say hello to Will. Go gentle."

Tony got down on his belly and wriggled forward.

Will extended his hand palm up. Even though his riding gloves covered most of his hand his fingertips were open to Tony's nose. "Remember me? Why don't you tell your lady friend that I'm okay?"

Tony looked up at Will, sniffed the bike tires, then nuzzled his leg in the canvas cradle.

Tiffany called, "Tony, come."

The dog pushed on its haunches, rose, then meandered back to Tiffany's side.

She lengthened Cleo's lead. "Cleo, say hello to Will. Go gentle."

Cleo repeated Tony's action. Will extended his hand. Cleo nudged his palm then bumped his side close to the seat belt.

Tiffany jerked the lead. "Cleo, gentle."

"It's okay she's fine." Will ruffled the fur between Cleo's ears, then ran his hands over her back. "Good girl," he murmured. "They're well trained." Will looked up at Tiffany.

"One of the other many things that happen in a small place. Pat couldn't handle both pups during a training class, so I helped. They're large dogs and we don't want anyone to be frightened of them, nor do we want anyone to hurt them."

"So you're not afraid of cougars while running the trail?" He was running his hand down Cleo's front legs.

"If cougars are in town, it's because Rockwell is disturbing their natural habitat." She clicked her tongue, and the dogs came to her side.

"Are you sure? You've been away." Will's posture changed, as if she had insulted him. "Change comes at a cost."

"Sometimes the price is too high." Her shoulders squared and she stuck her chin forward.

"There are always consequences for actions." He straightened his helmet. "The world needs fertilizer for food. Everyone will have to do the best they can to adjust."

"Why are you so high and mighty all of a sudden?" With the dogs at her side, she watched him put his hands on the pedals. He looked as if he could crack a few molars the way his jaw was set.

"Much of what is going to happen is good. Why can't you see that?" Will began to pedal his trike along the path.

"Because I'm scared," she called after him, then turned to run in the opposite direction.

"Wait, Tiffany. You carry a cell phone. Can we exchange numbers for emergencies?"

She stopped. "I suppose." While he attempted to pedal backward, she and the dogs moved forward, closing the gap. "Especially with tales about cougars." She gave him her number, which he added to his contacts. She entered his number. The dogs strained at their leads.

"Gotta run. These guys have been patient." After half a block, Tiffany turned and Will was moving slowly along the path. She wondered what made him expend so much energy just to ride. He couldn't see much beyond the vegetation on the edge of the trail. His rhythmic push of the hand pedals continued until the bike slid into a pothole. She considered running down the path. With her help he'd be on his way, but she didn't. Instead, she allowed the dogs to sniff at the roots of bushes.

The harder he pushed, the more it dawned on her that he wasn't very experienced. He was like her. They were both struggling to move forward with the tools and talent they had. He wanted to be in the outdoors so he was. She wanted to make art and now she did.

Tony and Cleo spread out on either side of her, their noses in the air, but so very well behaved. "You have been so very good." Tiffany reached into her pocket and handed them another treat. When the chomping stopped, she said, "Ready, set, go."

Bits of gravel scattered as they ran along the path.

"This is some pot hole," Will said to the birds rustling in the bushes. He flexed his abdominal muscles and engaged every inch of his core power, leaning and pedaling out of the hole. He swiped the back of his hand over his forehead, heard happy dog yelps. When he turned, Tiffany continued running away from him. He no longer heard her feet on the trail, and it was as if Sprite Tiffany flew in the opposite direction. While he pressed his palms on the pedals again and picked up speed, he heard the dogs' barking fade in the opposite direction.

Clouds of dust drifted above the bushes flanking the trail. Will heard the roar of diesel engines before he reached the hill and saw the convoy of vehicles crossing the intersection of grid roads ahead. He always knew that an architect had to get on the ground level to understand what was happening. The serenity of the trail was broken.

He had a choice. Either he could take his chances and cross the path between these heavy, moving trucks and risk being squashed, or he could turn around and go back home. Unless they saw him, his chances could be slim to none.

He thought about the bikes in the city with their long whipping antenna flying the red-alert flag. He should have every piece of safety equipment available. He knew that today his thoughts were running with the woman with black spikes in her hair who ran with the dogs. While he surveyed the trail and calculated his method of turning the cycle around, he laughed at the idea of running with wolves. Tony and Cleo were nothing like their wolf ancestors. The sparrows were kind enough to mock him from the cover of the trees.

The tires on the heavy vehicles sent vibrations through his handgrips. The economic growth driven by the large-scale potash mine impacted the community, even though Apex's mayor and councillors worked with Rockwell and Nosh developing the appropriate infrastructure, policies, and regulations. The elected officers wanted what was best for their community. They did their homework and trusted. Trust. Something that was hard to come by in the big cities.

Why did he think that just because the town was small that it would foster trust? He pedaled harder. That was almost like saying that all differently abled persons were the same. Generalizations caused trouble.

A ground squirrel ran ahead of him. *Don't worry, little fellow, you're a whole lot faster than I am.*

Will turned back onto the street, signaled, and cycled back to his apartment.

Once inside, he stripped off his clothes. He bumped into the bathroom doorframe, again. Yesterday's bruise was blue, and the previous day's was purple. The mural of stormy skies on his thigh was quite striking.

The pressure from the hot shower gave him a good massage. There wasn't much more he could ask for, except to be in Tiffany's company again. He was intrigued by her. He liked the way her black hair spiked all over her head. They say you choose a partner who resembled the image that you viewed in the mirror. Other than the black hair, they did not look alike. Her eyes were a perfect cloudless summer day.

He imagined cradling her heart-shaped face in his palms. His fingers ached to touch her full lips.

His stomach rumbled. His late breakfast was hours ago. He had to deal with real life. Did he want to cook? His phone beeped a message. It was from Paula. She thanked him and asked him to check out the restaurant for her. She had filled out an application online and crossed her fingers for an interview.

Could she stay with him if she scored an interview? He had the spare room. She'd been a friend since summer camps. *Of course,* he texted back. He dialed Lacy. "Can you spare a few minutes and drive me to the hotel so I can have dinner?" He listened to her list of chores. "Whenever you can . . . an hour is perfect. See you then." With a cold beer by his side, he answered emails and listened to the local news.

He retweeted the town's announcement about the Saturday information meeting, then he read his Facebook news feed. While he strolled through the common room and out the front door, he heard dogs barking. Tony and Cleo were jostling for attention on the ends of their leads but it wasn't Tiffany trying to control them, it was a teenage boy with a thin sheen of a potential moustache. "Hello, Tony, Cleo." The dogs assumed the down position. Will extended his hand to the young man hanging onto the leads. "Will Cleaver."

"Andrew. Sorry, can't shake your hand, don't want to let go. If anything happens to these two, I'll be the one sleeping in the doghouse. Not that these two do." He shuffled from one red Converse sneaker to the other.

"Are you a skateboarder?"

"How'd you guess?"

"The worn parts on your sneakers could be from kicking. Not that I've ever accomplished it but I've seen many boarders in my day."

"You've designed that new part of town. Would you consider a proper skate park for us? You know, part of the building new facilities and users will follow philosophy?" He smirked.

"Great idea. Why don't you come out to the town meeting on Saturday in the community hall and you'll see if I've come up with the right ideas."

"Can't, I've got drum lessons."

"Then drop by tomorrow sometime and you can give me your suggestions."

"Man, that'd be cool but the old fogies here will never agree. They make us move our half-pipes every time we get too noisy."

"We can try. You never get anywhere unless you try."

Just then Lacy tapped on the horn. She had parked her brown nondescript car along the grass road allowance. While she crossed the street to his SUV, her ponytail swung like a metronome.

"My ride is here." Reaching into his wallet, Will removed a business card. "My cell number is on here. Call me. We'll set up a time, Andrew."

Andrew tried to reach for the card but the dogs stood and tugged on the lead. "Could you put it in my jacket pocket for me?"

"Absolutely." Will reached round and tucked the card into his jean jacket pocket.

"Hi, Lacy, be right there."

"Boss, you don't even look where you're walking." Lacy held the door open, and Will climbed in and cinched up the seat belt and turned to Lacy. "Don't need to. These sticks and I are a team."

Lacy started the car. "You do know that you won't get much more then burgers and fries? The cook left in a huff so the waitstaff are cooking."

"Perfect." He waved to Andrew who was being led down the street by the two large dogs. "You know most people in town, Lacy. Any ideas about who will hire new staff for the hotel restaurant?"

"Probably the owner. I just wish we'd get a good cook who'd make some of those recipes I see on TV. Don't suppose all those people coming to build houses and work in the mines want that kind of food, though."

"Lacy, don't assume. With the Food Network many people want to expand their taste buds' experiences."

"Here we are. I can come back in an hour. My wash will be done."

"An hour will be fine. If I find another ride, I'll let you know."

"Oh no, please don't do that. I really want to be your driver."

"Okay, you got it. See you in an hour."

Chapter 12

Will climbed the wooden plank steps, opened the heavy glass door, and entered a room that held on to its frayed elegance in the flocked wallpaper, copies of the old masters paintings, and crystal chandeliers. Now the dark tables with carved legs were bare except for condiments and smudged serviette holders. The menu was on a chalkboard. When he thought of Paula, his lips smacked together by reflex. He recalled her cordon bleu, her spinach pie, and her decadent brownies. Residents of Apex would be in food heaven if Paula were hired.

Will sat at the far end of the dining room and surveyed the other diners. He didn't recall meeting the owners, but perhaps tonight would be the time. He could gauge if they would be receptive to minimal adaptations. The lodge had a great common kitchen, and he wondered if he could find a way to have basic short order or prep cooks trained and the residents could benefit by sampling the prepared meals. He needed community support for this type of undertaking. Yes, the mine was bringing commerce but he wanted to generate soul. *Sure, there I go again. Will the Soul Whisperer.*

Will photographed the dining room and pressed 'send' on a message to Paula. If only he could get a photo of the kitchen. *If I don't ask, I'll never know.* He hung his leather jacket on the back of the chair and maneuvered between the tables. He said hello to an elderly couple sipping coffee with their cookies. He knocked on the kitchen door.

"Come in," a young woman called.

He entered, immediately noting the flour on her face, the frazzled expression. He understood the pressure of a busy kitchen. "Maybe I can help you. I can chop and clean up. I worked in a kitchen when I went to high school."

"Be my guest." She swept up flour. "The guys in the bar want burgers."

"I'm Will Cleaver." He held out his hand.

"I've heard about you. My mother's been talking about your big ideas."

He raised his eyebrows. "And?"

"I don't listen when she yaks about that stuff." She shrugged. "She said you were a handicapped guy who thinks he can change our town."

Will tapped his crutch on the floor. "At least people remember me." He reached for an apron hanging on a hook, then scrubbed his hands in the sink. "Let's get those burgers made. I'll assemble the buns, lettuce, pickles, cheese, and you fry the meat." He looked around. "Let's put some packaged potato chips on the plates instead of fries and that way we'll get the food out faster."

"Good idea. Not sure what Mrs. Leman will say, but, hey, what can she do? Fire us." The young girl snickered when the meat patties splattered grease on the hot grill.

Will leaned his crutches in a corner, he held on to counters on his way over to the cooler. "What's your name?"

"Sydney, like the Australian city. People call me Aussie though, cuz I'm going there one day real soon."

"Okay, Aussie, I need you to promise that you'll open the cooler for me if the door closes. I'm not the steadiest when carrying things, and I'm assuming the fixings are in here."

"You got it, man."

Will stuffed a couple of tomatoes and an onion into one pocket, a jar of mayo into the other, and with a head of lettuce under his arm like a football, he stepped over the ledge and closed the door behind him. "I'm out."

"Good, now hurry up. These babies are done."

Will wielded a knife and sliced, then spread each bun and assembled them ready to receive the meat patties. "Ready when you are."

"Wow, you're good." Aussie flipped the burgers onto the buns.

Will ripped open bags of potato chips and piled them onto each plate.

Aussie balanced the plates on her arms and headed out the door.

While she was gone, Will took out his phone and snapped a couple of pictures. The place had potential.

He heard the door open.

"I just knew this would happen. More orders. Can you stay a while longer?"

"Sure, if you make me one of those burgers too."

Aussie brought eight patties out of the cooler. "These are double burgers. And they want a dill pickle. Jeez." She rolled her eyes. "I sure hope you're planning to add a restaurant to that plan of yours. If more of these working guys come to town, I'll never keep up."

"Not in my plan specifically, but again if there are customers and a permanent base then someone will open a restaurant."

"Don't let my boss hear you say that, she'll throw a hissy fit."

"Aussie!" A shrill voice reverberated over the sizzling and chopping.

"Mom, it's true. You always say there isn't room for anyone but you."

Will put his knife down. He couldn't chop onions without his full attention.

He turned slowly and leaned against the counter, watching the woman in her exercise gear stride into the kitchen and stay well away from the grill. She stopped in front of him, put her hands on her hips, drew her eyebrows together. "And what are you doing here, Mr. Cleaver?"

"Mom, what does it look like? He's helping me out. Ryan didn't turn up again and there are all those construction workers wanting to eat. I called your cell but you must have been in the middle of your meditation. Will, the burgers are ready." Will slid the plates evenly along the counter. Buns piled with lettuce, tomatoes, and onions. Mounds of chips and dill pickles on the side.

"You know who I am but I'm at a disadvantage." He wiped his hands on a towel and extended it.

"The owner of this hotel. Mrs. Leman and obviously Sydney's mother."

He waited for her to continue. He wasn't sure which way this conversation might go. And he didn't want to antagonize her.

The door banged open again. "Will, I'll make your burger now. There's only one order and mom's here to help, so you may as well eat."

Will untied his apron, then retrieved his crutches. "I look forward to this. You're good on the grill, Aussie."

"Obviously you've filled a spot for Sydney but you must realize that we can't allow just anyone to come into our kitchen."

"Of course. I have had experience or I wouldn't have offered."

"Mom!" Aussie said .

Mrs. Leman stepped aside. "When you have a few minutes, I'd like to hear about your business and how you see the future."

He looked at his watch. As soon as he sat down, he dialed Lacy. "Lacy, I'll need another forty-five minutes if that's okay?"

He listened to her talk about her schedule. She had said forty minutes, tops. She wanted to be back home because the new episode of *Bones* was coming on.

"Got it." He hung up and chuckled.

Aussie brought out utensils and a plate piled high with a double burger and chips with a pickle on the side. Will's stomach rumbled. "Sorry to bug you, but could you bring me a large beer, please?"

"Roger in the bar will bring it. I'm not old enough."

A man with a round belly placed a beer stein on a coaster. "You weren't specific so I just brought you what's on tap. You should have come into the bar and saved us all some steps." He turned and hurried away.

"Never thought of it. Next time," he called before taking a deep swallow of his beer.

Mrs. Leman came into the dining room and checked her reservation book. She had changed into a long skirt, sparkly top, had styled her hair and transformed into the hostess. She approached his table. "Sorry, Mr. Cleaver. I was taken by surprise." She threw up her hands. "That daughter of mine."

He dropped a chip back onto his plate. "Have a seat."

She sat, half-turned toward him and half toward the door. "If I can't hire a chef soon, I'm afraid I'll have to close the restaurant."

He cleared his throat. "That would be too bad especially since the town is going to get even busier." Will eyed his food, getting colder by the minute. "Mind if I eat?"

She waved her hand, giving him permission. "I can't keep staff. The trades are paying more than I can afford."

"Soon families will move here and that will open up the possibilities."

"I've put up advertisements." She twirled the saltshaker. "I've had a few inquiries but there isn't much suitable housing for a family. I've got a small place in the hotel but it's for one person."

"We're working on housing for families."

"Yeah, but not for normal people." Her lips formed a tight straight line.

"Of course they're normal." Will tossed back the last of his beer.

"The way my sister told me, they are a bunch of cripples."

Will's chin went up and he took a deep breath. "There are more appropriate descriptions required these days."

Mrs. Leman reached over and touched his elbow. "I apologize."

"Thank you." He pushed his plate to the side. "I have a friend I've told about your advertisement. She is a graduate of the Culinary School in Ontario."

"Why would she come out to a back water like this?"

"I'll let you ask her those questions. Check out her CV. You might be surprised." He heard a car horn. "My ride's here." He put money on the table. "Tell Aussie to keep the change for her travel plans."

Will concentrated on his gait on his way out the door. He wished others didn't look at a person with a disability as stupid. Sometimes he still felt like the six-year-old boy with other kids watching him leave the classroom ahead of everyone else so he arrived at the library or the gym at the same time as the rest of the class.

"Get a move on, Mr. Cleaver, I haven't got all night," Lacy called out of the car window.

"Lacy, I might have to buy you a personal video recorder or find another driver." Will climbed into the seat.

"What's that?" She tapped her fingers against the steering wheel.

"You can tape and then watch programs on your schedule rather than during the TV timeslot." Will settled into his seat.

"All I need is for you to buckle up." Lacy put the car into 'drive' and only paused at the stop sign.

"Lacy, that was a stop sign."

"Do you see an RCMP car anywhere around here?" She frowned at him. "I know they've left town. I just passed the cruisers."

"Is there anything you don't know?"

"Hmmm, let me see? Why don't you drive?"

"I can drive. Most often I prefer not to because my reflexes aren't quick enough at high speeds and I like to save my energy for other things."

"You work well with your hands. I had a picture message from Aussie and you were chopping onions."

"There really aren't any secrets." Will shook his head.

"Oh, is that supposed to be a secret? Like the confidentiality you talked about?" Her voice shook.

"No, Lacy. We're good." Will unbuckled. "Here we are." He opened the door, turned, and slid out of the vehicle. "You'll make it home even if you stop at all the stop signs. Drive carefully." He closed the door.

Chapter 13

The secondary highway and its distance to the city provided Tiffany with time to think. The traffic was sparse. She was picking her brother Eric up at the airport and then taking him to the hospital. She thought about how to prepare him for what he would see. Was there a way? She should have snapped a quick photo to show him Dad's present condition. Too late now. Eric would have to experience the changes in their dad as she had.

She loved the light in the afternoon with its play of shadows. The leaves on the trees were bright green. Their stems were strong, indicating they could resist a stiff breeze.

Tiffany missed her brother. He had been there when she created paintings and sculptures. He hadn't played hockey or football. His asthma made running outdoors tough for him. They played school or store. Eric had imagined grand schemes to increase their sales. He could make change faster than the computerized toy cash register, and even though he was two years younger, he played the role of the math teacher while she taught art to their dolls and stuffed animals.

Tiffany had always followed her father around while Eric stayed in the house with their mom. Whenever he tried to accompany their dad, he needed his rescue inhaler. Long before Apex had established the First Responders, Eric had forgotten his inhaler while on a plumbing call. Dad panicked and called 911. Mom arrived before the ambulance and brought him around. Eric had to go to hospital for observation anyway and was banned from future plumbing jobs. After that, Tiffany was Dad's helper and the unspoken heir to the plumbing business.

It was Eric who had begun doodling a design for the fasteners after listening to the frustration over damaged furnaces and hot water heaters because of flooding. His designs, along with Tiffany's innate understanding of metals and plastics and their father's courage and determination, led to the bracket fastener prototypes that were designed. It seemed that even though it appeared relatively easy, engineers hadn't made the connection. They just kept trying to keep water out of places rather lifting the important mechanics off the floor. The George Family prospered, and Eric went off to the university and became a marketing guru.

Tiffany signaled toward the airport road and parked. Glancing at the time, she jogged into the arrival area and waited facing the escalator that would bring Eric to her side. She waved at him while he descended then raced toward him.

"How's my little sister and all of her fish and sea creatures?" He wrapped her in a bear hug.

She snuggled into his chest. He may be her younger brother, but he was taller and since he'd been away, he'd filled out. For a few short moments she felt as if she wasn't alone. That things would work out. As a family they would find a way.

She took a deep breath and said, "The aquarium is on hold. My mentor, Owen, has been texting but I haven't answered him. I wanted us to have a plan."

"Don't worry, Tiff, we'll solve this. We'll move step by step toward a resolution." Eric reached behind her and folded his fingers into the palm a brunette, standing close. "Rebecca, meet Tiffany. Tiffany, Rebecca."

Tiffany recognized the total absorption of a woman in love. Rebecca's eyes followed his every move. "Hello, welcome to Regina," Tiffany said.

"Hi, Tiffany, I feel as if I know you. Eric has told me so much about you."

Rebecca giggled, and Eric kissed her on the forehead.

"Thanks for the heads-up." Tiffany punched Eric on the shoulder. "There's your old duffle bag coming down the shoot."

They shuffled toward the carousel. Eric slipped through people guarding their turf at the front of the line. He quickly snagged his duffle bag and then a green hard-shelled case. "Tiff, we've rented a car, so we'll pick up the keys and we can get going. If you wouldn't mind meeting us at the hotel, Rebecca and I will register and then you and I can drive over to the hospital together. Rebecca and I talked about this, and we both feel it is better to introduce her after I've had a chance to see Dad and Mom."

Rebecca went up a notch in Tiffany's eyes. "Sounds great. Especially since you are going to be a total surprise. Have you chosen a hotel?"

"The Holiday Inn Express. Rebecca can walk to the mall until she's familiar with the city."

Tiffany grinned. Her little brother had grown up. He was going to be in a hotel with someone who cared for him, and she was going home to the business alone. She plastered a smile on her face. "That's nice."

Eric raised his eyebrows at her. "Rebecca's important to me. She's supporting me and by extension you and our parents."

"I know," Tiffany said. "I thought that you and I would go over Dad's contract details. I don't know if George and family can honor the tender or if we should just back out now." A sense of loss seemed to hover over her head.

Eric laid an arm across her shoulders. "We will. I promise I won't let you handle this all alone. I know you finally have a new life away from Apex, and I'll try my best to help you resist the urge to return just because of family responsibilities."

She knew he meant what he said but he hadn't seen the scope of the plumbing job or met Will Cleaver or saw the hope in some of the locals' eyes now that they knew prosperity would be coming to Apex. It was a whole lot easier to say that all would be well when you just flew in from Calgary with someone who adores you than it was to have witnessed your father spitting up blood and lying in a hospital bed with monitors tracking his every breath and heartbeat.

"Okay, Eric," she said, "I accept your assurance that I will be able to return to my life as I know it. Let's get this show on the road. You remember the way?"

"This is Regina." He smirked.

Tiffany thought about Eric, and now Rebecca, and she included Will in the armature for the future of George and Family Plumbing. Tiffany George, as metal sculpture artist, would weld the pieces together, similar to attaching fins on her sculptured school of fish for her mural.

Tiffany drove to the center of downtown and parked in front of the hotel doors. The gentle rock music soothed her while she waited. When her phone binged a text, a knot of guilt formed in her stomach. She was a lot later returning to the hospital but she had wanted to surprise Mom and Dad. She opened the text. Will. How did he do that? How did he know that she was considering him as part of the skeleton of their plan? She read the text: *The dogs like me. I rode and they ran beside me but not too far. You are not the only dog whisperer.*

She smiled and texted back. *How many treats did you toss their way?*

Aren't we supposed to give them the whole bag?

She could imagine Cleo and Tony rotund when Pat came home from hospital. *No, and I'm assuming you are joking.*

That I am.

Waiting for Eric to go to the hospital.
Eric?
Brother.
Nice to have family at a time like this.
Yeah.
When you see Aunt Pat tell her the dogs are well loved, he replied.
Thanks. She'll be pleased. TTYL.

Tiffany leaned against the headrest and thought about her artistic use of an old technique with a modern twist. Her childhood friend Cheryl had badgered Tiffany to use her artistic ability with metal after Collin had broken their engagement. While Tiffany worked with copper out of discarded hot water heaters and sculpted with her ball peen hammer, she pictured Collin's finger with the promise ring they exchanged. She had thought about his big teeth being popped out of his mouth when she used a punch hammer. She had imagined his heart stopping when she used a dead blow hammer. But mostly she had recalled feeling as if he had hit her heart with the tools of her trade. Now she could thank Collin for being the catalyst for her new life.

There was a rat-tat-tat on her window, and Tiffany jumped.

Eric called, "Let me in, or I'll blow your door down."

Tiffany hit the unlock button. "You frightened me."

"I stood here for a minute, hoping you'd feel my vibration but, alas, you were somewhere far away."

"I was in my happy place." She stretched and touched the interior roof of her car.

"Art again?" He buckled his seat belt.

"You got it." Tiffany started the car and drove down the street. "Back to reality. Mom's going to be miffed because I've taken so long to come to the hospital and haven't texted her." She passed him her phone. "While I drive, would you text Mom and tell her I'm on my way? Ask her if she'd like anything from the coffee shop."

"Are you sure you don't want to tell her I'm coming with you? We don't want other emergencies." Eric began texting.

"If there is an emergency then Mom and Dad are in the right place." Tiffany snorted.

"Black humor prevails."

"Sometimes it's necessary for survival." Tiffany glanced at Eric's thumbs tapping in the message. "How long can you stay?"

"Surprisingly, as long as I need to." Eric put the phone on the dash.

"Really, why?" Tiffany glanced quickly at Eric. Was there something he wasn't telling her? Did he lose his job?

"I can work anywhere in my type of business. I've brought my laptop, tablet, and of course smartphone. I'm not an artist who needs a whole shop full of equipment. Are you sure you wouldn't want to work with something smaller, say pencil drawings?" He chuckled.

"Eric." Tiffany hoped he was teasing. "I work with my hands and my body. I love moving around the shop, pounding and shaping objects out of materials that end up totally different from when I started. I've made beautiful copper flowers, sea creatures, and underwater plants from scrap pieces of copper and steel."

"You always did like handling all that pipe and welding or gluing them together. Maybe all the fumes changed your brain." He punched her arm. "Just kidding."

"So who is Rebecca when you aren't the planet she revolves around?"

"The woman who said yes when I asked her to marry me."

She heard the happiness in his voice. "Whoa, you really are her planet. Congratulations, little brother." Tiffany reached for Eric's hand and squeezed it.

"She is my sun. Tiff, I got lucky when she came into

my life. But that's a story for another day. There's a parking space."

The phone binged a text.

"Are you expecting anyone else to be texting you or can I check?" Eric reached for the phone.

"You can check. Could be Mom. I don't have any secrets, like a fiancé." Tiffany parallel-parked.

"There's a text from someone called the Dog Whisperer."

"Someone must have the wrong number. No, wait, give me the phone." Tiffany shut off the engine.

Eric held it out of reach. "Tiff's got a boyfriend. Does he kiss you? Does he hug you?"

"Eric, what are you, eight years old? Okay, open it." Tiffany opened her door and slammed it shut. "Brothers."

"Settle down." Eric closed his door and handed her the phone. "Do we need money for the meter?"

"Yes, and it's only two-hour parking." She dug into her pocket for coins. Another *bing* from the phone.

Tiffany opened the phone and read the message. "Mom says she'll have a hot cup of tea and a biscuit. This could be good news. She hasn't been eating much."

"She never does when she's worried."

"I hope they'll be pleasantly surprised to see you. They never want to bother anyone. I didn't even know that Dad bid on the job. He must be bored." Tiffany swung her purse over her shoulder.

"They'll take it in stride, though, and not be totally surprised because they know that we Georges always close the circle when trouble comes our way." Eric reached the hospital front door while Tiffany was trotting behind him on her not-long legs.

Eric slowed his stride until they reached the doughnut counter. Tiffany gave the server their order and after having it filled, carried the tray with the cups of hot beverages to their father's room. Eric entered the hospital room first.

Tiffany stayed at the doorway, holding the tea and biscuit for her mother and coffees for Eric and her.

Her mother gasped, jumped up, and then ran into Eric's outstretched arms. Her father seemed to melt into his sheets as if the need to hold everything together could be freed for a while.

Tiffany felt her phone vibrate again, drawing attention to her unread message. She felt a rush of warmth knowing that Will was reaching out to her. She'd read the message in a bit. She watched Eric and her mother separate and then Eric leaned over the side rail and gave her father a kiss on the lips. She was stunned. She had never witnessed this type of intimacy between them. Her father stroked Eric's face, then closed his eyes and fell asleep.

Tiffany whispered, "Mom, do you know that Aunt Pat is here somewhere. She broke her hip. She might like to see you for a minute. If you do, tell her the dogs are well taken care of. I'll stay with Dad."

"Eric, Aunt Pat would love to see us. Dad will sleep for a bit."

Her mother tucked her arm into Eric's. She was supported and could leave the room, even though she glanced back toward the bed every few steps.

Tiffany held up her coffee cup in a salute. After they left, she settled into the visitor's recliner and watched the hypnotic change of the flashing numbers and the waves floating across the screen monitoring her father's condition.

The cellphone in her pocket vibrated again. This time she opened the texts. The first text was from Will. *Can you bring me back some doughnuts please? A couple of dozen should be good. Thanks.*

What was Will thinking? She was with her father who was lying in a bed with leads and electrodes recording his state of health and Will wanted doughnuts? Doughnuts!

The second text was from Darryl stating they'd had some trouble again and were digging up the line. Tiffany ran her fingers through her hair. She didn't want to be involved in this anymore. Her dad seemed to pick up on her discomfort. He shifted and moaned.

She texted her reply to Darryl, *Do you need me? I can be there in an hour or so.*

His reply was swift. *Yes.*

"Dad, there's another water break. I need to go back to Apex. Sorry," Tiffany whispered in his ear.

Her father, without opening his eyes, nodded. She glanced over her shoulder before leaving the room. Her father slept soundly. She knew he would want her taking care of business rather than watching the flashing lights on his machines.

Now she could guess about Will's request for doughnuts. Apex residents always fed the staff who worked during their time off.

Tiffany stopped at the desk and told them she had to find her brother. She heard Eric's mellow, comforting voice. She peered down the corridor. Eric was leaning on the doorframe.

Tapping Eric on the shoulder, Tiffany placed her finger against her lips and motioned for him to follow her. Eric pointed toward the bed against the window in Aunt Pat's room. She was surrounded by staff and visitors. Her mother was involved in a conversation.

Eric followed her down the corridor.

"I have to go back to Apex," she said. "There's another water problem. Can you get a cab back to the hotel? Or maybe Mom could drop you off."

"Aw, sis, I'm sorry. Yeah, you go ahead. I'll tell Mom, and don't worry, I'll get back to the hotel and Rebecca."

"Tell Mom goodnight. I'll talk to her tomorrow."

Tiffany stopped at the coffee shop in the hospital. After getting in line, she replied to Will's text. *Picking up doughnuts. What's your favorite?*

She thought about the little she knew of him. She

looked over the display of confections. He seemed caring, intelligent, and athletic. She chose a maple glaze for him. Not too sweet but a unique flavor. She added a couple of honey-dipped doughnuts for herself. Then she added a mixture of choices. Just as the server was taping the boxes closed, her cell binged again with a text from Will.

Glad you can help me out here. The men have eaten most of the ladies' baking and they still have work to do. Drive carefully. Maple-dipped or double-dipped chocolate are my favorite. Thanks for asking.

Tiffany congratulated herself on her assessment. She knew her family's favorites. Dad was an old-fashioned, Mom, a jellied center, and Eric, a turnover. She wondered about Rebecca. If her art didn't make a go of it she could always become a doughnut reader. She could set up shop and tell people which doughnut they usually ordered and if it matched their personality. She would guide clients toward the confection that could ensure a balanced life.

Leaving the hospital, she juggled two boxes of doughnuts, and managed to open the trunk, and set them on a flat surface. Here she was again, reversing and driving back to Apex. She wondered what had happened to the water line.

Chapter 14

After texting Tiffany, Will tucked his phone in his shirt pocket close to his heart. He helped himself to a coffee from the urn the women's church group had set up on Willow Lodge's patio, near to the town crew's worksite. He admired the skill of the backhoe driver as he squared off the hole and the man on the ground as he directed the trench shield into place.

So many vehicles were moving around, Will hadn't been paying attention until one of the men gave a long, wolf whistle when Nikki stepped out of her car. She wore knee-high leather boots and her flowing dark cape set off her long blond hair. She strode effortlessly with her shoulders back over the uneven ground to the back of her SUV and opened the hatch. Reaching into the cargo hold, she bought out two cases of pop. Nikki must have heard that there was trouble and here she was. She was an asset to getting things done on time. One of the men ran to her side and relieved her of her burden. She smiled at him as if he were the only man in the area. The poor man. He was half-infatuated with her before he had both cases in his hands. She focused all of her attention on the man carrying the drinks, "Please tell everyone to help themselves. We appreciate their dedication to our community."

Wow, she sure had nerve. No one snickered. Will had been here longer and he wouldn't presume to insinuate that he was part of their town. He was an outsider. He was comfortable on the outer edges whereas Nikki assumed she belonged. Will had hoped that Tiffany would arrive with the doughnuts and he would be the hero. Will knew all about hospitals. There was always a coffee shop with doughnuts. Guys usually ate whatever was offered anyway. Will looked toward Elm Street. The vibration of a backhoe dropping a boulder shook Will in his loafers. Now he hoped that Nikki would leave before Tiffany arrived. Nikki might infer to everyone the he was interested in Tiffany, as more than a potential contractor.

Tiffany drove up in the car he had worried wasn't substantial enough to rescue him. He made his way over to her door and opened it. "I thank you, and the guys will thank you. The repair is almost completed." He didn't want to share the suspicion that someone had maliciously cut the line again. "The pipe seems to be developing leaks. They've decided to take it back to the next juncture."

Tiffany raised her eyebrows at him while accepting his hand to help her out of her seat. "Natural leaks? Or . . .?"

He leaned low and whispered in her ear, "There will be an investigation."

Tiffany's eyes opened wide. She understood his cautioned reply. She sidestepped him and popped the trunk. Without a second thought, she passed him the boxes of doughnuts, which glistened under the streetlamp.

He leaned against the side of the car and held on to the boxes for dear life. He didn't want to drop his treat to the workers. "I hope I didn't call you back from your parents when it was important that you stay."

She looked him up and down. "If it was important that I be there, I would have stayed." She turned and leaned into the car and lifted a takeaway tray. "I brought you coffee too. I took a gamble and decided on milk."

"Good call."

"What would you rather carry, two coffees or the doughnuts?"

"I'll look after the coffees and that way if I have a mishap then it is only you and me who will be the losers and not the guys." He placed the doughnuts onto the hood of the car.

"Now it is my turn to say, good call." She passed him the coffees securely held in the tray.

He shook his head. Tiffany was some woman. She had given him a choice, hadn't just assumed that he couldn't do certain things. He watched her move through the employees like an old friend, while she carried the boxes to the makeshift coffee station.

Darryl called out, "You're a saint, Tiffany."

"I'm the delivery person. The idea guy is leaning against my car drinking coffee."

"Way to go, Will."

"My pleasure." Will lifted his coffee cup.

"Not so fast. It isn't his pleasure until he pays me." Tiffany tilted her head to one side.

"This man never has cash. If there isn't an ATM machine then anyone with cash pays."

Nikki stepped with long and controlled movements toward them, her blond hair drifting around her face. "I'll take care of reimbursing Tiffany."

"I was just having a bit of fun with the guys." Tiffany returned and leaned against the car next to Will. "They can't expect to have goodies appear, even if they are working long and hard."

"Please give the bill to Rockwell and we'll make sure that you are reimbursed." Nikki held up her palm.

Tiffany shrugged and reached into her back pocket and held the receipt out, forcing Nikki to reach and grasp it with long fingertips.

"Nikki, that's not fair. I'll pay Tiffany and give you the bill. You know how long it takes to make it through the accounting channels. I don't want anyone to be out of money that long."

Nikki scanned the receipt. "Will, that's so thoughtful." She put her hand into her pocket and extracted bills and coins. She counted out money and put her hand on his sleeve.

"This is what we owe you." She extended her hand toward Tiffany.

Tiffany accepted the cash. "Thank you."

Will moved closer to Tiffany. "Your coffee is probably lukewarm, but it's right here."

"Thanks."

Will wanted to touch Tiffany. His fingertips brushed against her small, calloused palm when he handed her the takeaway cup.

"Nikki, I would have brought one for you too, if I'd known you were here."

The men seemed to be watching the interplay between the women. Will felt comforted knowing that Tiffany could be magnanimous. Nikki, as usual, created her center of attention.

"Will to earth." Nikki was waving her hands in front of his face. "Where did you go?"

He shifted his weight. "That quiet little place inside where you try to understand the big questions."

"Find any answers in there?" Tiffany asked. "Cuz if you did, I'd like the address."

"There are a few bright bulbs in some of the corners but the center is still dark." Will gulped his coffee.

"Good, because when the center is clear you'll be all grown up and sitting in your rocker on some porch somewhere." Nikki saluted with a bottle of water.

The revving motors thrummed against his eardrums. Nikki waved as the work crew left the site. Tiffany smiled, nodded, and gave a thumbs-up signal.

Nikki stood with her shoulders thrown back and seemed to be waiting for him.

"Do you need to speak with me tonight?" he asked.

"No, nothing important. I thought perhaps we could debrief like we usually do after a job." She put her hand over her mouth to cover a yawn.

Tiffany's eyes widened. She checked the time on her phone clock. "Wow. It's late. I'll just run into the lodge and make sure the water is running at capacity and then I'm going home. Tomorrow is another new day." She turned on her heels and marched to the front doors.

Will watched as the motion sensor lights lit her way.

Nikki sauntered over to the recycle bin and dropped her bottle inside. "You've changed."

"After you left, I stopped trying to prove myself." He turned toward Nikki. "I paid closer attention to family and friends."

"Then you owe me big time," Nikki said.

"I do." He nodded. "Thank you. I'm told I'm a better friend, son, brother, and co-worker."

Nikki moved away from the sticky bin and brushed her designer jeans before returning to position herself in front of him leaning on Tiffany's car. "That sounds ominous and old." They both laughed. They may no longer be a couple but they were colleagues who had worked together for years.

"Let's try our best to enhance what's important in Apex," Will said.

"I agree, but we have a mandate and there is always fallout when money comes to town," Nikki said.

"We'll help each other stay on track." Will casually extended his arm toward Nikki. "We're a good team."

"Just not a team for pleasure." Nikki spread her legs wide ready to stabilize them both, as she had in the past when they had embraced, but Will reached for his crutch and balanced on the balls of his feet.

"Thanks for coming out tonight, Nikki. You made a good impression on the crew who will be impacted the most by Apex's future."

"You too, pal. I know you work differently and you've been here longer. You're making inroads too. I can read it in their gestures," Nikki said. "Time for me to go back to my beautiful mobile home and for you to go into your sterile room in the lodge." She shuddered. "Goodnight, Will." She flipped her cape around her as if warding off a chill in the air.

"See you tomorrow. Drive carefully," Will called to her.

Will watched Nikki's taillights disappear around the corner.

When he turned, Tiffany was standing in the foyer of Willow Lodge. She opened the door and came toward him. "You didn't eat any doughnuts. I bought a couple of extra. You can take them home." She shuffled from foot to foot. "Or if you'd like to sit on the bench and enjoy the crisp spring evening we could have a starlit picnic."

"I'd like nothing better. Bring on the sweets." He was exhausted. He dropped heavily onto the bench across the street from the lodge. He leaned his head back. He felt Tiffany sit beside him. He heard the rustle of a paper bag. "Did you know that most of the stars we see are two-star systems? The stars in the Milky Way would add up to hundreds of billions I would think."

"Ah, a mathematical mind," Tiffany said, her head turned toward the sky and her feet stretched out along the cement walk.

"You might say that." Will's crutch clattered off the bench. She moved to retrieve it. "Leave it for now."

He heard her sigh. "How much will all this new development change the complexion of my town?"

Her profile outlined by the streetlight created the feeling in him that he wanted to protect her. He wanted to tell her everything would be taken care of. "I know my company will do its best to meld the old and the new, and if Nikki has her way, Rockwell Mines will do the same."

"You know each other quite well." She offered him first choice of doughnuts.

"Hmmm, maple. I watched those guys devour them but they worked hard so I couldn't begrudge my favorite topping. But I'm having one anyway. Thanks." After he'd taken two bites, he said cautiously, "Nikki and I go back a long way. We attended the same university and have worked on projects together. We were even a couple for a while."

Tiffany dropped a partially eaten doughnut into the bag. "I wondered. She seems to be very familiar with you."

Truck headlights illuminated them sitting shoulder to shoulder and thigh to thigh on the bench.

"The dining room must have closed," Tiffany said. "There goes Sydney."

"I met her and her mother at the restaurant tonight."

"Yup, if you stay here long enough you will meet everyone, and their dogs. By the way, thanks for taking the Tony and Cleo for a walk."

"My pleasure. My parents wouldn't allow us to have a dog." As if on cue, a distant bark drifted across the evening.

"I've put a schedule up on Facebook and in a weatherproof container on Pat's deck. Friend me, and you can add your name to the calendar."

"We're going to allow service dogs in the complex. I think I'll get one. He or she can pick-up after me." Will didn't want to leave. He was enjoying her company.

"If that's what they do, put me down for one too."

"Even with these legs, I'd probably be way down on the list and you'd be old and gray before you'd qualify. We'll have to do our own picking up after ourselves."

"Too bad." Tiffany stretched her arms over head. "On that note, I should go home and get ready for bed."

Will felt as if he was back in elementary school, when boys stretched and then put their arms around the girl who sat beside them. But Tiffany, in her bedroom, reaching for PJs filled his imagination. He changed the subject quickly. "How's your dad?"

"We don't know much more but I'm glad my brother is here. He's so good for my parents." Tiffany stood. He watched her push her fingers through her hair. Remnants of spikes appeared. "Why is it that a son seems to be the guy that can fix everything?" Her hands clenched and unclenched. "And to be honest, I'm hoping he can."

"What about the tender?" Will leaned forward, watching her expression change.

"I've glanced at it." She sounded weary. "Eric and I will look at it in detail. We'll assess if we can complete the plumbing bid. Are you okay with that? I know you have deadlines." Her eyes glistened in the streetlight.

"I can wait a day or two. But anything beyond that and I'll have to make other plans. We need to be ready to work inside all winter." Will picked up his crutch, stood, and stepped closer to her. "Are you coming to our general meeting tomorrow?"

"If we have time."

"Bring Eric. The information might help make your decision." He touched her arm. She turned toward him and placed her hand on top of his.

With her other hand she traced the lines on his face and brushed her thumb along the stubble on his jaw. "I'm going to draw you one day," she said. Closing her eyes, and flickering her fingertips over his eyebrows, his eyelids, and traversing the length of his nose, before gently prodding his nostrils. Will had learned patience during many doctors' and physiotherapists' measurements, but his heart picked up speed when her fingers drifted along his lips. He lifted his hand from her arm and wrapped her close to his chest. His exhaustion dissipated when her head rested on his shoulder, imprinting her body and this moment in his memory. Holding her like this all night was definitely on his list of important things to do.

The warm breeze, the street shadowed with soft lights, dogs barking in the distance, and Will's hand gave her hope. Her father would recover and her career as a mixed-media artist was safe, while she ran her fingers over the contours of Will's face capturing it for society's enjoyment and of course her own.

When a car honked, she jumped, banging her head against Will's chin. She grabbed Will when he tipped backward toward the bench and steadied him. "I'm sorry."

He flexed his jaw. "I think my teeth are intact." Then he smiled. "See."

"Your teeth are Hollywood perfect." She closed the short distance between them and her fingers lingered on his lips.

He groaned. "Any chance you'd like to kiss these lips again?"

Leaning in decisively and turning her face up confidently, on tiptoe she closed the distance between their height difference and pressed her lips to his. Her eyes closed as if controlled by a switch. The night was theirs.

She wrapped her arms around his neck. He wrapped both arms around her waist and drew her closer. A few seconds later, she slowly drew her lips away, lingering but not touching. She wanted just a little bit more. He accepted her kiss and she opened her lips slightly and then explored his lips with the tip of her tongue. They swayed closer. Their lips parted as he swung his arm backwards and braced himself against the bench. He dropped onto the seat. "Sorry."

Tiffany snuggled down beside him and reached for him. "I'd like to finish that kiss, if you don't mind. You have a maple flavor I'm fond of."

"Not at all, be my guest."

She ran her hands through his hair as he eased her next to his thigh. Her breasts flattened against his chest. She drew her lips away from his, lowered her hands from his hair, and slowly opened her eyes. His eyelids were half closed.

"Hmmm," she said. "Next time I'll bring you a double, double chocolate."

"Any time." He wet his lips.

"The first time we met we kissed." She slowly slid out of his embrace.

"I remember that kiss, and the kiss in the lodge. This one I'll dream about." He leaned back. "I like the thought of many more."

She raised her eyebrows and handed him his crutch. "We've got full days ahead of us." Walking backward toward her car, she laughed. "Watch for bags containing doughnuts. Your lips are lovely to relax with."

Will put his fingers to his lips and blew her a kiss.

Will had a special way that helped her accept the present and excited her about the future. His kisses released the knots in her stomach and heated her core, like a piece of malleable metal. The remaining heaviness in her breasts and her comforted warmth freed her thoughts.

Tiffany wasn't her father's little girl any longer, and hadn't been for a long time. She used to need her father to be proud of her ability to be like him. But she was changing. An uncertain voice inside cautioned that she didn't want to change too much, that her acceptance of those around her was a part of who she was, but she needed to carve out some time for herself and become more of the person she was away from here. Later she could use her plumbing skills again, but right now her life was in Winnipeg, with her fresco and where she'd be establishing her career. She had to break away to become more of the artist she discovered.

Driving back to her childhood home she said to the night sky, "Thank you, Soul Whisperer Will Cleaver." She blew a big kiss in the direction of the lodge.

Unlocking the summer door, Tiffany wondered what Rebecca did when she wasn't revolving around Eric. Perhaps she could take over the plumbing business. Eric said he could work anywhere. If he stayed, then Tiffany knew she could definitely grow into the artist she wanted to be. While hope coursed through her entire being, she wandered through the living room picking up family mementos. Dad's condition couldn't be as serious as it appeared. Great medical advances occurred daily.

Her phone felt heavy in her pocket. One way to find out. She texted her brother. *Any changes?*

Eric answered, *Yes, sent Mom to Aunt Beth's. Dad insisted. I'm staying until Rebecca picks me up.*

Tiffany replied, *Thanks.*

Eric sent another text. *Dad resting. Filling me in on business and his personal finances.*

Tiffany tapped out, *Great. Need all the info you can get.*

Tiffany searched her beating heart and not a jealous spasm surfaced because Dad was confiding in Eric rather than her. Perhaps that had been part of the problem way back when. Eric had his asthma. And as a child she had needed something to feel special. *Such silliness, but who knows what motivates families?*

She added one more text message to Eric. *Tell Dad I have the town covered.* Then she added a kissing emoticon.

Next she texted her mother, *Goodnight, Mom.*

This was her opportunity to become someone she hadn't been before. With her art and she would have different reasons to be loved.

Tiffany thought of her life as the *before* sequence, when she would have taken over the company and lived in Apex with her sweetheart Collin and their children, and *after*, when Collin no longer wanted a woman who dressed in coveralls, wore steel-toed boots, came home emitting all kinds of odors, and who hammered metal for recreation, to the allure of skirts, revealing tops, and home-cooked meals. Because business for George and Family Plumbing had been slow, it had been the appropriate time for change. It became her opportunity to become the woman she hadn't known she could be.

Tiffany made herself a hot chocolate and sat down at the kitchen table with her sketchpad, pencils, eraser, and with her phone in her pocket. Drawing always filled the lonely hole that at times formed in her middle. Some people read, some knit, and some just like her drew images of things in their world or people they met. Even though the plans for her mural were firm, she could sketch small design changes in the underwater life or fish. But the aquarium fresco will be in Winnipeg, away from Apex. The architectural design for the business center provided direct sunlight in the morning and indirect for the rest of the day through large windows and a skylight. The copper fish she had cut and welded in her studio would glimmer and when the copper aged it would take on the undersea appeal of greens and blues. The plaster fresco would mature over time, giving it the appearance of tiny ceramic tiles.

Tiffany's phone rang. Her hand jerked a line through an intricate drawing. "Darn."

Reluctantly she reached for it and read the caller ID. "Hi, Owen."

"If you hadn't answered, I was going to get on an airplane, rent a limo, and find Apex."

"I haven't answered because my dad's sick." She doodled an underwater monster.

"I'm sorry to hear about your father." She heard his children in the background. "But you need to return on schedule. This is important, to your career and to me for recommending you."

"I'm working on it. I want to create this mural, too."

"I have your commitment." His voice was low and firm.

"Yes." Many bridges might burn, but she had to complete this commission.

They said goodbye, and Tiffany pumped her fist in the air. She promised. She would return to Winnipeg and to her art. Pressing her fingers to her lips, she swallowed a lump of loneliness for Soul Whisper Will.

Right now, she would have to maintain her life in manageable pieces as she did the parts of her mural. And these glitches, like a fresco, built upon layers, were part of the whole. Today she was glad that Eric was home and that she had acknowledged her recent accomplishments and goals in life. After the aquarium mural was completed, perhaps she could return to Apex and design something for Will's neighborhood.

Tiffany chose her B sketch pencil for its softer, darker shade and a clean piece of paper. Her diagonal and curved lines shaped Will's eyes, which had experienced a great deal in life and her hand shaded the upward laugh lines and the downward curves of the teacher lines. When she shaded his pupils, her stomach fluttered. *There you are, Soul Whisperer. Thank you.*

With her H pencil for lighter lines, she captured Will's knuckles when they curved around his crutch handle. She recalled his hand splayed across her thigh while she drove. *Will, you have a light but powerful touch.* Tiffany carefully placed the sketching pad into her portfolio bag and carried it to her bedroom. The red digits on the clock indicated the end of another day.

Chapter 15

The rumbling of a train rolling past Will's window shook him out of his dream about Tiffany. Rubbing his eyes, he knew there wasn't a train track next to the lodge. He threw back the tangled blankets, then held on to objects as he walked to the window. A massive, yellow earth-moving machine with wheels the size of a one-story house inched down the street.

He slipped on sweat pants, tied his housecoat, then gripped his crutches and opened his door to the hall where he saw Dorothy and Mac tucking their arms into sweaters on their way toward the picture windows.

The sight of the enormous piece of equipment brought the development of the mine into perspective. This could either help or hinder his plans. Right now he marveled at the technology that manufactured this machine and the man who was driving it down the middle of Elm Street in Apex.

"I can't believe the size of those tires. The driver looks like a pimple on a hill. I sure hope he has more in his gray matter than a pimple would have," Dorothy said, opening the door. The roar of the engine pulsed through the common room.

"They take classes and graduate just to be able to climb the ladder to get up into the cab," Will said.

"Some of the local farmers are going to feel that their combines are puny," Lorraine said.

"The price on that monster must be the GNP of a small country," Mac, one of the few men in residence, said, holding the door for Will.

"If not this particular one then it and a few more the mining development uses." Will breathed in the crisp morning air.

The town truck whizzed by followed by the mayor's car. Time for him to put on his business pants. "I have to join the action," Will said. He punched the button, which automatically opened the door. "Mac, Lorraine, Dorothy, I'll see you later."

Once inside his apartment, Will looked longingly at his coffee maker, but there wasn't time. He quickly showered and lathered his face for a shave when someone knocked at his door. He wrapped a towel around himself, then checked the peephole. Nikki. There weren't any secrets between them. He opened the door. "You're up early and looking fantastic, may I add."

"You may. But get a hustle on. You've got to be down there to promote the neighborhood and the mine." She tapped his bicep and then lifted her hand to his chin, and ran a finger through the lather. "Or we could keep everyone waiting." She lifted her eyebrows and wriggled them.

"Nikki leave before you cause more talk than that dump truck. It was your idea, wasn't it?"

She leaned against the doorframe as if she had all the time in the world. "Of course. And calling that piece of machinery a dump truck is like calling this"—she spread her arms wide—"a luxury suite." She shrugged. "It would have been easier for the operator to drive down the highway, but last night I decided that the people of Apex needed more proof."

Will turned toward his front window. "It's a brilliant idea."

Will heard two women talking. "Go, now." He gestured toward his towel-covered body. "I don't want them seeing me like this. I have a reputation to hold on to."

Nikki gave a little whistle, turned, and closed the door.

After he finished his shave, he put on a crisp white shirt, charcoal jeans, black leather loafers, and his casual sports jacket. While he locked his door, his text message beeped. A quick check told him Lacy was waiting to drive him to where the machine had been parked.

When Will arrived on the street, men were admiring the size of everything from the tires to hauling capacity. Women were busy holding on to little boys' hands to keep them from climbing onto the tires. There was a table with doughnuts, muffins, and coffee. The mine managers in suit jackets with open-necked shirts were weaving in and out of the crowd, pointing out features of the earthmover. The driver in blue coveralls used technology to show off the inside of the cab with a big screen set up on the flatbed of a truck.

Will wove around the man who delivered the newspapers, past the woman server from the coffee shop, and two councillors, making a beeline to the table with the coffee urn. Many awed exclamations filtered through the growing crowd. Nikki was busy talking with the men in suits.

Cars streamed past Tiffany's parents' home. Was there an emergency? She didn't smell smoke. The fire phone hadn't rung or she'd be driving too. Just one of her many duties when she was home and her father wasn't available, because she was a qualified First Responder and Firefighter. Tiffany drove to Aunt Pat's and clipped leads on Tony and Cleo. They walked west, toward Miss Tate's who lived outside of the town limits. Her sixth-grade teacher had always encouraged Tiffany's artistic talents and had been saddened when Tiffany chose community college for her plumbing certification rather than furthering her art career. Tiffany's pulse raced. She could now share her artistic success with Miss Tate.

While she and the dogs jogged toward her destination, a stream of cars with people waving placards out their windows honked their horns. The placards read: *Save our water, Save our town,* and *Boom is eventually Bust.*

She was tempted to flag down one of the cars and ask what was happening, but she promised herself that the community could wait, it was important to have time for herself, do what she needed to do, and allow the others to do what they needed to do.

When she passed Apex's town limits, fields stretched across the highway where a convoy of gravel trucks spewed dust in their wake. Half a mile off the highway, in Miss Tate's yard, a layer of dust covered the pink flamingos strutting their metal legs across the lawn and muddied the water in the birdbath.

Tiffany rang the doorbell.

Miss Tate peered out the window. She smiled and the curtain fell closed.

Tiffany heard two deadbolts release and then the chain.

"Come in, my dear. Come quickly before the dust follows you in." Miss Tate coughed into a handkerchief.

"I have Pat's dogs with me. I thought we could visit outdoors."

Tony and Cleo stood by her side.

"Bring them too."

Inside, Tiffany heard the whisper of an air purifier. Miss Tate's furniture was covered with sheets, all except a recliner in the corner, which faced a flat-screen TV.

"I'm so happy you came, my dear. People from town don't drop in very often but I do have businessmen who want to set up shops on my property come almost hourly. They want to supply all and sundry to the mine."

"I thought the mine was on the other highway. At least that's the way I was shown just the other day." Under her feet, Tiffany felt the vibration of vehicles traveling down the road.

"It is, but the mining company purchased all the farm property in this square mile and then some, I'm told." Her breathing grew labored as she struggled with a flowered sheet covering a love seat. "Please, sit down and stay a while."

Tiffany picked up the other end of the covering, and they folded it. "I'm so sorry. This was always a special little place. I often dreamt of living here and enjoying the solitude but being close enough to town." Tiffany felt the grit under her feet, then sat on the royal blue velvet love seat.

"Yes, it was. But don't worry too much about me, my dear. I won't be here long if everything works out." The older woman sat heavily beside Tiffany.

"What do you mean?" Tiffany turned toward Miss Tate.

"A nice Mr. Demerse is going to rent my property and park twelve four-season mobile homes on it for the workers. He tells me that not everyone wants to live in the company camp." She swiped her handkerchief across the coffee table. "Some employees want to live on their terms and he's going to provide that. He's giving me enough money so that I can move to the city."

"I thought you loved it out here." Tiffany looked at the empty shelves that had been filled with books. The wall had faded where her framed awards for Teacher of the Year had been. Her photos of past students in graduation gowns, wedding gowns, or with children by their side were no longer on her mantle.

"I did, my dear, but so many of my friends have moved to the city, and of course there is the whole getting around, and doctor appointments that need taking care of." She held her hands toward Tiffany. "The arthritis has really taken hold. I need to go."

"Have you heard about the adaptive housing neighborhood with physiotherapists, doctors, and even a dentist coming to town?" Tiffany leaned toward Miss Tate.

"I have, but I want to leave. There are so many changes. I'm not sure I will like our town." Miss Tate wrinkled her nose as if a bad odor had wafted into the room. "I may just want to start all over again. I'm not too old to try." She clasped her hands together, "I have hope."

"You're not too old." Tiffany noticed dust on the window frames and floating in the air.

"I could take art classes again at the Life-Long Learning Center through the university." Her eyes sparkled. "Passions might hibernate but they don't leave you."

"I'm a pretty good example of that. You've encouraged me since elementary school." Tiffany watched Tony and Cleo curl up on a throw rug. She noticed boxes perfect for storing paintings stacked in one corner.

"Can I make a coffee, tea, get you a juice?" Miss Tate stood and wiped her hands down her slacks.

"I'd love a juice, please."

Miss Tate dashed out of the room, and Tiffany heard a refrigerator open and close followed by ice cubes being dropped into a glass. The dogs lifted their heads when Tiffany stood and meandered to the kitchen doorway. "Could I have some water for the dogs?"

"Of course." Miss Tate bent to her bottom cupboard and brought out two big mixing bowels, which she filled.

"When do you plan to go?" Tiffany asked while Miss Tate placed the water on the floor for Tony and Cleo.

"Mr. Demerse doesn't take over until July, but I have a condo in the city for the beginning of June."

"That's only a few days from now. My parents didn't mention this." Tiffany accepted a glass of red juice.

"Cranberry," Miss Tate said. "Actually no one knows, except my lawyer, and now you. I didn't want to have the whole town thinking I was abandoning the new boom, but if the truth were known, I've been hoping for this opportunity.

I thought I'd be stuck here until my dying days when they took me to hospital."

Tiffany shook her head, trying to make sense of what she was being told. "I thought this was your home."

"It is. But that doesn't mean that I don't want to leave." Miss Tate spread her arms. "This tiny piece of property is my nest egg for the next stage in my life. And now it has given me the money to do what I need and want to do." She brushed her feet against the floor in a soft-shoe shuffle.

"I've heard very little about the boom. I came home for a short break before starting my fresco commission."

Miss Tate put her hands over her mouth. "Oh my. Congratulations."

"I'm going to be working with sand and lime, just like Michael Angelo." Tiffany clasped her hands together.

"Are you working inside a church?"

"No. A new mall. It will be on a feature wall between the office tower and the shops."

"Climate controlled. Wonderful. Do you have help?"

The constant rumbling of trucks past the driveway couldn't distract them from their happy, creative place.

"I'm not sure. But I'm up to mixing and skimming the plaster coats." Tiffany flexed her muscles.

"I'm sure you are. But that process is time sensitive. You have to move quickly while the plaster is at the right wetness."

"I know. I hope you'll be able to come to Winnipeg and see it someday." Tiffany looked up at the kitchen clock.

"You can email me pictures," Miss Tate said.

"I will. This conversation has meant the world to me, but now I have to return to reality. You've heard about Dad?"

"Yes I have." Miss Tate patted Tiffany's back. "Everything will work out. Just don't let others determine what's important for you."

"You say that with a great deal of emphasis."

After placing the empty glasses in the sink, Miss Tate turned slowly and said, "Our lives are similar in some ways, except I came to Apex when love abandoned me."

"I'm sorry, I never thought about why you moved to Apex because I loved it and I couldn't understand why anyone wouldn't want to live here." Tiffany saw a woman with a past instead of just her teacher. "Good luck. I hope you find the adventures you need in the city."

"I'm going to try. Now go, and don't tell anyone about me leaving. That will come out soon enough. I just don't want to deal with everyone saying stay, when I know it is time for me to go." She gripped the door handle.

Tiffany wrapped her arms around her past teacher's thin shoulders. "Thank you for your support all through these years."

Tiffany snapped the leads on both dogs. "Tony, Cleo. Walk."

The door flung open, and she and the dogs were back in the dust-filled yard. Tiffany held the dogs' leads tight while she jogged back toward town through clouds of truck dust. This boom was changing so much.

On a different route back to Pat's, Tiffany noticed two-story homes where her friends used to live with new outside fire escapes installed and living quarters were being added above garages. Spring. A time of hope. Everything had to work out.

When she returned home, Eric's rental car was there. She wasn't sure how much she wanted to share with Rebecca, a stranger. She had to trust Eric's judgement but then she knew how love could make sound judgement disappear.

Tiffany opened the door and called, "Hello, I'm home."

"Back here in my old bedroom."

Tiffany strolled down the hallway of the ranch-style bungalow. Eric had one arm around Rebecca, and in the other, he was holding one of his chess trophies. Because he couldn't play sports, their parents had made special efforts providing other challenges. They hired tutors who helped him advance and, therefore, he was usually the science and math star in the classroom. When she was younger, she had often wondered if Eric was scamming his parents when he coughed and sucked back on his puffers. She had conducted her own experiment and tucked some moldy bread under his bed. He didn't have an immediate reaction but day by day he had become weaker and weaker until he had to spend a night in the hospital.

While he and their parents were in emergency, she had stayed behind and cleaned up the evidence. To this day, only she knew the terrible thing she had done. She had almost killed her brother. If her mother hadn't been a nurse, he might have died. After he came home from hospital, she gave him anything he wanted, but he hadn't ever taken advantage of her generosity. When he left for college, she was at a loss and missed him terribly.

"Hi, Rebecca. Congratulations, soon to be sister-in-law." Tiffany held out her hand.

Rebecca smiled and displayed the diamond clustered ring on her left hand. "I wanted to come along and see where Eric grew up." She smiled up at him, and he drew her closer. "Eric explained that while you two discuss business I can explore around town. Are you okay with that?"

"Sure."

"We brought lunch." Eric led the way to the kitchen. When he opened the oven door an extra-large vegetable pizza was baking to a golden brown.

"Smells delicious."

"Let's eat on the deck. No ceremony, just napkins and cans of pop," Eric suggested.

"I love the deck." Tiffany rubbed her hands together.

They sat with their faces toward the sun. Eric leaned back and stretched his feet. Tiffany recognized vestiges of

Eric's youth in his relaxed face. Tears pooled at the corners of her eyes. She swallowed quickly and blinked. Rebecca gave her an understanding smile.

"Tiff, we'll work it out." Eric stretched and touched her foot with his own. This gesture had been their signal of support while they were growing up.

Tiffany answered with a touch to his foot, and then bit into the pizza and hummed with delight.

"Tiff, did you see the demonstration against the mine and the boom?" Eric tapped his finger against his lip.

"Why wouldn't everyone want to grow?" Rebecca asked, gazing at the clouds floating across the sky.

"This morning, I saw changes to the community first hand." Tiffany stretched her neck from side to side, relieving built-up tension. "The dust from the heavy equipment covers everything in its drift path." She took a quick sip from her can of pop. "The backyards are filled with lumber. Residents are adding suites to their houses and garages. The density will change the neighborhood."

"Yes, but there will be increase in taxes and an increased customer base for businesses. The community building just has to be controlled." Rebecca formed a steeple with her fingers.

"Wonder why Dad bid on the boom?" Tiffany frowned.

"You know how he always likes a challenge." Eric clasped his hands behind his head. "He told me he believes in the urban expansion and in the lead man, Will Cleaver. Dad has advertised for immigrant laborers and his suppliers are lined up."

"He's a good businessman." Rebecca winked at Eric.

"He is," Eric said to the sky.

"But it's all changed." Tiffany wiped her clammy hands on her jean capris. "I'm scared that he won't be able to do this."

Rebecca clasped her hands to her chest. "Perhaps we'll move here and you can help your dad, Eric."

Tiffany's heart jumped as she felt a spark of hope. "You'll have to find a place to live." Her eyes widened.

"I checked out the basement before you came and with a little renovation and a lot of redecorating"—Eric jumped up and put his arm around Rebecca—"we could stay here."

"Have you run this by Mom and Dad?" Tiffany's thoughts raced. *What if Dad doesn't get better? Mom will need help.*

"I thought we'd go over Dad's business plan and see what is available around the town." Eric brushed Rebecca's hair behind her ear. "There's so much going on and Rebecca's skill as an interior designer is always in demand."

"I've worked on new developments, and if I can get in on the ground floor with some of the developers I can help decorate with flare." Rebecca kissed Eric's cheek.

"I'm sure Mom and Dad will be pleased." Tiffany clasped her hands together. *Please.*

Rebecca picked up the car keys. "Eric, I'll take the car and explore on my own. See you in a couple of hours." She briefly held his hand, slipped on her sandals, and slung her camera around her neck. She skipped down the stairs and then backed out of the driveway.

"Okay, big sister, let's see what we have to do." Eric bumped against Tiffany while he recycled the cans and pizza box. "Let's do this."

"I've looked over Dad's plan briefly." Tiffany stopped at the doorway. "Will Cleaver wants the building closed in before the snow flies. I told him we'd give him our decision tomorrow."

"Dad will have his test results today. We'll know what is ahead of us." Eric sat in their father's office chair.

Tiffany leaned against the desk. "Can you really move here?"

"Yes I can. Rebecca and I were planning a move out of the city, we just hadn't decided where." He turned toward the backyard. "This seems right."

"How did you know about the development here and I didn't?" Tiffany reached for a roll of diagrams.

"I'm in business, you're not." Eric shrugged.

Tiffany punched Eric's arm. "But I was. It didn't even cross my mind that Apex would change. That it would grow and be a powerhouse in feeding the world."

Eric opened the file with the tender and the plans. "These blueprints aren't contingent on a mining boom."

Tiffany smacked her forehead with her palm. "Actually, I forgot there is a public meeting about this development this afternoon. We should go."

"I'll text Rebecca and ask her if she is close by . . . where?"

"The community center on Chestnut Street. As soon as possible." Tiffany patted her pockets for her keys.

Eric pushed his hand through his hair. "I wondered why everyone was drifting in that direction."

"It will be a hot time in the old town this afternoon." Tiffany led the way down the hall and out the door to her car.

Eric slipped the front seat back as far as he could. "This will give us some perspective too." His phone binged. He read his text message, "Rebecca is outside the building. She says lots of people. She'll save us seats."

After they parked the car, they walked up to the community hall, placards declaring, *Save our water*, *Save our town from drugs and druggies*, and *Motorized scooters are vehicles too* were stapled to stakes and pounded into the ground around the front door.

Rebecca stood up and waved her scarf at Tiffany and Eric who squeezed through the crowd at the back of the hall. She had saved two seats in the middle of the row near the stage.

"Excuse me, Mr. Roberts, Mrs. Roberts." Tiffany stepped across legs, around purses on the floor, and knocked over a water bottle. She bent to retrieve it and handed it back to a woman she didn't recognize. "Sorry."

"Some people should come on time," she heard from behind her.

Eric stopped to chat with Mr. Cornwall, their former neighbor. They discussed her father's condition. Most of their friends probably guessed Dad's condition was potentially serious because Eric had come home.

The meeting was called to order, and Eric sat beside Rebecca.

Tiffany turned and focused on Mayor Robert, who introduced the head table. She saw Will looking in her direction, and she waved. He acknowledged her. Someone harrumphed behind her. Tiffany turned and tried to guess who had been displeased with her wave. She heard someone say in a stage whisper, "So her man dumped her and now she's after the rich stranger even if he is handicapped."

Tiffany clenched her fists. *How could anyone even think this? This town. I won't have to worry about it much longer. Maybe pigs will fly.*

Chapter 16

Will placed his palms on the table. His full height, squared shoulders, his readiness to defend his position were formidable. He announced that a slide show would begin with a virtual tour of the building and grounds, showing off the different configurations of the units plus the common areas, the pool, track, and gym. "And here is the area for the doctors, physiotherapist, nurse practitioners, and a psychologist."

Someone yelled from the back, "How about a dentist?"

"We're working on it," Will said.

The murmurs seemed pleased throughout the seven-minute presentation. When the question period opened the first question, from a man in suspenders, was, "Why this piece of land? Why not somewhere else in town?"

"This parcel was on the market and is zoned for a high-density joint-residential and commercial-land use," Will said clearly.

"That's not true. No one in our family would sell that property for anything other than a business." Mr. Russo stood in the aisle.

"It was on the market, we made a bid, and it was accepted. Our development will not be a hotel but it has rental units and it will have businesses. The conditions are met." Will's voice was strong but he felt a strain on his wrists where he leaned on the table. He was tiring.

The questions continued. "How long do you think it will take to complete this project?"

"We have our contractors in place," Will said. "We're informing you as good neighbours so that we can all work together."

"Yeah, typical. Tell us when it is a done deal. Where do we get to voice our opposition?" Mrs. Russo called from her chair.

"Right here, if you like, or speak to any of the councillors, or to your MLAs, or MPs. But perhaps I can help you out now or any other time. My door is always open."

Will felt his shoulders caving toward his chest.

"I don't want to have to lock my car doors when I'm out driving around. I don't want to have to look at every new person and wonder if they are friends or foes," Mrs. Russo said with a hiccup in her throat.

A voice from the back said, "You're talking about different colors of skin, aren't you? Or how about his turban or her head scarf?" Heads turned toward the back. A man with a well-trimmed beard, dressed in a white T-shirt and jeans spoke. "James Pritchard. I run the used bookstore." People nodded. "Just because we were a small community doesn't mean that most people who come will be anything other than friendly. They want to be friends, neighbors, and want to be treated with respect and be safe, too." His voice grew stronger. "We have no idea about their backgrounds, or where they came from. Some of them have had to struggle just to stay alive and here is an opportunity for another life. So let's not take that away with our narrow-mindedness." There were a great many heads nodding, and a soft applause grew louder, and more supportive.

"Well said, James. Anything else?" Will now leaned with both hands firmly on the table's edge.

"I'm a doctor in my homeland. I like the idea of being of assistance when I have written the exams," said a tall woman with a lilting cadence to her speech.

"My babies need to learn to speak English as another

one of their languages. I hope the town is ready for this," said a woman with a baby swaddled to her chest.

"We will definitely factor in language classes in the community," Will said, and Nikki seconded that sentiment.

"I would like to introduce myself. I am Rajni Patel. My brothers and I purchased the old lumberyard. We are going to turn it into a bazaar."

"Pardon?" Mrs. Parker's teeth flashed in a wide mouthed gasp.

"You call them Buck stores here. We call them bazaars. We have something for everyone at very cheap prices," Mr. Patel said, "where everyone is welcome."

"There goes the neighborhood," someone said again in a loud stage whisper.

"Well if you don't like it, you can always leave. Someone will buy your property," a male voice answered.

Will stood up. "If there are no further questions about the new neighborhood, I'm done. Does anyone have any questions for Nikki, the planning engineer for the mining portion of the community?"

"Are you going to hire men and women?" a woman with a blond ponytail asked.

"We are going to hire the most qualified," Nikki answered. "Rockwell Mining is committed to their policy that all employees are entitled to equal opportunities."

"Locals too?" a man in a cowboy hat asked, then put his hands back in his pockets and sat down quietly.

"Again, the most qualified. Many of you have witnessed the movement of machines, similar to the big yellow earthmover out front. More of these will be coming daily. We've been interviewing for heavy-duty mechanics and machine operators. If you have the experience, pick up an application right here or complete one online. The surveying is completed. We'll bring in temporary housing but we also need crews for the pre-constructed homes. We're encouraging new infill in the main part of town. But my meeting will be next week. This is all about Mr. Cleaver and his inclusive plans." Nikki pointed toward the screen with the neighborhood design.

"If there are no more questions, please help yourself to drinks and baking from Shawna's Bakery. We've set up electronic tablet stations where you can go through and see the layout as we have planned. If you have knowledge about past usages of the land which may not be recorded, please contact me." Nikki strode off the stage toward the tables with her shoulders back, her head held high.

Although the neighborhood was a well thought-out design, there was also a great deal of work. Months, in fact, or perhaps a year or two. Tiffany felt the energy in the room. This was her community, her friends, and her neighbors. Yes, there was opposition to the program but new developments needed opposition if they were going to be done correctly.

Tiffany glanced down at her hands. It seemed as if the callouses were flaking off her thumbs and forefingers. She smoothed her jeans down to her knees. *I must think about me and what I want and need for a happy life. Everyone else is doing it, so why not me?*

The room was hot. She felt clammy and her skin tingled. The old doubts clawed to the surface of her mind. *Or because sometimes I wonder about spending hours in a studio creating art when only I like it. I could be part of Apex and be part of the new growth. Why shouldn't I be?* If her art commission was closer to home, she could do both. But it wasn't. She had a contract to honor and she was being well-paid for her work.

Tiffany planted her feet firmly on the floor. She needed to break free, leave and come back on her own accord. Better for her to want to be home rather than be here because she felt trapped.

Will's eyes sparkled. He was doing what he wanted to do.

But perhaps after the mural is complete, I could plumb part-time, create part-time, and participate in the growth. Who am I kidding? I don't multitask well. I'm sticking with my plan. I'm just feeling left out because Eric and Rebecca have something special.

With those thoughts, Tiffany returned her focus to the presentation. Eric was intent on taking notes. Yes, he was ready to come home.

Tiffany scanned the room. Besides people she knew, there were other nationalities and cultures present, identifiable in their dress and whispers in other languages. Up front, a person interpreted with simultaneous sign language as well as a screen with closed caption. This architectural firm didn't just walk the walk, it talked the talk. On the left wall was a screen with French translation. All of a sudden, Tiffany felt as if she was in the middle of a United Nations conference right here in Apex. How had she missed all of this? Was it any wonder that her father wanted to be a part of it?

At the end, a smattering of applause broke out. Chairs scraped against the linoleum floor. Tiffany waited. She, Eric, and Rebecca remained seated for a few minutes, allowing others to find their way to parts of the hall. The restless children in attendance started to play tag. Tiffany felt a tap on her shoulder.

"Thanks for coming." Will leaned on his crutches.

"I almost missed it. Will, I'd like you to meet my brother, Eric, and his fiancé, Rebecca."

Eric stepped forward and extended his hand, followed by Rebecca.

Will shook hands. "Pleased to meet you, Eric, Rebecca."

"How is your father, Eric?" Will asked.

"We'll know later today," Eric said. "This is pretty impressive and a big undertaking for George's Family Plumbing, which is really a one-man shop."

"Fred impressed us with his plans and the momentum he made in applying for international workers. He also agreed to allow some of the residents with disabilities to shadow his team." Will leaned against a chair. "I'd sure hate to re-tender at this time."

"I'm glad we made this meeting. The scope of the mine, its employees, and the integrated complex has been brought into perspective." Eric looked down at his notebook.

Rebecca stepped forward. "Will, I hope I can be of assistance. I'm an interior designer. I'd enjoy working with you."

"Individual owners will have complete control of their living space. I'm sure there will be call for your services."

"I am always looking for new opportunities to expand and this seems just the right place," Rebecca said.

Tiffany finally had a moment to talk to Will. "Your presentation was great."

"Hmm, which part did you like best? You seemed to drift off there for a while in your own little world." He shifted his body closer to her.

Crossing her arms, Tiffany said, "I was not that obvious."

"I'm used to reading people." Will grinned.

"You caught me. I have a few things on my mind." She felt a flush creep across her cheeks.

"I wasn't criticizing, merely teasing you. You looked as if you had the weight of the world on your shoulders." He seemed to sway toward her.

"I've made decisions that will affect others." She reached into her pocket and felt for her keys.

Eric tapped Tiffany on the shoulder, "We'll meet you outside."

"Be right there."

"Your aunt informed me that you are on the way to fame and glory." He tilted his head, looking at her curiously.

"She's a little premature about the fame and glory. She's biased." Tiffany needed her supporters.

"I'd like to see some of your work one day. Perhaps we can use some around town." His brown eyes seemed to look deep into her center.

She flooded with warmth. "I'll show you some slides." People were asking them to move because they were piling chairs. "When we have time, of course."

Will remained close to Tiffany. "I'll take care of Tony and Cleo this afternoon. I need fresh air and a walk or ride should do the trick." Will pressed the automatic door opener.

Will and Tiffany reached the street. "You'll have trained Tony and Cleo to walk with Aunt Pat while she recuperates."

"You're smart." He waved to Lacy, who had parked in the designated handicapped space.

Tiffany ignored the placards pounded into the ground beside the walk.

Will reached for the door handle. "We can trade stories. You can show me your artwork and I'll tell you about the philosophy of rehabilitation."

"It's a deal," Tiffany said quietly. What had she just agreed to?

Eric held up his hand, calling her.

"I have to go. I know that you understand how tenuous everything is right now. Eric and I will get back to you as soon as we can about the plumbing contract."

Will opened his arms to her and it felt right for her to step into them. He closed both arms around her and held her briefly. Needing someone's body pressed up against her, offering and accepting support, seemed the right thing at the moment. Then he opened his arms, and she stepped away. While she hurried to Eric, she wondered where Will's strength came from. He seemed to find a way to be cheerful, and positive. She could learn a lot from Will Cleaver.

Tiffany found Eric and Rebecca huddled over Eric's phone screen. Tiffany bent and read the message from their mom.

Mom had written that *the pneumonia is on the road to recovery. Dad has to stop smoking but he seems ready.* They read that Dad would be available to head up his team. *She* wouldn't have to be the responsible one. Eric was here to help for the time being.

Tony and Cleo barked wildly when Will came toward the fence.

"Cleo, Tony. Sit."

Both dogs obeyed. They waited patiently while Will entered and latched the gate, gathered their leads from the hook, and signed out the dogs. He wrapped the leads around his waist, then clipped them onto the dogs. With a crutch on each arm, he called, "Walk."

The dogs sauntered, one in front of the other, on his right side. They did practice rounds in the yard, allowing Will and the dogs to establish their pace. The last thing he needed was for him and the dogs to be found in a heap.

He hadn't imagined that he could walk two dogs, but here he was. He thanked his resolute mother. Because the research recommended standing for muscle development, he had had to stand in an upright metal standing frame during family pictures, in restaurants, in school, and on vacation.

Will nudged the gate open and all three of them exited the yard in single file. "Sit." Will latched the gate. The trees were green, the lawns were lush, and the flowerbeds were a cornucopia of potential color.

Tony barked, his chest trembling when he saw a squirrel scurry up a tree.

"Steady, boy. If you run after that little one, you'll have a hundred and eighty pound anchor to tow."

Cleo turned toward Tony and gave him a look that made Will burst out laughing. "I'd better be careful or I'll want you for my own. Then what would Pat do?"

Cleo turned toward him and raised her head and licked his fingers gripping the handle.

"Thanks for the kiss, but I know you are devoted to Pat. Now pay attention. Come."

Both dogs' tails wagged while they snuffled along the grass with their noses.

All of a sudden, a half-ton truck squealed around the corner on two wheels. It looked as if it was out of control.

"Left turn," Will commanded.

The dogs turned toward the neighbor's lawn, and kept moving out of the range of the truck if it should jump the curb. He heard it accelerate down the street. He turned in time to get the license number. "Sit." Will spoke into the microphone on his smartphone. "R7J 5X2." He'd report the incident to the RCMP. There were children on these streets.

Tony and Cleo looked up at him with anticipation in their eyes.

"Walk."

A woman poked her head up from behind a Caragana bush. "Pardon? Were you talking to me?"

"No, ma'am, I was talking to my four-legged friends," Will called over his shoulder.

"Hi, Cleo and Tony. I've heard the most remarkable things from behind my hedge," she said.

"I'll be careful about what I say to them when we're out and about." Will felt comfortable talking to the dogs while they snuffled their way to the next tree.

Another shrill voice called out, "Don't you let those beasts urinate on my tree! It'll kill them."

"Hello," Will called to a pair of eyes peering through a gap in the fence. "They're sniffing the last calling card. They are well-behaved dogs." Will tightened the leads. "Tony, Cleo, come."

"Just make sure they don't in the future," the female voice bellowed. "Pat knows trees are necessary on the prairie."

"I know, too." Will felt strange talking to a set of eyes peering at him through the pickets in a privacy fence. "I can guarantee you that when they are in my care, we'll take care of your trees."

"Thank you. Have a nice day," the mysterious voice called.

Wait a minute, Will thought, *by the height of her eyes she could have been in a wheelchair.* He made a mental note to pay attention to the yard. There was so much he didn't know about this town. His new mission was to discover and meet as many residents of Apex as he could.

He, Tony, and Cleo rounded the last portion of the four-block square.

"Sorry, guys, I'm bushed. I wish I could let you run loose but if anything happened to you, for example with that speeding truck, I'd never forgive myself and neither would Pat or a certain plumber/sculptor. So patience. You can chase each other around the yard. I'll throw balls for you. I can sit and do that." His walking companions seemed to understand.

Will nudged open the fence with his hip, unclipped the leads, and the dogs ran into Pat's yard toward their water bowls. With the gate latched, Will looked around and found the outdoor hose and filled their bowls and leaned over and drank his fill from the cold water before he turned off the nozzle. He found balls in a basket on the steps. He tossed the balls into the air. The dogs barked wildly and caught the balls mid-air, and then ran them back to him. Will let the sun warm his body until he felt rejuvenated enough for his walk back to the manor.

"See you again."

The dogs nudged him and watched until he closed the gate.

"Be good! Someone will be here later. You are very lucky dogs."

Down an alley, Will surveyed the backyards with building materials, empty paint cans, and piles of old wood. The community was getting ready for the influx of people. He had witnessed this type of renovation prior to an Olympic Games. People added bedrooms and bathrooms to their homes to accommodate bed and breakfasts, wanting to be part of the economic boom.

When he approached a retaining wall, he noticed a mural on the cinder bricks of a green valley populated with deer, rabbits, and bears. The trees were lush and a man was fishing in a river. Someone's way of beautifying a necessary space. Good idea. Perhaps more people would consider doing this to some of the buildings in town. He wrote down the address. He would ask at the town office about the artist. He had read about this outdoor art being used for tourism. He knew that some of the clients who registered to live in the neighborhood were emerging artists. Perhaps he could convince them to help out.

He never knew what he would discover on a slow walk, rather than driving or riding his handcycle. He was making lemonade again. He chuckled to himself. He'd have to convince the town council and the population that just because they were going to have a potash industry did not mean that they were limited to that. They could develop all kinds of industries.

Will breathed in the air of newly mowed grass, the earthy smell of a garden, and heard the birds singing in the trees. He couldn't tell what kind of bird, but its song was cheery. In the city, these sounds and aromas were lost. *Care must be taken to retain the feeling of spaciousness. We can't lose this important commodity.* Will saw poplar poles stacked in the form of a teepee. The community had a rich heritage as well. Although he was only a small part of the new development, he knew how to help keep the important things on the burners for committees' consideration. Yes, everyone was going to be busy with the new potash mine, but there were other priorities, for instance a pretty sculptor and plumper who understood art. He was looking forward to seeing Tiffany's creations. What would they be like?

Hmm, when he got home he was going to Google her name. Perhaps he'd find images of her work. No, he wouldn't, he'd wait until she showed him. He'd just make sure it was sooner rather than later. He didn't mind a little mystery. His phone rang. He checked the caller ID. It wasn't Tiffany. The universe had not sent out that call. "Hi, Nikki. What can I do for you?"

"You can invite me for a drink. It's boring out here in the middle of nowhere with only bobcats and grader operators working away."

"I'm not home. I've been out for a walk. Give me half an hour and come on over. I'd like to share some insights I've had on my walk. Maybe the company will help out."

Nikki sighed. "Oh, Will, don't you ever leave work?"

"It's my passion, as it is yours. That's why we are friends."

Nearby, a lawnmower roared into action.

"Sure would like to be a friend with benefits." Her voice was playful.

"Sorry." The lawnmower seemed to be keeping pace with him. "But yes, let's have a drink."

"Let me pick you up and bring you back to my place." He heard the pout in her voice when the mower moved further up the yard. "Your place is so visible and plain."

"No, thanks. Visibility is fine with me."

A cat ran up a tree after a squirrel.

"You just don't trust me to take you home when you want to leave."

The squirrel scurried along the power wire, and the cat pawed the air.

"That too. I've had a big day."

"I'll see you in a bit. I'll bring the wine." She sounded resigned.

"See you soon." He ended the call.

The conversation had lasted half a block. He could see his back door. His feet didn't move as easily as they did on his way to Pat's house. But he was stronger for being outdoors. He opened his gate.

Dorothy called, "Hi there."

"How's it going?" Will stopped and waved at her sitting on her patio.

"Good. You?" She stretched her neck and shifted her glasses. "You look whacked."

"I am. I could do with a rest for sure." He leaned heavily on his crutches.

"Want to rest with a beer?" She held up her bottle. "This one was for the slugs. I have more."

"Sounds inviting, but will you come on over to my place? I'll provide the libation. My friend Nikki is coming over with a bottle of wine." He straightened.

"You don't want an old lady when you entertain your friend." He heard the loneliness in her voice.

"I like company. Come on over and have whatever you like. Besides, you've lived here since the ark landed and you might just have the information I need."

"All right then. Just let me put on my lipstick. It's getting chilly to be outside anyway." Dorothy went into her unit's back door.

Inside, Will splashed water on his face and changed into a fresh golf shirt. He picked up his papers and stuffed them into the side table drawer. He fluffed the pillows on his sofa and blew at the dust on the coffee table. *I need a cleaner to tidy up after me. I'm sure Lacy can provide some contacts.*

Will popped in a CD of easy-listening music, placed a few grapes, cheese, and crackers on a plate. After a quick knock, Dorothy stepped into his apartment. She wore a skirt, blouse, fashion shoes, and her eyelids were streaked blue and her lips ruby red.

"Nice lipstick." Will smiled. "Have a seat. Nikki should be ringing the doorbell momentarily."

"Are you sure she won't mind?" Dorothy smoothed her skirt over her knees.

"She won't." He sank heavily onto a sturdy kitchen chair. "She wants to get to know the community, too. You are a wealth of information."

Chapter 17

In their dad's office, Tiffany and Eric paged through blueprints and the tender contract.

"Dad has this worked out. I'm proud of him," Eric said, while making notes.

Rebecca browsed the books on the shelves.

"Can you help?" Tiffany asked her brother after a while.

"Rebecca and I want to make a change, and I've been thinking a great deal about this community, Mom and Dad, and the family business."

Eric reached for Rebecca's hand. "We're going to get married and start a family and we'd like to do it right here. It seems as if it is the right time."

Tiffany swiped the back of her hand across her eyes.

Eric put his arm around her shoulder. "You've carried the ball for a long time and it's my turn to receive it and carry it further down the field. I can't work with the pipes but I can provide other support."

Tiffany rolled the chair away from the desk. "Wow, guess you'll have some good news to tell Dad and Mom when you go to see them."

"Yes, let's go now. I'll drive." Eric drew Rebecca to his side.

"I need to pick up a few things while I'm in the city, I'll take my own car and meet you at the hospital." Tiffany stepped out of the summer door, waved, and said, "Till later." Her purse banged against her thigh while she sprinted to her car. Couples need time alone.

She drove out toward Elm Street and looked over at the Lodge. She recognized Nikki's vehicle. She banged her hands on the steering wheel and then looked at her calloused palms and fingers. The spaces in her family and friend's lives in Apex were filling up fast. Soon there wouldn't be room for her even if she decided to stay.

Did she have to remain here or could she return to Winnipeg, now? Dad seemed to be organized. After their visit today, she would know more. Her breathing quieted as she soaked in the landscape with the expansive horizon. There was a whole world out there for her to explore.

Her hand itched for a pencil and sketch paper. She thought about the landscape and the design of large pieces of mining equipment she had seen at the site. The scrub brush along the side of the highway, the stream of water that glistened in the newly planted corn, the blue plastic hives that provided protection for the bees that pollinated the crops were inspiring.

Before her education, her designs had been freer and cruder but she had enjoyed her time in the garage away from her family and friends. It was just her, the copper pipe, and the propane torch. The sound of solder paste sizzling was her type of music.

Collin had thought that Tiffany should have been happy with him, selling porcelain sinks, toilets, copper, and PVC pipe, not actually working in the stench of broken water or sewer pipes. His world was Apex. His family had been here since the first settlers arrived. She too might have been happy-ish with that life if Miss-Dolly-Parton-look-alike hadn't strutted down the beach one day with her assets on display. What made her think it would be any different with someone else? Will for instance. Even though she wasn't in sewage sludge anymore, she was usually covered in paint, sand and lime and emitting fumes from a cutting torch.

Tiffany signalled toward the parking lot. She found herself behind eight vehicles waiting in line. She checked her watch. Eric and Rebecca would have shared all the good news with her parents and Tiffany would receive the happiness leftovers. Her mother would be beaming at the thought of another woman in the family. Dad would be polishing his PJ buttons because he was so proud and then she, Tiffany, would walk in.

Waiting was useless. It was a beautiful day. She wore good walking shoes. She parked in the first available spot and then jogged back to the hospital. She took the stairs and sped down the hall, stopping outside Dad's door. She took a deep breath, then ran her fingers through her hair, attempting to have it stand on point. She slid in through the partially open the door. Mom, Eric, and Rebecca were wrapped in a group hug.

"You finally made it." Her father beamed. "Where have you been?"

"Trying to find a parking spot. You'd think this establishment would provide more parking spaces for visitors."

"We were the last car through before the 'Full Lot' sign went up," Eric said.

"That's my parking angels looking out for us," Rebecca said.

"Next time, I'll phone you so you can talk to your angels for me," Tiffany said. "Mine must have been on their coffee break."

"She's not kidding, sis. I don't know how she does it but a car will leave just as we are circling. It's uncanny."

"Glad someone has positive vibes hanging around them." Her father winked at Rebecca.

"I'd say you've got some pretty positive vibes. You had us really scared." All of the monitoring equipment stood as a silent sentinel beside the bed.

"Yeah, me too. I had a lucky break." Her father pushed the button on his bed and he sat upright. "Let's talk about the contract. I assume that is why you are all circling my bed."

"Fred," Mom said.

"It is okay, Mom. Dad is right." Eric took his notepad from his jacket pocket. "Tiff and I went over the contract and tendering process with broad strokes. It's pretty tight."

"Did you think your old man was losing it?"

"You said you were retiring." Tiffany stepped toward the bed and rubbed her father's shoulder.

"But then you bid and win the biggest job to come to town. Yes, as your children who love you, we have a right to question your judgement," Eric said.

"At least Tiffany didn't have to voice that concern. Instead of being straight forward, she'd have beaten around the bush and then chewed on her fingernails about completing the job," her father said. "Men know how to talk about what's important."

Tiffany jerked her hand away from the bed. "Guess I know where I stand. You obviously have it all handled and worked out. You've made my decision a whole lot easier." Tiffany felt nausea crawl to the back of her throat. She needed to get out of here. She felt the same way when Collin left her. She wasn't needed anymore. She wasn't worth consideration. She could be left behind when others found someone they liked better. Now that Eric was back, her father could let go of his substitute son and everything she thought she meant to him.

"I'm glad you're better, Dad." Tiffany felt as if she had been shoved out of the room. "I've got to run. See you later in Apex, Eric. Rebecca, good luck with those angels."

Outside the room, Tiffany stopped in the hall with its baskets for laundry and its charts for registering pain. She pushed herself off the wall.

"Tiffany," her mother called, "wait." She put her hand on Tiffany's shoulder. "You can't run away." Her mother blocked her path. "This is important to the family as a whole. Dad won't be in shape to handle it all."

"Mom, he's always wanted Eric to be by his side and now he has the chance for father and son to be in business together. I get it."

Her mother stepped back. "You need to find a way to fill that hole you've been digging for far too long."

"Guess I'll go out and find myself some dirt." Spittle flew from Tiffany's mouth with her hissed stage whisper. "I'm going." Tiffany punched the elevator buttons willing the doors to open. She did not want to talk to anyone. When the elevator doors swished open, the occupants crowded together, making room for one more on a non-stop descent.

The elevator jerked before the doors slid open on the main floor. Tiffany blinked, rapidly clearing her tears. Among the people gathered around the door was a brown-eyed man with blue-black hair and broad shoulders in a black polo shirt and beige jacket.

"Tiffany."

"Will. What are you doing here?"

"Quick trip. Doing my community duty. You?"

"Getting my priorities lined up for me." Tiffany balled her fists at her side.

"Whoa, that doesn't sound good." Will leaned on his crutches. "You should always be in control of your priorities."

"Easy to say when you're the boss man. Hard to do when you're the helper." Tiffany didn't want to talk to anyone, not even her Soul Whisperer.

"Come on, I know a great coffee place just around the corner. I think you need to talk with me." He touched her arm.

She brushed off his hand. "What are you, a counselor?"

"I've had enough therapy to qualify for one. Do you think growing up with gimpy legs and walking with crutches or pedaling a handcycle is something every normal young man wants to do?" He steadied himself. "Do me a favor?"

"Depends, I'm not in a very generous mood right now. In case you haven't noticed."

"Just put your hand on my forearm"—he pointed to his left arm—"here, and walk with me."

Tiffany placed her palm on his left arm. She felt his muscles flex.

"I know you are nimble and quick but could you just pay a little attention to where the sticks land." His stance was straight, his arms through the cuffs and resting on the handgrips. "I always move my right leg and left aid and then left leg and right aid. You might have to do the opposite. I haven't done this since my mom used to walk with me."

"Is it a bit like a three-legged race?" She almost felt a smile slipping through her resolve to run away and hide.

"Let's just not tumble. Not too sure what the visitors would think looking down and seeing us wrestling on the marble floor." Will gripped his handles.

"I could not hold your arm, you know," Tiffany said, but she wasn't sure that was the solution she wanted.

"I'd prefer if that wasn't an option." He seemed to read her mind.

"Ready. My right, your left." He moved toward the electric eye, which slid the hospital doors open to a crowded walk filled with people being picked up or dropped off.

Tiffany concentrated on the motion. She felt the slight breeze in the dusk gently weaving its way through the gelled spikes in her hair. Even though the cement was pockmarked and crumbling in places, Will moved steadily forward. She stumbled.

"Concentrate," Will said, as he adjusted his stride. "Look toward the corner, we're almost there."

Tiffany breathed in the aroma of fresh-roasted coffee beans. They skirted car bumpers parked in front of large windows with light spilling onto the sidewalk. "This place is popular."

"Don't let the parking lot fool you. Remember how close

it is to the hospital." Will lifted his crutch and poked at the button, which automatically swung the door open.

Tiffany could have stepped away but she felt comfort in their connection. She slid in sideways allowing room for each of them to wait in the narrow space between the doors. They moved in rhythm toward the counter.

"Hi, Will. Your usual?" The young man with one pierced eyebrow turned to reach for a cup.

"In a minute, Mike. I need to ask Tiffany what she'll have."

Tiffany stared up at the menu while feeling and hearing the people behind her shuffle.

Will waited patiently for her to make her decision. "I'll have a decaf café latte with low-fat milk, please."

"And yes, my usual, Mike." Will passed his debit card.

Moments later, she turned and surveyed the available seats.

"How about the one in the corner?" Will wiggled his eyebrows up and down.

Tiffany nodded.

"Are you up for another favor?" Will asked while they made their way to their seats.

"Depends." She tried to hold on to her sadness.

"Would you sit with your back to the wall and observe the servers and clientele?"

"Of course." Tiffany broke contact with Will's arm, shimmied around the outside chair, and slid into the chair in the corner.

Will settled into the seat next to her and propped his crutches against the wall.

"Do they call a number or our name or just the type of drink?" Tiffany asked. "By the way, what is your usual?"

"A double espresso."

"And you sleep at night?"

"Why do you ask?" His eyes seemed focused on her lips.

Tiffany felt a giggle sneaking up on her. She cleared her throat but not before the telltale smile slid across her lips.

"Don't ever do that, please." He leaned forward and touched her cheek.

"What?" She frowned. Someone else was telling her what to do.

"Hold back laughter. It is so important in our lives." Will dropped his hand from her cheek and covered the hand she had placed on the table.

"Who are you? Some sort of guru for a good life?"

"No, I'm Will Cleaver. I've just moved to Apex. I've designed a neighborhood to accommodate differently minded gurus."

This time Tiffany did laugh. "Great. The residents will really like that." She drew her eyebrows together. "Did you meet my father before he put in his bid?"

A woman with a tray clamped to her walker was at their side.

"Hi, Crystal. How's it going?"

"Pretty good, Will. I'm getting faster every day."

Will passed Tiffany her coffee, with a wonderful design in the foam, and he picked up his tiny cup and saucer. "I'm glad. Thanks for bringing our order."

As Chrystal pushed her walker toward the counter, Tiffany noticed there were wide aisles between the tables. The walls were covered with paintings and small shelves with sculptures or pottery.

Will brought the cup to his lips and sipped the thick liquid. "You asked a question about your father?"

Tiffany picked up her cup and sipped carefully around the foam, attempting not to disrupt the design. "Yes, but let's talk about this coffee shop first."

"What would you like to know?"

"Tell me the story, Guru." Tiffany sat back and wrapped her palms around her mug.

"About a year ago, I had a few people come to me with an idea. They loved coffee and wanted to work in the industry. However, in the other coffee shops, if you think about the design, the counters are high and all of the stock is kept in cupboards even higher." He stopped talking for a sip.

Tiffany watched the light from the window behind them cast shadows through the planes of his face. "And then?" she prompted.

"And then we sat down and with our group knowledge we made it accessible for those with physical and mental limitations."

"But why is the parking lot full and the seats are almost empty?"

"It's still visiting hours at the hospital. We allow patrons to park and walk to the hospital."

Tiffany really began to look around. "Where does that hallway lead?"

"There are booths along the wall for those who don't want to feel too exposed. A hospital is a hard place to be sometimes."

"How many staff?"

"Not sure. I leave the running of the place to the group." He twirled the cup in its saucer.

"Let me guess, you're a silent partner." She watched him carefully.

"I'm a partner and mentor."

The hiss from the steam machine broke through a moment of silence from the chatter and clanking of cups on saucers.

Tiffany took a big gulp. "Are there other partners besides you?"

Will seemed to be looking deep into her eyes. "Of course. We need all sorts of expertise."

The music was a mix of easy rock, classical, and country. "Someone has chosen a good play list and the music doesn't seem to just hang around the ceiling."

"We consulted persons with a hearing disability, and they requested background noise control especially for those who use hearing devices." Will pointed to a wall where the visual words were being screened. "If a customer asks, we can turn the speakers off for a particular table." Will sipped his coffee. "This is what I mean and why I want to give everyone a chance in the new industry at Apex. Disabilities do not take away from our talents."

A group of teens came in, boisterous and juggling for chairs. One bumped Will's crutches and they tumbled to the floor.

"Sorry, man." The young man's asymmetrical hair fell away from his face when he bent to pick them up.

Tiffany glimpsed a face that hadn't aligned properly. The long hair covered one misshaped eye.

"No problem." Will shifted. "Thanks."

Tiffany didn't know what to think. Was she the only totally abled-bodied person in the place? No, there were many others. Some had slumped shoulders and drawn faces, while others had the quiet glow perhaps caused by relief of an averted tragedy.

"Any chance you want to talk about your priorities that have been realigned for you?" Will turned his cup in his saucer.

"No, not now. Thanks, though." She was used to working out her feelings with drawing pencils and a sketchpad, or pounding metal. "I'll tell you another time."

"In that case, do you want to sneak back into the hospital and visit Pat with me?"

"But visiting hours are over."

"Come on. What can they do, kick us out?"

"Yes," she said, suddenly feeling mischievous.

"Then we'll leave if they ask us to. But we really need to be in sync so we don't cause any calamities."

Tiffany stood and waited for Will. Her palm on his left arm feeling the play of the muscles beneath his jacket felt as if it were in the exact right place.

They strolled down the sidewalk, through the hospital's double-doors, and across the marble floors, over the caduceus, the medical insignia.

Tiffany paused. "This symbol has many myths attached to it."

"I like the one about the Greek god's wand being used to separate two fighting snakes and then they coiled around it to live in harmony," Will said.

"I'm not surprised that's your favorite. My favorite is the shedding of skin seen as rebirth."

"I see." He stopped. "Is this the new or old skin?" He ran his finger across the top of her hand.

"A little of both. It's hard to shed the past totally." She looked into his eyes.

"How did we get so serious? Pat will think we are bringing her bad news." Will gave her a little nudge with his shoulder.

They stopped in front of a room. The nursing staff seemed to be carrying out their duties without any notice given to the two intruders.

"You go in before me, just in case she is in a compromised position," Will whispered.

Tiffany entered the room while Will stood in the partially open doorway. The woman in the first bed was asleep.

"Knock, knock," Tiffany said quietly.

The "Come in" was faint.

Tiffany went to Pat's open arms and closed her eyes while Pat wrapped her in a big hug and patted her back. "I'm so glad to see you."

"Oh, Pat, I should have come sooner, I'm sorry." Tiffany bit her lip.

"No need to be sorry. You're here now. Have a seat." Pat pointed to the chair.

"Just a minute." Tiffany slipped past the curtain. She curled her finger. Will followed her.

"My boy. I knew you wouldn't forget." Aunt Pat extended her hands toward him.

"Of course not. Just a small change of plans." Will winked at Tiffany.

"Tiffany, you delayed him. I've been waiting." She bunched the sheet in her hands. "How are my babies?"

"They are just fine. I took them for a walk, then as I was leaving town, someone in a cowboy hat had them by their leads." Will unlocked his phone. "I took pictures."

"They'll be spoiled. I don't know what I'll do when I get home with this gimp hip."

"You'll walk them," Will said firmly. "And I'm sure the rest of the dogs' walkers will continue even after you return home." Will leaned against the side rail of the bed. "Since walking Tony and Cleo I've experienced for the first time in my life that animals have a way of adding pleasure to a normal day."

"You're right. Tony and Cleo have their antics," Pat said. "They've certainly brought me back from some dark places over the years."

Will reached into the inside pocket of his jacket, brought out an envelope, then gave it to Pat.

"Thank you. I've been waiting for this for so long, I didn't want to miss it. And when you described it to me this evening. . ." She swallowed tears and clutched the envelope to her chest. "I knew it was from my cousin, Cynthia. I've been waiting to find out how she's been feeling after her surgery."

"You're welcome. We have to thank Lacy and Postmistress, Irene."

"Irene knew I was waiting for this. Thank goodness for friends who care for each other," Aunt Pat sighed.

"And Apex residents care about our Town. There was standing room only at the community meeting. Will provided positive information and calmed some of the concerns residents have," Tiffany said. "There are so many people interested in growing our town for the future."

"What about you? Are you going to stay and help your parents?" Aunt Pat shifted her weight and closed her eyes against discomfort.

"Eric is home, Dad's on the mend." Tiffany swallowed hard after that statement. She felt stifled. "I have a contract in Winnipeg. I have to return."

"Your mom is right. You have changed," Pat said.

A nurse came in with Pat's medication.

Will checked the clock on the wall. "Sorry, Pat, I have to go. I promised Lacy I'd be ready to leave."

Pat reached for Will's hand, and kissed it.

Will shifted his weight and the muscles in his free arm braced him against the bedframe. "Steady there, Pat, or I'll be joining you in bed, and then what will these good nurses say?"

"I'm so happy and I'm thankful you called me and kept me informed about my precious babies and brought my letter." Turning her watery gaze to Tiffany, her Aunt Pat said, "I know you've become too busy to think about such a little thing."

"I'm sorry. I'll try harder while I'm here," Tiffany touched her aunt's cheek with her hand. It was as if she'd traveled through a portal into an altered universe. She had spent hours with Pat, Tony, and Cleo before she moved away. Was this what happened when someone left? Their place was filled by others.

"Mind if we hurry, Tiffany? Lacy needs to get back to

Apex for something or other and I promised her I wouldn't keep her from it." Will moved with agility and speed.

Tiffany stepped up her pace. In the elevator, she said, "Thank you for sharing some of your time with me and showing me the coffee shop. I hadn't realized I kept you from Aunt Pat."

"You needed me. Besides, Pat knew I was coming." He leaned close to her. "The staff and eventual owners of the coffee shop are working toward their goals." He looked down at his legs. "I learned a long time ago, that realigning my priorities has to be my choice to be able to move fearlessly toward my destiny."

The elevator gave a little bump. The thought of being stuck in a confined space with Will seemed like a good idea. She imagined them leaning against the wall with her arms around him. "I could drive you home."

"Thank you but Lacy was kind enough to drive me here. She went shopping while I visited. She'll be waiting."

Tiffany felt a sense of relief. She wasn't ready, wasn't even sure where she belonged anymore. "You're right. My choices. My destiny." After a deep breath, she continued, "I'm returning to Winnipeg as I had planned that first day we met."

"If it's what you want to do." The framed art along the wall, the unattended information desk, and vending machines blurred together as she raced toward the doors that would separate them.

The doors spread wide, and they walked out side-by-side. "Goodnight, Will. Thanks."

"Lacy's right on time." He motioned to his car, parked in front of the building. "Goodnight."

He opened the door and the interior light lit up Lacy's face.

I'll miss you, Will had wanted to reply when Tiffany told him that she was leaving. But he wouldn't be the kind of person who asked her to give up her dreams and stay behind. He would find a way to be in her life.

"Thank you, Lacy, for breaking into your evening. You helped make Pat's day. She was touched to receive her letter." He locked his seatbelt.

"That's good, but now can we go straight home?" She turned and looked at him with her direct gaze.

"Yes."

"We're outta here."

Will watched the city lights flash by. If the new facility had been ready, Pat would be able to be back in her community almost immediately after surgery.

"Lacy, what do you think of the mine coming to town?"

"I see a lot more men in town and that's a good thing for me and my single friends." She giggled.

"Do many people talk about the changes that will be coming?" He pressed the button that reclined his seat so he could watch Lacy's expression.

"Oh yeah. Everyone is talking about how much money they are going to make and then how they will become a snowbird and sit in the sunshine instead of shovelling snow." Lights from oncoming traffic flashed through the interior.

"What about you? Are you wanting to run away to someplace warm for the winter?" Lacy heard a lot of chatter and didn't seem to have a filter like many others.

"I wouldn't mind, but only for a little while. I like the winter. I've never driven in a snowstorm. I sure hope you stay here long enough to let me."

"I'll be here. If you aren't teaching in daycare, perhaps you'll be a driver for other residents."

"I never thought of that. I know there are lots of seniors who could use a ride. But some people say you should get a bus to run into town or have the railroad bring back the train. I've never ridden on a train."

"I have been working on those two items. I think they're necessary too."

"Now can I drive instead of talk? I'm going to be late." She glanced at him again.

"I promised to pay you overtime tonight."

"I know. I really like to play bingo, and tonight the big prize is an iPod that clips to your jacket while you're working, running, or walking. I'd like to listen to music all the time. It makes me happy."

"If you have a few more jobs with time and a half, you'll be able to buy your own."

"Yes, I know. I calculated my time and the cost while I was waiting for you. But I like the chance to win."

"Don't we all?" Will thought about Tiffany and her black spiky hair. He wondered what had caused her face to be so drawn and sad when he saw her. When he first met her at the seniors' home she was confident, but as the days went by her shoulders seemed to curve in on her. Now she was a boat just floating with the currents. Perhaps with her brother home things would work out.

"We're here, Will," Lacy said.

Will roused himself from a half sleep.

Lacy ran around the car, opened the door, "Here you go."

Will got out of the car as fast as he could, took himself away from the door, and Lacy slammed it. "Goodnight." She tapped the automatic lock on the keychain. The lights flashed.

"Go, and good luck. Good night," he said to her back while she ran to her compact car.

He let himself into his apartment, and saw his phone message indicator flashing. Pressing the button, he heard, "Will, Eric George here. Can we set up a meeting for tomorrow afternoon and go over the contract?"

Will checked his electronic calendar. He sighed. It had

been one busy, very long day. People were counting on him. He sat in his armchair, and dialed.

"Eric, Will here." He listened to Eric at the other end. "Three-thirty in the town office will be fine."

He wished he had someone who would bring him a nice cold beer.

He lay his head back against the cushions. His phone vibrated. He had a message from Paula. It informed him that she was arriving tomorrow to check out the bar facilities. She wondered if he was free?

Any time before three-thirty, he texted back.

Things seemed to be falling into place quite nicely. He hoped it wasn't a calm before the storm. He closed his eyes and rubbed his arm where Tiffany's hand had rested. She was a puzzle but he enjoyed puzzles.

While Will expended enormous energy when he was speed-walking on his crutches, Tiffany realized that this was one of the reasons Will had muscles that rippled through his arms, back and neck. Will was in control and he didn't need anyone to help him feel confident. She tried to shake off a feeling of sadness that began to wrap around her heart. What would a man like him need? Not someone as indecisive as she'd become.

After Lacy and Will drove away, Tiffany returned to the coffee shop and ordered a sandwich and coffee. She sat at the same table she had shared with Will. While observing the servers, baristas, and the patrons, she understood that this group of people had a good idea and followed through to realize their dream.

She opened her purse and brought out her sketch paper, then laid her colored pencils in a row and doodled. Will's forearm took shape under her pencil. Shading the vibrating strength seemed to bring it to life. She had sketched an eye, lips, and a calf. The man was in pieces to her. She didn't know him well enough to construct a whole portrait but she'd like to. She was in the glow of creative energy and she didn't want it disrupted, yet she needed to return to Apex.

On her way home, she spoke into the message portion of her phone. Her idea was still too new. She loved the glow of beginnings. After she completed the fresco, she'd be paid well. She would have more funds to sustain her while she began designing a new piece of art.

Tiffany drove into the driveway of her parents' home. Her childhood home? To hell with whatever it was, it was where her bed was tonight. She held her satchel tight to her side.

Eric and Rebecca were cuddling on the sofa watching TV when she entered.

Tiffany made a beeline for the fridge, grabbed a bottle of water, and quickly passed through the living room. "Good night." She opened the door to her old bedroom. With the extra toss cushions, and the organized bookshelves, this was now a guest room.

She lay on her bed in the dark. She wanted to understand why she couldn't embrace the idea that Eric was home with his love, Rebecca. They would share the responsibilities of their parents' needs. She heard a paper slide under her door and smiled. Their family had decided notes under the door worked best when either she or Eric wanted some space. She'd read it tomorrow morning. Now was not the time. While she stared up at the dark ceiling with the glints of fairy dust in the paint, she thought of Will and life choices.

Tiffany needed to create the spaces she would fit into. She would be a daughter, sister, soon-to-be sister-in-law, and a very good plumber and an artist.

She thought about the fresco aquarium mural, she had kept it simple but tonight she added diversity into the design.

At the shrill sound of the emergency phone, Tiffany jumped out of bed. She ran down the hall and picked up the receiver. "George here." She listened. There was a fire at the mining camp. Eric and Rebecca turned on the lights in the hall while Tiffany took notes. She hung up the phone. Because she had fallen asleep in her clothes, she was ready, except for her runners. "Fire, have to go."

"What can I do to help?" Eric asked.

Tying up her sneakers, she said, "Sorry, you have to be trained."

She drove to the Fire Hall. When she got there, other firefighters were in various stages of dressing in their safety gear. The Deputy Fire Chief started the engine. She and five firefighters jumped into the truck, with the siren wailing and lights flashing. The adrenaline ran high. She could see it in the volunteers' eyes. Would there be injuries? Where were the hydrants?

The truck sped out onto the highway. The firefighters spoke quietly. The red lights flashed across the fields. "Smoke on the horizon," the driver shouted.

The truck stopped. A group of sheds was fully engulfed in flames. Tiffany and her partner, Sharper, unrolled the hose and ran toward a man in a hardhat standing beside a hydrant. The pump man started the engine. The chief gave directions. The sprayed water hissed when it hit the flame. The heat flowed out in waves. Men from the camp were out with shovels, putting out embers when they dropped in the long, dry grass. A Rockwell water pump truck attacked the fire from the other side of the Apex crew. The water smothered the flames. The black smoke filled the sky and burned her eyes, the acrid odour irritating her nostrils. Men in hardhats were moving machinery away.

Tiffany continued to survey the area. Nikki waved at the RCMP vehicle which sped onto the scene with the blue lights flashing to join the group of white hardhats on the sideline.

The First Responders attended to an unknown injured person on the ground.

"George, Sharper, roll up the hoses. Let's get back to the hall and dry things out," Chief Gordon called.

The injured person was helped to stand and his crutches were given back to him. Will! Tiffany started toward him.

What was Will doing here? How did he get here?

Ahead of Tiffany, Nikki strode over and put her arm around Will. Tiffany swallowed her jealousy. She didn't have any reason to feel a propriety for Will Cleaver.

"I'm fine, Nikki." Will lifted Nikki's arm from around his shoulders. She stomped back to the other men in white hardhats.

Will was in the same clothes she had seen him at the hospital. "Hello. Are you okay?" Tiffany asked.

Brushing his trousers, he said, "Darkness and uneven ground can be my enemy and set me back on my rear."

"Your rear. You'll survive."

He lowered his eyebrows, giving him a dangerous look. "Is there anything you don't do in this town?"

"We all do what is necessary to keep our community safe."

"Good job."

"George, stop chatting. This isn't a social. Pack up," Chief Gordon barked.

"Yes, sir," Tiffany answered. "Give a man the title of Chief, and he takes over the world."

"Someone has to lead," Will said.

"I know." She looked him up and down. "Looks like you fell asleep in your clothes."

"Yes." He looked at his watch. "Not much time of the night left. How much do you have to do before you go home?"

"There is about an hour of work and debriefing. I'm lucky I don't have to report to a job at a specific time like some of the other volunteers."

"The challenges of a small-town volunteer firefighting unit." Will stared at Tiffany.

"You said it. We were glad of the assistance of the mining crew. This could have been so much worse." Tiffany moved along with the hose as it wound onto the truck. Will followed beside her.

"George," the chief roared.

"Talk to you later."

"Looking forward to it," Will said.

Tiffany worked in tandem with her partner Sam Sharper. They'd been in the same grade throughout their school years. She had been a bridesmaid at his wedding and did the plumbing in his new house. "Glad that's over. I might get a few hours of sleep before I have to work," Sam said.

He covered his mouth with his hand, hiding a long, drawn-out yawn.

"Let's keep the debriefing short," Tiffany whispered.

"From your lips to the chief's ears." Sam nudged her.

The equipment was loaded and the truck was ready. The other firefighters settled into their seats and closed their eyes for the drive back to the station but Tiffany searched for Will on the other side of the caution tape until she could no longer see him.

"This fire might slow down those potash guys with their big money from buying big boats and churning up our fishing grounds. Then their snowmobiles will tear up our trails over the winter and scare all the animals. Everybody just looks at the money, money, money, but what about quality?" Mac, the longest-serving firefighter, slapped his palm against his leg.

"I didn't see you at the community meeting," the Fire Chief said.

"Not everyone can go to meetings during the day," Mac said, and looked away.

Another firefighter spoke from the rear. "They're going to have more meetings to report the mine's progress. I hope you can make it."

"Only if they do it on a day when the homecare is scheduled to be there for my kid, Ben," Mac said. "Unless one of you want to come over and babysit while I go to a la-de-dah meeting."

Frank, Mac's neighbor, put his arm around Mac. "Let's talk about this later. I'll help."

"Maybe I'll bring my son. This town needs to be reminded who lives here. Yes, that's what I'll do."

The truck was parked in the fire hall and the equipment was put in place. It was ready for another emergency.

"Everyone, it's late. Gary, if you could write up your report and email me. Same for the rest of you. I'll collect all the reports and email them out to you. If you had a concern, let's hear it in an email," Chief Gordon said. "Now go home and sleep while you can. Tiffany, I'd like to see you for few minutes. I'll give you a brief rundown of the new response equipment."

The men and women disbanded to their vehicles.

"Thanks, Chief." Tiffany looked around the building, recalling the times the crew had saved buildings and people's lives.

While the sun streaked the horizon through the open office window, Fire Chief Ron Gordon showed Tiffany the new communication system. "Your father should have one of these new phones."

"You do know that Dad's in the hospital?" Tiffany would have been shocked if Ron didn't know.

"Yes, I heard at coffee this evening that he's doing okay. Not cancer," Ron said.

She shook her head. "I love this town's communication system."

"That way you don't have to tell me and waste too much time and tears." Ron put his hand around her shoulder. "What's with the black hair? I didn't recognize you without your name on your helmet."

"New system too. Not everyone is up to speed yet." She nudged him with her elbow.

Tiffany spent time looking over the new alert system that recorded every responders experience when they called in. It helped the fire chief know if he needed to call in backups. "This is incredible. How did you hear about this advanced system?"

"That guy, Will Cleaver, who rides around on a hand cycle and more often than not maneuvers on crutches. I know you've met him. It doesn't take long until Will makes himself known."

"I hadn't realized he'd been here long enough to change so many things."

"He has scouted things out off and on for months." Ron put his feet up on his desk. "We were having a practice one day and this guy hobbles up and asks if he can join the department." Ron took a sip from his coffee. "You can imagine what everyone thought. He can barely keep himself upright never mind carry a hose. He sat in the back and listened and the next meeting he came back with this program, a price, and the mayor."

"Wow, you know how long we've had to wait for improvements over the years. He sounds like a good man to have on the team."

"He's our new consultant. That's why he was on the fringes. He watches. He'll send his report in to me and we'll add it to the firefighters' and First Responders' notes." Ron yawned.

"And I thought he was just one of the concerned neighbors." Tiffany hid her yawn behind her hand.

"Don't get me wrong, he is that too." Ron's eyes closed for a moment.

"Thanks, Chief. I'll encourage Dad to keep you in the loop with his physical changes."

"I appreciate that." Ron stood and slipped his baseball cap on over his graying hair. "See you around town."

Chapter 18

After the fire, Will stripped down and crawled under the covers. Without sleep, his body would fight him at every turn. Later today he needed to be alert and focused in a meeting with Fred, Eric, and Tiffany to review the George and Family Plumbing bid.

Usually he thought only about the business at hand but he felt an affinity to Tiffany and wanted her to be happy, even if it took her away from Apex. She'd always return, her family was here after all.

He fell into a deep sleep and woke to his alarm and daylight cutting around the edges of his blinds.

After his shower, he dressed in his dark-blue jeans and favorite casual button-down checked shirt. His phone rang.

"Boss, are you going to need me today?" He heard country music in the background.

"Good morning, Lacy." Will cradled his phone to his shoulder while he buttered his toast.

"It's actually afternoon, boss."

"Right, Lacy. Yes, I need you to take me to the office at two, please. Then perhaps pickup at five."

"Perfect. I'll see you in twenty minutes." No small talk for Lacy. She loved to drive and this job gave her experience.

Tiffany woke with a start. She rolled her neck, then shaded her eyes from the room bathed in sunlight. Her heart beat in her throat. Today she needed to clarify her responsibilities to George and Family Plumbing and to her career.

While filling a cool glass of water, she saw the neighbor's cat on the fence then she realized that Eric and Rebecca's rental was gone from the driveway. She remembered the note that slipped under her door last night. The house was quiet. She went back into her room and found the note next to her office chair. She read it, then looked at her clock radio.

A meeting with Will and the family about the tender in forty minutes.

Showered, dressed with hair spikes in place, her blue jean shorts were almost at her knee.

At the office, she took her spare cardigan from her car trunk covering her short-sleeved blouse, attempting an appearance of competence, even if she no longer felt confident.

When Sylvia showed her into the boardroom, Will was in dress jeans and a casual shirt and Eric was in golf-length shorts.

It wasn't her appearance that mattered but the knowledge she brought to the discussion. The responsibility gnawed at her. She should have reviewed the plans in greater detail.

Eric gave her a little wave, and Will spoke into his computer. "Fred, Tiffany just walked in the door. I'll turn the screen and you can see everyone and we can all see you.

After they said their hellos, Fred started the conversation. "You chose a very intelligent woman, Eric. She has me all set up for this meeting."

In the hospital room, Rebecca smiled over Fred's shoulder.

Tiffany was struck by how relaxed her father was on the camera. All of the medical equipment had been removed. "I'm fine. In case you were wondering."

"Thanks for sending the file, Eric," Dad said.

Will's papers were organized in front of him. Eric opened his file on the oak table and slid it closer to Tiffany, allowing her to follow along. Tiffany felt the heat moving up her cheeks. She wasn't prepared and she didn't like it.

Because she hadn't studied the tender in detail, she would have to listen intently.

While her father directed them to pages, she scanned the figures and the plans. Eric asked questions. Will asked questions. Soon it was evident that her father continued to be a competent manager. Orders for materials had been made.

"Tiffany, a great deal will depend on you. Are coming back to work on this job?" Dad asked.

One quick switch and she was in the hot seat. "Hmmm, Dad since you seem to have everything under control and since Eric is home to be of assistance, I will not be on your work force."

Her father frowned. "I wasn't counting on you when I made this tender, and I won't be needing you now."

When had her father become so uncaring? Not even an Are-you-sure? crossed his lips. He cleared his throat. "But I want you to be available if I have a relapse. Just until I can get a foreman in place."

She squeezed her eyes tight. She had just finished breathing a sigh of relief that she would be free. But here it was again, the coiled plumber's snake spiraled to snag her again. "Sorry, Dad." What else could she say? "I'm going back to Winnipeg, I have a deadline."

Eric squeezed her hand. "We'll be fine."

Will doodled on a piece of paper. He handed it to her. A happy face with half a frown and half a smile.

"Thank you, Will," Dad said. "Eric and I felt it was important for you to see that I'll be able to continue.

Will nodded.

"Thanks, Eric, for bringing the modern technology along with you, and Rebecca for hooking it all together." Her father slung his arm around Rebecca's waist.

"Tiffany?"

"Yes, Dad."

"See you next time you're back in town."

Tiffany watched him pat Rebecca's hand.

Had she had it wrong all along? Did her father really want a daughter too, like her mother always seemed to throw at her, instead of a tomboy helper? Tiffany felt her resolve waver. She bit her lip. "Good luck, Dad."

Rebecca gave a little finger wave.

"See you soon, Rebecca. I'm marinating the steaks for dinner," Eric said.

"On my way." Rebecca blew a kiss to Eric.

Will closed the Skype program.

"Would you like to join us for a steak dinner, Will?" Eric gathered the papers from his file

"I'd like to, but I have a friend coming to town. She's applying for the chef position at the hotel."

"Bring her along. There's enough." Eric stood. "Unless of course, you won't have the time."

"Her interview is scheduled for tomorrow." Will leaned on the conference table. "She can get to know you and you will be able to give her a better feel for the community."

"Tiffany makes a mean Caesar salad," Eric said.

"I can purchase a loaf of garlic bread and I'll bring a bottle of wine," Will said.

"Rebecca ordered a dessert from the bakery this morning," Eric said.

"Sounds like you have everything planned, Eric. Do I need to shop for the salad ingredients?" Tiffany felt left out.

"No, big sister. I did that while you were sleeping this morning." Eric put his arm around her. It felt good to have others in charge, but it also made her feel boxed in. There wasn't anything special she could do.

Eric accepted Will's hand. "Thanks for the meeting. I'm sure George and Family Plumbing can complete the job."

Will smiled back. "I know you can. You just needed to discover it for yourself."

Eric gave Will the address. "See you around six-thirty. If your guest is late just let us know. Nothing is time sensitive."

Will closed his laptop.

Tiffany turned to leave.

"Tiffany, can I talk to you for a minute?" Will asked.

"Sure."

"I'll wait for you in the parking lot, sis."

Tiffany put her hands in her back pockets. "What can I do for you?"

"Come into my office, please."

She followed him out of the boardroom and toward his office. "Have a chair."

While sitting, she looked around at the maps on the wall, the diorama on the table, and the binders of material on the bookshelves. "You've acquired a lot of material in the short amount of time you've been here."

"I moved here a short time ago but I've been coming back and forth for months." He settled into his chair. "But that's not what I want to talk about."

Tiffany crossed her ankles and leaned back.

"Paula's an old friend. I'm glad you're going to meet her." He moved closer to her chair.

"I should be going. I have a salad to make." She stood.

"I saw you struggling during the meeting. You seem to be realigning your own priorities."

Tiffany felt the knot in her stomach loosen. Someone understood her.

"Thanks, Will. I'm conflicted. I'm selfishly pursuing my own goals when I should be helping my family."

"You heard your dad. He planned the job without you."

"I know but you don't know how hard it is to not be his right hand person. I feel as if part of me has been cut off." She shrugged. "And he seems to have accepted it so well."

"You've been gone for a while, haven't you?"

"Eighteen months. And not much use for a few before that."

"Then he has had time to adjust."

"Yes, and sonny boy is home, so good-bye Tiffany." The bitterness almost gagged her.

"Sibling rivalry?"

"No, it's more than that, a feeling of loss."

"But the other side of loss is found."

"Where do you hide Pollyanna?" Tiffany stretched her neck to look behind him.

Will tapped his chest. "Right here. She has a permanent spot in this man's heart."

Tiffany watched Will's eyes go soft and languid before he closed them. He opened his eyes a few seconds later. "She fought a hard battle to open a chink and nestle in. She doesn't have to come out too often anymore. I think she's getting lazy." Will smiled.

He reached for her hand and placed her palm above his heart. "Pollyanna will be right here whenever you need her."

Tiffany swayed toward Will, wound her other arm around him, then put her forehead against his. "Promise."

"Promise." He lifted her chin up then leaned and kissed her on her lips.

She felt the gentle pressure and wanted more. She opened her lips for a deeper, more sensual contact. The phone rang in the outside office. She felt Will withdraw from their intimacy. "Tiffany. Remember Polly is here when you need her."

Tiffany stayed in his arms for a minute longer feeling his heart beat behind her palm. She nodded. "I'll have to add doubter to my list of inadequacies." She stepped out of his reach.

"You can do that or you can change and believe." He looked deep into her eyes. "Who tore you down so low?"

"If you're in this town long enough, you'll hear the story." She turned. "See you and Polly around." Straightening her shoulders, Tiffany closed the heavy glass door behind her.

Chapter 19

After Tiffany left the office, Will covered his heart. He had learned when Nikki left him there were certain things that couldn't be changed. He couldn't change his parents and the love they gave him. He wouldn't change his wellness team that had been by his side through many rough spots. He couldn't not have cerebral palsy even if he had all the money in the world. And now he was going to convince the residents of Apex that a disability was a part of a person. They weren't special, or an inspiration, they were people getting on with lives.

Lacy tapped then opened his office door the same time his cell phone binged with a message.

"Be right with you, Lacy."

He ran his thumb over his phone and read a message from Paula. She was half an hour away.

Meet me at my house, he texted back.

Positioning his crutches and slipping his canvas messenger bag over his head to sling across his body, he said, "I'm ready" to Lacy standing in the doorway.

He moved toward the door, and Lacy held it open for him.

"See you tomorrow, Sylvia," Will said.

Lacy was in the driver's seat buckled up when he tossed his bag on the seat. "I need you to make a couple of stops on the way. The liquor store and the bakery."

Lacy in her usual no nonsense way, did as she was asked.

Back at the lodge, Will slid out of the front seat.

"Need me again tonight, Will?"

"No, thank you, my guest will drive." He walked quickly toward the front door of the lodge with his key ready.

Will lathered his face and ran the razor over his five o'clock shadow. He had just put on his clean Hawaiian sports shirt when his phone rang, indicating his guest was at the security door. He could hardly wait to see Paula again. She stepped into Will's open arms. Their history had formed during summer camps for *crips* as they called it. This was when they practised answering the slurs, when words like spaz, gimp, and worse that were tossed at them.

Will heard someone behind him clearing her throat. When he turned, he saw his neighbor Dorothy, in a pink pantsuit. "Dorothy Murphy, I'd like you to meet Paula Day, who has come to apply for the position of chef at the hotel."

"Where'd you come from?" Dorothy clutched her three-pronged cane.

"Kelowna, British Columbia. You?" Paula asked.

Dorothy's eyebrows shot straight up. "Right here, of course."

"If I get the position, I'll ask you for local favorite dishes," Paula said.

Dorothy shoulders straightened. "I'd be glad to share my recipes with you, but I've got to leave now."

"My apartment is this way." Will pointed down the hall. "We can talk for a few minutes." His breathing relaxed. This was Paula. "I've accepted a dinner invitation on our behalf. BBQ'd steak."

Once inside, Paula turned slowly taking in his sparse surroundings. "Where are your sculptures? Your leather sofa, your paintings?"

"Toronto. My personal living space won't be ready for at least a year and I'm here."

"How can you create in this environment?" Paula sat on the sofa.

"No distraction?" Will ventured.

Paula punched him on the arm.

"How was your flight?"

"Uneventful."

"On that note, would you drive us to dinner? I gave my driver the night off."

"Still not driving?"

"Not when I don't have to. I've been stranded on the highway in a rental. I like to have someone else behind the wheel." Will pointed to a bowl on the counter. "There are the keys."

"Can I have a minute to tidy up?" Paula asked. "And where should I put my suitcase?"

"Of course. Sorry." Will looked around his suite. "There is a second bedroom down the hall."

"Perfect," Paula said.

While Paula was busy organizing herself, Will put the wine and the garlic bread in his messenger bag and lifted it across his shoulder.

"Ready when you are." Paula almost reached his height in her high-heeled sandals.

"Like it?" Paula twirled. "My prosthesis is a good match."

Will flipped the keys to Paula. "You are one amazing woman, Paula Day."

"I'm also a woman with a very supportive prosthetic and engineering team that can build a fantastic leg." Paula jingled the keys. Her passion was racing cars in her spare time.

"This town has a speed limit though." Mrs. Leman wouldn't stand a chance of not hiring this inventive, creative woman to be her chef. Apex wouldn't be the same after Paula began preparing meals. "After your acceptance for the position at the hotel, we'll talk about the modifications you will need in the kitchen."

"She seemed to like my Skype interview, however I'm not sure if any other qualified person applied for the position. She's hired local short-order cooks for a long time."

"You need to remember that Apex was standing still until just months ago. She probably didn't need much more."

"I'll have to introduce her to your mantra. 'Create the opportunities and people will come.'"

"Maybe we should just put a sign at the town entrance, 'The opportunities are here, come and stay'," Will said.

Chapter 20

Leaving the town office, Tiffany linked her arm in Eric's until they stood beside his car. "Eric, Tony and Cleo need a run and I'm scheduled. The salad isn't complicated." She batted her eyelashes. "If you or Rebecca have time, would you make it?"

"Sis, you have changed." Eric had his hand on his door handle. "You wouldn't let anyone fiddle with your recipe."

Tiffany placed her hand on her chest. "Thanks for noticing."

"Six-thirty."

Her face felt comfortably warm. On her way to the car, before inserting the key, Tiffany thought about Will's positive Pollyanna principal. *Where there was Will, there was a way. For her.*

With a renewed sense of calm, she drove to Pat's house. When she opened the gate, the yard was empty. The sign-out/in sheet indicated the dogs had been taken for a run three hours ago. She called the number beside the name Pearson. No answer. She quickly opened the Facebook page on her phone. There hadn't been a new entry.

Tiffany searched her purse for Pat's spare key. Perhaps the dogs were in the house. Opening the door, Tiffany heard the fridge running. "Cleo, here, girl." Nothing. "Tony, here, boy."

Kicking off her runners, Tiffany hurried through the rooms. They weren't there. Tiffany felt her stomach clench as she redialed the number of the last walker, Pearson. She tried the number for the walker next to the last. "Diane.

Tiffany. I'm at Pat's and the dogs are gone. Any ideas?"

Diane explained she had returned them at noon.

Tiffany wrote a note and asked the person named Pearson to call her when he or she returned the dogs. She had to believe in the system. No one would take two dogs who belonged to a woman in hospital. They were probably out and just lost track of time or Pearson could have taken them back to his or her home.

Tiffany felt a stab of guilt. She had been in charge. Her focus on her art and new life, her selfishness, had caused her to loosen the control she had usually kept under these circumstances. She had been called a control freak more than once in her life.

She sat on the step with her head in her palms. She should phone Owen and tell him to help the business center and mall designer find someone else to complete the mural. She wasn't the right person for the job. When she was away from all responsibilities, she could be an artist but here at home, she didn't have any right to put her dad's health, her aunt's dogs, and her family's economic security at risk. Who was she kidding?

After waiting a while, she latched the gate, scanning the street on her way to her car. Driving slowly up and down the streets of Apex she saw children playing street hockey, trucks pouring cement for foundations, and heard other dogs barking in yards. Her throat ached. Thinking about strangers in town, she shifted into drive and sped out of town to the Rockwell Mining office.

Tiffany went directly to the reception desk. "I need to speak to someone who has a list of employees, please." The receptionist made a call and then Nikki came out of an inner office. "How can I help you? Tiffany, isn't it?"

"Yes, Tiffany George. I need to find a person named

Pearson with this phone number." She passed Nikki a slip of paper.

"This is an unusual request. May I ask the reason?" Nikki pushed her long hair away from her face. "You may have heard we've had a fire and are very busy."

"I know. I'm a firefighter." Tiffany took a deep breath. "This is important. The woman you helped, her dogs are missing and the last name on the sign out sheet is Pearson. I've been calling the number and there isn't an answer. I'm worried." Tiffany pointed to the slip of paper she'd passed to Nikki. "I know there are privacy issues but if you would check and call me back, I'd appreciate the assistance. Please help a woman find her pets."

"I'll see what I can do and get back to you. Give Susan your number. They're probably just fine. They are dogs, after all."

"If they're sick or in trouble, they can't call for help but you can be of assistance." Tiffany printed her cell phone number on the back of a George and Family business card. "Call anytime."

"If we locate anything helpful, we'll call. We have hundreds of employees." Nikki piled her blond hair on top of her head and then allowed it to cascade in waves around her shoulders.

"Could Susan call and tell me the results? I need to explore all avenues." Tiffany tried to keep her tone professional and calm when she wanted to drag Nikki by her hair to the computer.

She pressed redial on her phone again. This time the phone message was that the number was unavailable. It was either out of the district or turned off. *Please let it be turned off.*

Tiffany scanned the horizon on her way back into Apex. Nothing. Driving past Pat's house one more time, she checked the backyard. No dogs. There was nothing more to do than drive back to her parents' house. Will would be there. Maybe he had an answer. Maybe he could ask Nikki for assistance. Nikki wouldn't turn him down.

When Tiffany entered the kitchen, she gave Eric a quick hug because he was mixing the salad. The steaks were marinating in the fridge. Tiffany twisted the cap off a cold beer and took a long drink. "Thanks."

"How were the dogs?"

"They weren't there." Tiffany put the bottle down. "I'm worried. I don't recognize the name of the last walker."

"A lot has changed in the time we've been away. A new family could have moved here."

"I agree, but it's been over five hours. If anything happens to Cleo and Tony, I'll never forgive myself and neither will Aunt Pat. She told Will and me that they were there for her when she was in some dark places."

"They're smart dogs. If someone has taken them, they'll find their way back. Relax."

Rebecca came into the kitchen in a vivid yellow shift dress with peek-a-boo-toed flats.

"Rebecca, you look like sunshine." Eric wore khaki walking shorts and a green T-shirt.

Tiffany ran her palms over her jean shorts. Perfect for a backyard BBQ, with Will and his friend as guests. She excused herself to the restroom and gave her eyes a smoky appearance, added dramatic red lip colour, and on a whim, flattened her spikes and feathered her fringed bangs. She was an artist who created within her limitations.

As she was returning to the kitchen, she saw Will's car in the driveway. A stunning woman with long dark hair flowing down her back and a dress of flowered confection stood beside the driver's door in high strappy sandals. She waited for Will to come round to the front of the vehicle, and then the smile she gave him was full of love.

Tiffany's heart sank. She would be odd woman out. Holding her head high, Tiffany opened the front door. "Welcome."

"Tiffany George, I'd like you to meet Paula Day," Will said.

Smiling at Tiffany, Paula's high cheekbones were prominent. "Pleased to meet you."

Will winked at Tiffany.

"Need a hand, Will?" Eric asked from behind Tiffany.

"No, thanks. Just admiring the beautiful women."

Rebecca had also stepped forward to meet Paula.

"Come on in, everyone, let's clear the deck for Will," Rebecca said with a chuckle.

They all moved around the corner toward the cushioned patio furniture organized for conversation on the deck. Will weaved around the furnishings until he reached a coffee table. He ducked his head out of the strap of his messenger bag and handed a bottle of wine and the garlic bread to Eric.

"Awh, so you didn't change your aftershave. I detected garlic bouquet but didn't exactly know where it was coming from." Paula sniffed the air.

"You have a chef's nose."

Eric indicated the cushioned furniture. "Have a seat."

Will sat in the chair while Paula fixed her skirt over her knees on the settee. Tiffany opted for a single chair. Rebecca bustled around with the appetizers and a jug of iced punch. "Non-alcoholic."

Paula nodded. "I love your dress."

"Thank you. And you look like a summer garden in full bloom," Rebecca answered.

Tiffany curled her bare feet under her chair.

"Paula flew in from BC today. She's interviewing for the chef position at the hotel." Will's chest puffed out with pride.

"Paula, would you like to grill the steak?" Eric asked.

"No, thank you. I enjoy tasting the different flavors used by others." Paula licked her lips.

The steaks were tender. The wine lovely. Tiffany had to grudgingly admit that Eric did a good job of the salad. Thankfully, the evening breeze kept the mosquitoes at bay.

Will sat back, patting his stomach. "Wonderful meal." He continued in a casual tone, "When Paula is hired, I'll help Mrs. Leman design modifications for a safe work area." Everyone turned toward Paula.

Paula laughed and lifted her skirt hem to show the top of her prosthesis. "I'm going to wow Mrs. Leman first and when she's convinced about my abilities we'll discuss the other aspects."

Tiffany checked her phone yet again.

"Are you waiting for a call?" Will whispered while the others chatted.

"Yes. I'm waiting for whoever has Cleo and Tony to call when they have returned them."

"They're missing?" Will's eyes widened.

"They weren't there when I dropped over after our meeting and they've been gone since two." Tiffany didn't need to check the clock on the wall. "That's seven hours now." She bit the inside of her cheek.

"But I thought you knew everyone who was on the walk list."

"I don't know this person." Her eyes filled with tears. "I've been preoccupied and didn't check. If anything happens, Pat will never forgive me. I've always been responsible."

"Take a deep breath." Will leaned closer. "What have you done so far?"

"I've called the number that was on the paper several

times. I've driven up and down the streets. I even went out to the campsite and asked for help. I was hoping that Nikki would call back with some information." She blinked back tears. "But there are so many strangers in town."

"I'll text Nikki and ask her if she's had a chance to check." He reached for Tiffany. "Why don't we drive past Pat's house?" Slinging his messenger bag over his shoulder, he said, "Tiffany and I are going to Aunt Pat's and check on Cleo and Tony. We'll be right back."

"Don't be long. I need my beauty rest," Paula said.

"Paula, you have the keys, you can return anytime. But I might need to call you to let me in, I don't have a spare key."

Once on the road, Tiffany drove to Pat's. She jumped out and ran to the gate. Everything was as it had been. The spring evening was warm and dusk was extending into night. She whistled. Nothing. She ran back to the car. "Should I check inside just in case?"

"Has anything changed on the sign-out sheet?" Will asked.

Tiffany shook her head. "No. My note is the last entry."

"I haven't thought about this before, but who has been putting the dogs in at night and letting them out in the morning?" Will's eyebrows drew together.

"Carol, Pat's neighbor, has a key. I'll call her. Perhaps she has noticed something unusual."

Carol hadn't heard them bark all afternoon and evening.

"Let's drive out of town," Will suggested. "I haven't received an answer from Nikki either." Will waited for Tiffany to start the car. "I'm sure the dogs are fine."

Tiffany recognized Pollyanna speak when she heard it. "I wish I could believe you."

Will's phone rang. "Nikki. Thanks for calling back." He listened. "Did you check on a Pearson for Tiffany?" She felt him tense. "Nikki, they may be dogs to you but they are important to someone else."

Pocketing his phone, Will turned. "Nikki just didn't think it was important to call you back when she didn't have anything substantial."

"At least she checked. Who could it be?" Tiffany turned toward Will and tried to smile but she blinked back tears. "Let's drive."

Chapter 21

"Art, that's what has gotten me into this mess." Tiffany pounded the steering wheel. "If I wasn't so hung up on myself, I wouldn't have let this happen. I would have taken care of Tony and Cleo by myself, except for allowing them to be taken for walks by a few, very close friends."

"Hold on there," Will said. "I own some of the responsibility too. I told Pat I would be there for her and the dogs."

"Yes but you're a . . ."

The word hung in the air while Tiffany swerved to miss a skunk crossing the road.

Will held his cool. Someone always thought he couldn't do the job because of his gimpy walk. "A . . . what?" He let the space hang in the air between them.

"Stupid skunk," she said, signaling for a turn. "No, not you. You're a stranger."

Will expelled a breath. "I am a stranger, but that doesn't mean that I don't want to belong or to be held responsible for commitments I make."

"I know, and I'm glad you're here with me." She turned and gave him a weak smile. "I really don't want to be out here, it's creeping me out. Something isn't right." She put the car in neutral.

"Turn on your high beams." Will leaned forward. "I've been hearing about wild boars in the area and they are nocturnal."

"If one of those boars runs across this goat trail, I'm going to freak."

"No, you're not." He rested his palm on her taut thigh until he felt it relax.

"Why are we here again?" she whispered.

"The better to seduce you, my dear." He waggled his eyebrows up and down when she turned to him, her mouth agape.

"If that's the reason, can we go back to town? The rendezvous for the petting party is just behind the water tower."

"Are you toying with me?"

"If it will get me off this road and take my mind off Cleo and Tony, I'm game."

He turned away from her direct gaze. "Tiffany, look." Six pairs of eyes reflected in the headlights.

"What should we do?" She glanced over her shoulder. "What if there are men hunting out here? We're sitting ducks."

"They've spotted us." Will saw the boars drop back and form a single file off to cause mayhem and destruction in fields where they foraged.

Tiffany's face was as close to the windshield as it could be without her unclipping her seatbelt. "They're sort of cute. They remind me of Wilbur in *Charlotte's Web*." She jumped and yelped when one stopped and rubbed up against her fender. "I have to leave now." She shifted into 'drive' and pressed her foot on the accelerator. The car jerked. Will bounced forward and his seatbelt jerked into locked position. He put his hand on her thigh again. "Steady, Tiffany. I know they are supposed to be the ultimate omnivore creating environmental and economic disasters, but I haven't read that they eat plastic and steel."

She drove toward the next grid and turned. "I'm going back to Apex," she said through clenched jaws. "Why did we come out here, again? Explain!"

Will's palm felt warm and connected with Tiffany. He didn't want to think about Pat, Tony, and Cleo. Will wanted to think about the petting rendezvous Tiffany had mentioned. He cleared his throat. "I'm following a gut feeling." He stretched out his legs. His left calf threatened to spasm. Taking his palm away from Tiffany's thigh, he leaned forward and massaged his lower leg.

"As soon as you can, will you stop Tiffany? I need to stand."

She braked and stopped on the side of the road. She ran around the front of the car. He had opened the door and stretched his legs over the ledge." She knelt down and began kneading his leg.

"We've been here before," Will said when the spasms became less intense.

"Is it something you ate, or is it me?"

"I'm going to stand." He held on to her hands. When he was upright, he wrapped his arms around her. "It must be you. My body didn't want to wait until the rendezvous spot, but needed to hold you now."

"You could have just told me." She chuckled and leaned against his chest.

"I think you were more concerned for your safety than being ravished." He placed his chin on her head and breathed in her scent. He heard a faint buzzing sound off in the distance. "Do you hear something, or have you thrown my hearing out of whack?"

"Hmmm?" She turned her head so one ear was lifted toward the sky. "A swarm of bees coming our way?"

"This doesn't sound good. Let's get in the car." Will sat and positioned his legs under the dash. Until Tiffany was settled, he listened and scanned the horizon. Dark objects swooped from the sky with what appeared to be laser lights flashing. "Hurry."

"What is it?"

"I think they are hunting drones. Someone is determined to kill the boars and anything else that moves." He turned his head and watched through the back window. He needed to find out what was happening and who was in charge.

The car's speedometer pushed over the speed limit, and bushes, fence posts, and power poles flashed by. When they passed the welcome sign to Apex, Tiffany let out a huge sigh. "Two dangers averted. We need to let the residents know about this. What if someone was out stargazing? What if they were just out camping for the night?"

"I agree." He stretched his legs as far as they would go, and pushed his seat as far back as possible. "Tiffany, why don't you try that last phone number on the sign-out sheet again?" She drove to the side of the road. "No, wait. I have an idea. Give me the number. Whoever is at the other end won't recognize my number."

He dialed the number Tiffany had memorized.

"Sorry to disturb you so late but I'm missing two dogs." Will listened.

"You signed them out with this phone number."

"That's true. Where are you staying? We'll notify the RCMP. There is a dog-knapping alert."

Tiffany clutched the steering wheel. "Tell him I'm dialing 911," she whispered and reached for her phone.

Will shook his head.

"Motel 6 in Pleasant Ville. Thanks."

"Are you up for another road trip? I could call Lacy."

"Are you kidding? We're going. What did he say?"

"He said he doesn't have them and anyone could have used his name because it is on the side of his truck. He's going back to sleep."

"Are you really going to call the police?"

"Yes. A truck with the same company name he answered the phone with almost ran the dogs and me off the road, and the driver sped away so fast I didn't get a good look at him."

Will dialed the local RCMP detachment. "Will Cleaver. I would like to report two chocolate-brown Labradors missing from Apex." He listened. "Yes, they are Pat Morgan's." He nodded. "Pearson was the last person to sign out the dogs.

We've located and contacted him at the Motel 6 in Pleasant Ville. Tiffany George and I are on our way there now." He acknowledged the caution 'to be careful.' "Thank you." Turning to Tiffany, he said, "They are going to send over the highway patrol car as soon as it comes off the road. They will meet us at Motel 6. We are not to do anything until their arrival. They know Pat and how much the dogs mean to her."

"The benefits of a small community. The detachment knows us." They passed the sign that read 'Exit to Pleasant Ville, ten miles.'

"Will, what are we going to do if something terrible has happened?" Tiffany's knuckles grew white against the steering wheel.

"Let's not get ahead of ourselves. We need to find the dogs and then we'll take the necessary actions." Will reached over and ran his thumb down her cheek. "You and Pat trained them well. They are also a good breed. They'll find their way home."

The Motel 6 was at the end of Railway Avenue. They parked behind the half-ton truck with the magnetic sign advertising Pearson Land Developer.

"I've seen this truck around town," Tiffany said.

Soon the police arrived. They shone their flashlight in the back of the truck. Will recognized one of the tennis balls he had thrown to the dogs in Pat's backyard. The ball had Canadian Tire Jump Start Program written on the side. "That's the dogs' ball."

"We'll take it from here," the older officer said. "You two stay out here and we'll go in and question Mr. Pearson."

Will paced. He needed to keep his legs moving if he didn't want to seize up like an old rusted spring. He would have preferred to sit on the outside picnic table next to Tiffany while they waited. He saw her clenched fists. "Tiffany, walk with me?"

"Are you sure?" She moved toward him. "I really want to pound something right now, rather than wait helplessly."

"Tell me about this pounding thing you'd like to do," Will said as she followed him down the end of the parking lot and back.

"It's part of my art. I use different types of hammers and bend metal to my design." She held her chin high while she pounded one fist into another.

Before he could ask for more specifics, the police officer came out. "He did sign out the dogs. Apparently he heard about the walk program from a potential client. He wanted to help. He took the dogs out to a field and they didn't come back when he called. He thought they'd probably gone back home."

Will held Tiffany close. She molded herself to him like a piece of Silly Putty. "Was it Peterson's field?" she asked with a tight voice.

"Yes, but you won't see much until first light. It's a pretty big field," the younger officer said.

"There are wild boars out there. We saw them tonight." Tiffany shivered.

"And we heard what I suspect are hunting drones flying in that field," Will said.

"We've heard similar stories." The older officer took out his notepad and made a notation. "We're checking into it."

"Oh, Will." Tiffany collapsed into his arms.

He almost toppled but stabilized himself, wishing he had the strength and x-ray vision of Superman. He'd also take the power to fly right now too. He could scour the area and know if Tony and Cleo were safe.

"Do you have any suggestions, Officer?" Will asked.

"We'll have to wait until dawn. There isn't much we could do tonight," the younger officer said, turning toward his patrol car.

Tiffany straightened and wiped her eyes. "Yes there is. I'm going back out there. I'll drive slowly and whistle. If they are there, they'll come."

"I'm coming with you."

"You have to because I'm not driving you back and then coming back here. You're stuck with me."

"Call us if you find anything," the older officer said. "Take care out there. I'll tell the night patrol to keep an eye out for the dogs and you."

"Thanks. And will you look into the boar situation?" Will asked.

"Yes and I'll check for hunting licenses. Sometimes they are issued. I wouldn't be surprised with Rockwell Mining trying to establish a camp. Those beasts can wreak havoc," the officer said, tucking his notebook back into his pocket.

Tiffany opened her driver's door and jumped in, then began revving the motor. "You ride shotgun, Will."

Will threw his crutches into the front seat and hoisted himself inside.

As soon the door clicked shut, she reversed out of the hotel parking lot. "If one of those pigs or one of those drones hurt one of my aunt's dogs, I'll take out a hunting license."

"Can you even shoot a weapon?"

"No, but I can learn. I can learn to do anything perhaps even love again."

"What did you say?" He turned toward her.

"Will, eyes on the road." Gripping the steering wheel, she sighed. "Collin jilting me must be old news if you haven't heard about it." Anything to keep her mind off of the possibilities of what they could find in the morning.

"That explains the spikes." Will placed a hand on her thigh.

"My hair has nothing to do with it. This is the in-thing according to my stylist." Tiffany unfurled one hand and ran it over her head but the spikes weren't there. She had smoothed out her hair before dinner. Tiffany turned onto a road, her high beams illuminating the ditches. "If a pig comes in my path, I'll knock it to kingdom come."

"Please don't. It will damage your car and then we'll be stranded."

"Back to where we started, Mr. Cleaver."

"I wouldn't mind repeating the muscle massage and our kiss."

"If we find those dogs, you can have all of the muscle massages and kisses you want."

Tiffany slowed, then lowered all four windows. She leaned her head as far as it would go, and Will did the same on his side. She drove and stopped, listened, and then whistled. She continued this until her voice rasped and her lips could no longer pucker. "Even if we find the dogs, I think kissing will be out of the question."

"Let me take over while you rest your lips." He placed his fingers in his mouth and his whistle flew out into the night.

"Why have you been hiding that talent?" Tiffany slugged his shoulder.

"You wanted to do it all. Besides, I knew they'd recognize your whistle if they could hear it. I think we have to give up until morning. It's almost midnight."

"You're right. I'll head back to Apex and drop you off."

"You could always show me the rendezvous spot for my growing knowledge of the area."

"Ask around, someone will tell you." Tiffany yawned.

"I'd rather see it with you." Will slid his arm along the top of Tiffany's seat.

When Tiffany turned the car around the corner, she felt the passenger's rear tire blow. The steering wheel jerked to the right. "Hold on." She brought the car to a stop. "Can you believe that this night could get any worse?"

"You know your way around vehicles. I'm sure you have a spare." Will reached for his door handle. "I'll come out and keep watch. You'll have to do the heavy work."

"You're such a princess," she threw over her shoulder.

"I can call for help. Where did you say the nearest tow truck was?"

"They'll never find us."

"Yes, they will. I have GPS on my phone. I need all the help I can get. I even have a weak signal."

"Let's try to work this out together. If anything dangerous happens we'll use your technology." Tiffany turned on her four-way flashers. If anyone were out this way they'd see this signal.

Tiffany was concentrating on tightening the last bolt on the spare when Will tapped her with his crutch. "Shush."

She looked up, and he pointed his crutch behind her. She turned slowly to see eyes gleaming in the reflection of her emergency flashing lights.

"Get in the car," she whispered frantically.

"Not without you." He bent down and lifted the flat tire with one hand and clung to the car with the other. His crutches clattered to the ground. "Gather your things. I'll toss this at whatever it is."

"No you don't." Tiffany picked up the jack. "It's a three-hundred-dollar tire."

"I'll buy you a new set. Now hurry."

Tiffany picked up Will's crutches and handed them to him. "Get in the car, please. I'll toss the flat in the trunk and be right in."

When the trunk slammed closed, Tiffany heard a whimper. "Will, shine the flashlight toward the center of the road." Her heart slammed into her throat at the sight. She swallowed and ran. "Tony." She held her hand out to the dog. "Here, boy." Turning toward the car, she said, "Will, it's Tony. Hurry! He's injured." She knelt down and he put his head on her knee.

"It's okay, boy. We're here," Will muttered while he stumbled over the uneven ground. He dropped to his knees and crooned to Tony while Tiffany ran her hands over his body.

"You're safe. Will's here too. He knows how to help."

Tony looked up toward the car and barked.

She gave one final pat. "I'll get the car. Stay with Will."

"Where's Cleo?"

Tony banged his tail and turned his body.

"Back there, boy?"

"Will, what am I going to do? I can't see what's wrong. He seems exhausted."

"I have a bottle of water in the front compartment of my bag."

Tiffany hurried into the car and backed it toward Will and the dog. She brought the water and a plastic sack and fashioned a bowl. "Come on, boy, drink a little. We'll save some for Cleo. You need to get in the car, and we'll drive until we find her."

Tony followed slowly on his belly to the back door. Tiffany lifted his front feet in and Will pushed in Tony's back legs. Tony collapsed onto the seat. Tiffany jumped into the driver's seat.

Will crawled into the back seat beside Tony. "We'll find her, boy."

Tiffany drove slowly in the direction Tony had come, a mile down the road. Her life karma had her going backward again.

Tony started to yip.

"Are we getting close, boy?" Will asked.

Tiffany angled her car so the high beams spread across the field then shut off the engine.

Tony pawed the door trying to get out of the car.

"We're close. I'm driving onto the field." Tiffany shifted the car into low gear and maneuvered through the ditch and onto the field. The light reflected a few feet away.

Suddenly Tiffany braked and put the car into 'park.'

"Pigs be damned." She jumped out of the car and ran to a heap and buried her face in the fur coat. "Cleo, Cleo baby." She felt the dog's chest rise and fall. A faint heartbeat fluttered against her fingertips.

"She's alive," Tiffany called to Will.

The door opened. Will's movements were slow and cautious.

"Be careful," Tiffany called.

Tony stuck his nose out of the window, calling to Cleo.

"Two big dogs, two humans, and a sardine tin," Will said when he reached Tiffany's side.

"Use your talents. We can solve this," Tiffany said.

Cleo opened an eyelid when Tony whimpered again.

"Tiffany, I wish I could be more help, but right now all I can give you is a possible solution." Will knelt next to Cleo. "If you return the flat tire to the wheel well, lay the back seats down, there will be room for both dogs."

"You're a genius." Tiffany kissed Will's cheek while he spoke quietly to Cleo then ran back to the car, moved the tire, and sprayed the trunk and interior with bug spray.

"Sorry, Tony." Tiffany parked as close to Will and Cleo as possible, coaxed Tony into the trunk area, and then she brought out an old blanket, encouraged Cleo to crawl onto it and dragged it to the open door. On his knees, Will picked up the other corners, and together, they lifted Cleo into the car.

"Will, you okay? Do you need anything?" Tiffany asked as she closed the back door.

"Can you bring my crutches while I get in?" Will opened the passenger door and hoisted himself into the seat.

Tiffany snatched them from the ground, passed them to Will, and then slammed the door.

As soon as her butt hit the seat, Tiffany started the motor then stepped on the gas pedal. "Hold on, everyone, we're on our way to the animal hospital in Pleasant Ville." Passing her phone to Will, she said, "Call ahead and tell them we're coming, and we're not sure of the injuries."

After a brief conversion, Will said, "They're waiting for us."

Chapter 22

Will led Tony through the back door into a lit sterile room, where Tiffany was administering oxygen to Cleo while the veterinarian, in his stark-white lab coat started an IV.

Will moved confidently and quietly across an even smooth surface toward a sink and filled a large bowl of water for Tony. Holding on to the sink, Will placed it on the floor in front of Tony.

Will then sat on the chair beside the doorway observing Tiffany, wondering if there was anything she couldn't do.

Will closed his eyes against the overhead lights. He listened to the sounds of metal against metal, the swish of gowns. Opening his eyes slightly, he saw that the doctor and Tiffany had donned surgical masks. Will swallowed. He'd been in an operating room atmosphere many times, on the table, ready to be put under for surgery or just brought around. Tony lay at his feet. Will tucked one toe under Tony's paw and closed his eyes again.

Will woke with a start when his crutch crashed to the floor. Tony was on the examining table having gauze wrapped on his front upper leg. Tiffany's face was pale, her shoulders caved toward her chest, and her hands shook when she covered her yawning mouth. Will leaned against the back of the chair and watched out of half-lowered lids while the vet and Tiffany worked as a team. Who was this woman?

"Tony could go home tonight," the vet said, "but I'd like to keep him for support for Cleo." He removed his gloves and mask, showing off a neatly trimmed handlebar moustache.

"Jim, thank you." Tiffany put her arm around his shoulder. "Is there anything else I can do to help?"

"I don't have to tell you what the outcome would have been for Cleo if you hadn't found her when you did. Pat would have been devastated."

"We're not out of the woods yet, are we?" Tiffany asked, her voice hoarse with emotion.

Jim shook shiny bald head. "They've been pretty beaten up. The number and size of the bites on Cleo, it appears as if they tangled with small animal, perhaps a weasel."

"Should I call Aunt Pat?" Tiffany blinked back tears.

"Wait until morning. We don't want to worry her at this hour. There isn't anything she can do." The doctor washed and dried the surgical instruments and then placed them into a sterilizer.

"You're right." Tiffany brushed her arm across her eyes.

Will stood and stepped forward. "We haven't had the opportunity to meet. I'm Will Cleaver. I'm new to Apex."

Jim pumped his hand. "Pleased to meet you. I'm hearing great things."

"Thanks for everything you've done here tonight for Cleo and Tony."

"Let's go home." Will reached for Tiffany. "Can you drive back to Apex?" Will asked, noticing her half-closed eyelids, her slumped shoulders. You look done in."

"Do we have a choice?" she asked.

"I could drive, but we'd be driving slowly because my reaction time is limited by my fatigue." He wanted to sit and have her snuggle on his lap but there was a problem they had to solve. "Is there a hotel in Pleasant Ville?"

"The Motel 6, near the highway, where we saw Mr. Dognapper." Tiffany leaned against Will.

"I can get us there. We can sleep a couple of hours and then drive to Apex." Will looked at his watch. Three-thirty in the morning.

"Fine. Anything you say."

He guided her to her car and opened the passenger door. "In you go." He handed her the seatbelt. He talked to himself, "I can do this. I can do this." When he started the engine, Tiffany was slumped against the headrest. He eased on the gas, testing his strength on the brake. There wasn't anyone around to be annoyed by his slow driving.

When he reached the motel, he parked under the canopy, and then seemed to move at glacial speed through the doors and into the lobby. The night clerk, probably just out of high school, grinned when he asked for a room with two beds. There was one room left with one bed. "Take it or leave it. We got miners staying here."

Will handed over his credit card, collected the key card, and returned to the car. Right now he was grateful for the vacant handicap space, next to the doorway. He roused Tiffany. "Come on, sweetie. As much as I'd love to carry you, you'll have to walk."

She snorted and scrubbed her eyes with the back of her hand then shielded her eyes with her arm while he whispered directions to the room. He slipped the key card into the lock, the door swung open. She stumbled toward the bed and collapsed facedown. He had thought he would sleep in the chair, but the other half of the bed was too inviting. He laid down on the flowered comforter, tucked the pillow under his head, and closed his eyes. His exhausted legs shook against the mattress. He glanced over at Tiffany. She was in a deep slumber. He drifted off.

When he woke, the sun had created light bars across the bed. Tiffany had rolled into his back and her arm sprawled across his chest. He wanted to stay in this place for the rest of the day but nature called and so did work.

Before he lifted Tiffany's arm off his chest, he kissed her fingertips. She moaned and scrunched closer. With reluctance, he sat preparing to slip away without wakening her. His crutch fell and knocked the lamp.

Tiffany jumped out of bed. "What's going on?" She looked around. "Where are Tony and Cleo?" She shook her head as if trying to make sense of her surroundings.

"They're okay. Remember? We left them at the animal hospital last night."

She sank down onto the edge of the mattress and hugged a pillow to her chest.

"Just stay where you are for a minute. I need to use the bathroom." When Will came out, Tiffany had made a coffee in the coffee maker and handed him a cup. "Better coffee breath than morning breath." She leaned in and kissed his cheek, "My turn."

Will turned on the TV business channel out of habit. He sank onto the comforter when the news anchor announced that Rockwell Mining was halting production on the Apex mine because the world price of potash was falling. When Tiffany returned from the bathroom, he held his hand out to her and pointed to the scroll of news running across the TV screen. "We'd better get back to Apex."

"Right. I'll drive." Tiffany put her hand on his forearm as they progressed down the hall. "What are you going to do, Will?"

"I'm not going to jump to conclusions." Neither of them stopped at the desk. "But I can swing through these crutches and beat you to the car."

Tiffany removed her hand from his forearm and ran through the doors in her crushed and dirty clothes. Will reached the car door handle the same moment that Tiffany did.

Inside the car, she beat him buckling her seatbelt. "You're fast."

"I'm not just a pretty face." His eyes focused on her wide-open eyes. "You do remember suggesting I had more than passable features on the first night we met?"

"Of course. I've sketched the bits of you I've seen."

"I'd model for you one day, if you want." He reached past the gear shifter and placed his hand on her thigh.

She covered his hand. "I'd like that." While she backed up, she glanced at him. "You do know artists prefer nude models."

He swallowed a laugh. "I'm good with that."

"I'll check on Tony and Cleo's condition."

"No, I'll call. You continuing driving." Will noted the local news trucks passing them on the highway as he took his phone from his messenger bag. "I need to use your phone. Mine's dead." That might explain why Nikki hadn't called in a panic with the news.

"I won't speed but I will pick up the pace a bit," she said. "We'll take the back road into Apex. I'm sure there are many folks wondering what will happen to their plans now. They'll want to talk to you, but you'll have to change first."

When Will called the Animal Hospital, the receptionist answered. Tiffany spoke through the Bluetooth hands-free device. The receptionist told them that the Jim was in surgery but that Cleo was responding to her medications and that Tony was at her side. Jim would like to keep both dogs until tomorrow, unless there is an emergency and he needs the space.

Tiffany thanked her, motioned for Will to hang up, then groaned. "After I drop you off, I'll call Aunt Pat from home."

"Mind if I use your phone to text Nikki? I'll tell her to call my house phone in a few minutes."

"Be my guest. Or you can plug your phone into my jack. It's in the console."

"Thanks." As soon as Will plugged in his phone, missed calls and text messages scrolled across the screen. Nikki had tried to reach him all through the night.

Will contemplated sustaining the bubble of time he was sharing with Tiffany, but he knew it wasn't possible. He chose to text. *Phone battery dead. Will be available in thirty.* He turned off his phone. He needed to prepare himself for questions that he'd be asked from the community. And Nikki. He then used Tiffany's phone and called Nosh, Nosh, and Crane. He needed the company's response. "Hello, James, Will here."

Will listened intently while James spoke then said, "Thanks, James. I appreciate your support. We remain on schedule. I'll check the company statement as soon as I hang up."

"From your side of the conversation, your development will continue even though Rockwell is putting the mine on hold." Tiffany stared straight ahead.

He put his hand on her thigh. "Yes." Looking toward the patio outside his apartment, he saw Paula sitting on a chair reading the newspaper. "Paula's up. I won't have to worry about having one of the other residents unlock the main door."

He reached for the handle, turned sideways, and stood, holding onto the door. "Can you text me after you talk to Pat? I'd like to call and reassure her as well but I won't until I know you've spoken with her."

"With all that is going on, Mr. Cleaver, you amaze me." Tiffany's eyes were large and luminous.

"You wouldn't want to come out here and give me a hug, you know that hold where the whole of your body is pressed against mine?" Will held open his arms.

"Be right there. Don't move a muscle." She sprinted around the car.

She molded into him, reached her hand along his morning-bearded jaw. Tiffany patted him on his butt before she stepped away.

"Tiffany, you are the amazing one in this vicinity. It will take a long time to discover all your talents but I want to know." He winked at her, "An appropriately timed bum pat is appreciated, too."

"Get changed and beam all your positive power for the Apex hopefuls."

Tiffany returned to her car and waved before she continued down the lane.

Will needed to do one thing at a time. *Get changed, interpret official statements, and provide hope for the community.* He squared his shoulders and practiced continuous motion toward the patio doors. He nodded at Paula.

Paula glanced at him. "A little wrinkled this morning." She knew him well enough to allow him his space. They hadn't been friends since preteens without them being able to read each other.

"You're right," he called out to her. "Why is the phone off the hook?"

"I needed to sleep and Nikki called every two minutes last night."

"Did you answer?"

"No. I can read a call identifier as well as anyone. I didn't know where you were and what time you'd be home. You know Nikki, I would have been dragged into her drama and I chose not to go there."

"My phone battery chose for me," Will said.

"As if," Paula muttered back at him.

"I'm heading for the shower. The phone can stay off the hook for a few minutes. Nikki knows I'll contact her." Will put his cell phone on the charger, then checked his email. Finally he peeled off his dirty, bloodstained shirt and pants, and then kicked his loafers into a corner.

Naked, he held on to the memory of Tiffany's touch.

Chapter 23

Tiffany hummed along with a tune on the radio. The sun shone brightly. A rabbit hopped along in the ditch. For these few minutes before anyone interrupted it, she loved her life. She was proud of her planned fresco and copper sculptures and her life as a plumber, a daughter, sister and soon to be sister-in-law. But what excited her to the core was a tall, rugged man with warm brown eyes. Will had been there every step of the way with her last night. They were equals. He stayed because he hadn't wanted her to be alone in the search and he wanted to share the responsibility. Thank goodness for Tony and Cleo that Will had been with her. Jim thought the bite marks suggested the dogs had tangled with a weasel.

When Tiffany opened the door to the house, her mother got up from the table with her arms wrapped tightly around herself. "Dr. Thienes from the animal hospital called. He assumed that you'd be home. He told me you were with Will."

"Did he also tell you about Cleo and Tony?"

"What's this all about?" Her mother glared at Tiffany. "I don't care who you have a relationship with in Winnipeg, but this is a small town and our family is doing business with that man." Shaking her head, she continued. "I don't know what's happened to you but you just don't think about your dad and me."

"I need to clean up before I can talk with you." Tiffany shoved a chair under the table then pointed to the spots on her jean shorts. "This is Cleo and Tony's blood. Will helped me find the dogs and get them the help they needed."

"Does Pat know?" Her mother reached for the phone.

"Not yet. It was too early to call when Jim finished surgery. Then Will and I fell asleep." Tiffany wrapped her hands around her middle. "Mom, what are you doing home?"

"Dad felt so much better after his Skype meeting with everyone that he insisted I come home for a good night sleep. I'm just waiting for the hospital to call about his release." Her mom paced. "I don't know what will happen now the potash mine development will be halted."

Tiffany ached for a shower to rinse her body free of last night's tragedy. "I can tell you that Will isn't jumping to any conclusions and neither should we."

Mother looked at the digital clock on the microwave. "Eric and Rebecca will be back from their run shortly. I'd be happy if the whole thing was cancelled. Your dad could rest. He said you're going back to your art without regard for our needs."

"Yes, Mom, I told you I have a contract to honor." Turning toward the bathroom, she said, "I've got to get cleaned up."

"Eric and Rebecca will stay." Her mom's words followed Tiffany down the hall.

Tiffany tossed her clothes in a trash bag. The hot shower cascaded over her body. She scrubbed her scalp and then her knees of grit. Standing under a fine spray, she felt her core heating up remembering Will's hand on her thigh. When she lifted her arms, she recalled the strength in his back when she wound her arms around him.

Her stomach growled, bringing her back to the present. It had been a long time since they had eaten steak. Ever since she arrived from Winnipeg, it seemed as if life was in fast forward and everyday was made up of three. She wasn't looking forward to calling Pat, but at least she could tell her the good news. The dogs would be home tomorrow, and she wasn't letting them out of her sight again until Pat was home.

Tiffany bit back a sob as tears rolled down her cheeks and mingled with the water. This wasn't possible. She had to leave in a couple of days to make it back to Winnipeg on time. How the hell was she supposed to do all this and look after the dogs too? Her heart hammered in her chest. She toweled off and ran her fingers through her hair. She jabbed her fingers into a jar of sculpting gel and slathered and pushed until the black spikes were standing hard and straight.

Wrapped in her bathrobe, Tiffany sat on her bed and dialed Aunt Pat. When she answered, Tiffany shared the events of the last twenty hours.

Pat interjected an occasional 'oh no' sigh and sobs.

"I'm sorry, Aunt Pat, you put Tony and Cleo in my care and I failed."

"Yes, you did, Tiffany. I can't talk to you right now. I need to call Dr. Jim." Pat hung up.

Tiffany heard voices in the hallway. Eric and Rebecca were back. She was not going to think about what they would be doing now that the potash boom was a firecracker bang. She dressed for comfort in cut-offs and a sweatshirt. Her stomach grumbled louder, but she ignored it and opened her computer. The mural was her desktop background. It was vibrant with shimmering blues, greens, sea plants, fish, turtles and starfish. It was her creation. She knew what she had to do. Art was for many and lasting. Today's problems were immediate.

She put her computer into sleep mode and went in search of food in the kitchen.

Fortified with a fresh cup of coffee, a ham and cheese sandwich, she went outside to the deck. Before she took her first bite, she sent a text to Will telling him that she had spoken with Pat. She didn't say that she was crushed because her aunt hadn't thanked her, much less praised her for finding the dogs or for getting help.

Tiffany took a long sip of the coffee. Did she really belong here anymore? Eric was staying. *Tiffany George, you've been kicked to the curb.*

But what about Will?

What about Will? He seemed to get along just fine. He had Nikki, he had Paula, he had his independence with Lacy, and he had most of the residents, including Aunt Pat, tied around his little finger.

With Eric's help, Dad could complete the tender because the complex will happen. She hadn't and won't mention Will's conversation she overheard on their return to Apex. Will would share the Nosh, Nosh, and Crane's decision, when it was the right time and place. That was the least she could do for him. Because of his example of how one's destiny could be accomplished by fearless choices, she had sent a text to Owen, telling him she'd be back and ready to start on time.

Stretching out her legs on the lounge, she reached over and turned off her phone. Changing the events of the world could wait for an hour while she slept.

Tiffany swatted at something tickling her nose, then her cheek. She opened one eye. Eric was there running a piece of broom grass over her face. "Don't you ever grow up?" She grabbed for the grass and threw it over the deck railing.

"Oh, and be all grown up and sour, like you were while you slept." Eric scrunched up his face.

"I was dancing and singing, I'll have you know."

"Then I wonder whose funeral you were singing and dancing at?" He sat at the end of the lounge and pushed at her feet.

Tiffany tried to push him off of the lounge.

"Stop it, you two," Mom called from the kitchen. "Tiffany, you are as red as a ripe apple."

"Then tell this brother of mine to bring me an umbrella. I had the lounge first." It felt good to be childish.

"What will you give me if I get the umbrella?" Eric taunted.

"A snake bite." Tiffany squealed and jumped off the lounge when he came toward her.

Rebecca rounded the corner carrying glasses, ice clinking against the sides. "Eric," she said, her voice lilting, "I made lemonade."

He stopped chasing Tiffany then darted toward the tray of frosty glasses. Mom joined them on the deck. Rebecca handed around the remaining glasses.

"Just heard from the hospital. Dad will be discharged tomorrow," Mom said, "but I think I'll go in for a visit this afternoon, just to keep him company and thinking positively about our future rather than about the mine curtailing its work."

Rebecca turned to Tiffany. "Looks like you can go back to your life in Winnipeg."

Tiffany rubbed the moisture from the glass onto her shorts. "Yes. I'll return right on time and begin my aquarium mural."

"Eric and I have found a house," she gushed.

Tiffany almost choked on an ice cube. "That's wonderful." *I'll return to my life, and the crisis of these few days will be a memory.*

"I'm glad this happened." Eric reached across the table and held Rebecca's hand. "We may not have come home and discovered that here is where we want to raise our family."

Mother's grin told it all. She hugged Eric and Rebecca. "I can expect to be a grandmother after all." She looked pointedly at Tiffany.

"I'm glad for you, Mom." Tiffany gulped her drink. Had all this really happened in less than a week? She'd drive out of Apex right on schedule. Eric was home. All was right in the George Family. "I'll even go back with a tan, thanks to a much-needed sleep in the sun."

Tiffany went back to her bedroom. Her phone vibrated in her pocket. Will's text said he talked to Pat and she wanted him to look after the dogs. Everything seemed to have fallen into place. Tiffany texted back and asked if she could help pick up Tony and Cleo.

His text answer was short. *Going now. Pat asked. Animal hospital overcrowded cuz of emergency. Dogs discharged. Lacy driving.* Will had what he wanted. He had the dogs undivided loyalty and apparently Pat's too. These last days should be a Hallmark ending for everyone but her.

While she was sorting her clothes, Owen phoned Tiffany. He was over the moon. The materials had arrived at the mall and Owen had hired two assistant artists. She sat at her desk and opened her aquarium file. Life in Apex would continue without her. Nikki and Will could console each other about the changes that were on the way due to the drop in potash prices.

Positive thoughts. She had what she wanted. So why did she feel so sad? She was tired, that's all. Perhaps she could go into Regina with Mom and say goodbye to Dad tonight, then she could hit the road bright and early in the morning and be at her apartment for dinner tomorrow. Back to her urban life where everyone took care of themselves. Just what she wanted. Yes, that was what she would do.

She closed the file and went in search of her mother. It was agreed that they would leave in half an hour and pick up something to eat as well as a treat for dad. Tiffany glanced onto the deck, where Eric and Rebecca snuggled in the swing. Mom and Dad were happy. Their son was home planning a wedding and a future generation of babies for the George family to love. With continued channeling of Will's positive Pollyanna principal, Tiffany decided that those nieces or nephews will have a famous artist for an aunt.

Tiffany stared out the passenger-side window while they drove to the hospital in her mom's tiny car because hers hadn't been cleaned from last night's tragedy. Tiffany didn't want to deal with any of that. No old blood or dog hair. She wasn't going to think about Tony and Cleo, since no one else wanted her to be responsible again. She still didn't understand why or how this happened.

Mom set the cruise control. "Tell me what happened last night?"

"Not much." Yes, she was pouting. She and Will were heroes, but no one seemed to care about her.

"I know you didn't come home."

"I lost Tony and Cleo. Will helped me find them. We took them to the animal hospital. We were too tired to drive home. We stayed in the Motel 6 until this morning."

"Tiffany, you should have come home. This doesn't do your reputation or our family any good."

"Mom, who I spend the night with is nobody's business but mine and the man I'm with." Tiffany swallowed bile edging into her esophagus. "I'm thirty years old."

Her mother gasped. "You haven't known Will very long. You did use protection, didn't you? I'm sorry that's how you feel about your reputation in this community. It's good for everyone that you're going back to Winnipeg."

If she and Will had conceived a child. It would of course be a scientific wonder because their clothes had covered the necessary parts for conception. But she wished they had.

"Mom, I'm not sixteen." Tiffany said, exasperated. "Besides, you seem pretty excited about Eric and Rebecca's surprise."

Her mother's jaw tightened. "You probably just acted out because Eric and Rebecca are in love. When you're back in the city, you can have your indiscretions."

Tiffany watched the landscape go by. "Thanks for the vote of confidence in my choices."

"Put on a smile. You're going back to your life away from us, back to a freer life where there aren't any neighbors or family to call attention to your behavior. What do you want to eat?"

"An A&W Teen burger and a milkshake."

"And I suppose you want me to have a mama burger?"

"If the burger fits, eat it." Tiffany skimmed her fingers across her hair. "How about subs? Dad always enjoys the ham and Swiss cheese with banana peppers."

"You always thought you knew Dad better than everyone else." Her mother drove into the fast food drive-through, then ordered their sandwiches into the intercom.

"Wait a minute. Of course I knew the Working Dad. The Boss Dad. The man who didn't tolerate a sloppy job," Tiffany said. "We spent hours together. I was his work partner."

"And I'm his life partner."

They drove in silence the rest of the way.

When they arrived, Tiffany allowed her mother to enter her father's hospital room first.

"You're a sight for sore eyes," Dad said as her mom gave him a kiss. "Hi, Tiff."

"Hi yourself, Dad. We brought you a sub, just the way you like it."

"You're going to have to save it and eat it tomorrow. The doc says I have to clean up my food choices, as well as no cigarettes, if I'm going to stay alive to see our grandchildren."

"What's this fascination with grandchildren all of a sudden?" Tiffany unwrapped her sandwich.

"The circle of life, Tiffany. The circle of life." Dad ate salad from the container her mother shared with him. "It makes all we've worked for worthwhile." He reached for her mom's hand.

Mom wiped a tear from her eye. "It's such good news." She gripped Dad's hand. "Remember all those evenings last winter when we thought having family and grandchildren living in Apex was over for us?"

"You flew in a few hours for Christmas and then you were gone." Dad patted Mom's hand. "We knew you'd never come back after your taste of city life."

"I was cramming to catch up and learn everything I could." Tiffany's heart hammered in her chest.

"Between Eric and Will, we'll do what we need to do."

"But, Dad, you encouraged me to go." Nausea threatened the back of her throat.

"You weren't much help at home, pounding your metal 'til all hours of the early morning. Collin and his new fiancée were planning a wedding. I'd hoped you'd take your little course and come to your senses," the Boss Dad said.

"I'm sorry you feel that way." Tiffany stood with her hands on her hips. "Dad, I have a commission. I'm creating a mural in a mall for thousands of people to enjoy. Doesn't that count for something?"

"But you're not in the family business and that's what's important now."

"Guess that's all for me, then. I'll pack up and leave." Tiffany wrapped up her leftover sandwich with care and tossed it into the trash.

Blinking rapidly, she turned and felt as if her life in Apex was similar to the leftovers she dropped into the trash. Excess. Not required. Skimming her fingers over her spikes, she turned and walked over to the bed. "See you, Dad. Take care." She gripped his hand and squeezed. "I'll meet you outside the front doors, Mom. I'm sure you would like some quiet time with Dad."

"I'll be a while. I want to stop in and see Pat, too."

"Say goodbye to her for me, will you?" Tiffany held up her phone like a shield. "Take as much time as you need, I have work to do. Text or call when you're ready to leave."

With her eyes focused down the hall to the exit sign, Tiffany knew she had to keep it together until she was in the concrete stairwell. No one would find her there. Biting her lips, she forced her feet to move at an even steady pace until her hand turned the door handle. Once inside the cavernous chamber, her first sob escaped. It reverberated off the walls and the concrete stairs. Stuffing her fist into her mouth, she swallowed deeply and sank onto the landing. Why wasn't she jumping for joy? She was free.

When voices entered the stairwell, she scrubbed her hand across her eyes. Then she found a tissue in her satchel, blew her nose, and started down the stairs. She'd been here before and she had survived. She'd do it again.

The voices were on the flight above her. Tiffany scrambled down the stairs and through the emergency exit into the alley. She would not allow her mother to see her like this. She quickly sent a text to her mother. *Pick me up at the coffee shop on the corner.*

A couple at the counter were leaning into each other while they ordered. The man had difficulty speaking, the woman's eyes were puffy, and her nose was red. They paid and went through the doorway into the place Will had said was for those who wanted to be out of public view. Tiffany saw the server pushing a tray with her walker. The barista's hearing aid squealed, and the cashier sat on a high stool.

Tiffany ordered Will's usual. "An expresso, please."

After paying, instead of going through to the private side, Tiffany scanned the seats and moved toward the table she had shared with Will. *Tiffany George, you will survive.* She had talent, she had a job to do, and she even had a place to live. "Fake it till I make it."

"Pardon?" the server asked when she placed Tiffany's expresso on the table.

"Just trying out a new mantra." Tiffany shrugged her shoulders.

"What was it again?" The server waited.

"'Fake it till I make it.'" Tiffany felt her eyes tear.

"Stay positive." The server roller her walker forward.

Of course there were people who understood. She only had to look around. Turning the tiny cup on its saucer, she said, "I'm okay."

Customers came and went. The milk-foaming machine blasted, the grinder blared, the country-rock music played, and the world continued to spin on its axis. Her phone vibrated, and she glanced at it. Her mother was on her way and had directed her to meet her across the street.

Outside, the leaves on the trees twisted in the wind. Instead of turning her back to it, Tiffany turned her face into it. Her mother stopped the car beside the curb. Tiffany jerked the handle, but the car door was locked. The wind pressed her spiky hair away from her face. After her mother unlocked the door, Tiffany slid onto the seat, and clicked the seatbelt.

"How were your visits?" Tiffany asked.

"Pat is really worried about Tony and Cleo." Her mom turned sharply toward Tiffany. "She was surprised at your carelessness."

"I'm sorry she feels that way." Tiffany bit the inside of her cheek. "I apologized this morning."

"Yes, she mentioned that. We both agreed that since you left Apex, you seemed to have lost your sense of community." Her mom signaled to merge onto the highway.

Tiffany watched the green wheat in the fields bending to the wind.

"Don't you have anything to say for yourself?"

Tiffany shook her head. "No." Watching the wind ripple through the grass calmed her and her fingers loosened their grip on the armrest. *Good deeds are just that. Not to be advertised.*

Her phone vibrated in her jean pocket. She switched it off. There wasn't anyone she wanted to communicate with now. "I'll be packed and ready to leave at daybreak, Mom." Tiffany faced the horizon. "I'll pick up some breakfast on the road."

"You always were self-centered." Her mother signaled the approach to Apex. "We just didn't recognize it for what it was."

"That's enough, Mom." At the stop sign on Apex's Main Street, Tiffany opened the door and got out. "I'll walk from here."

Her mother threw her hands into the air. "Fine."

Tiffany marched down the alleys. She hadn't felt this vulnerable since Collin left her. She was going to finish her laundry, hide out in her room, and hit the road as early as she could. It seemed as if no one would care. At the house, only her car was in the driveway. She didn't know where her mother, Eric and Rebecca had gone, or why.

Inside, Tiffany went to the laundry room, where she found her clothes were dry. She folded them, took them to her room, and packed her suitcase. She was tempted to leave immediately but she wanted to speak to Eric, to reassure him that she would come back if he needed her, really needed her but otherwise this was all his baby. She had thought she had understood the George family relationships. Yes, it was made up of different layers, and yes, the picture had been added to but it felt as if chunks had fallen off it. She had a life to lead and she was going back to the place where she mixed sand and lime. She knew the sand made the fresco porous and the lime was caustic. It seemed to her as if the lime measurements had become skewed in her family dynamics.

Chapter 24

Will sank onto the chair in the corner of the accessible shower. He couldn't stay vertical any longer. The doctors and his care team had warned him about over extending himself. It had consequences no one was sure about. Cerebral Palsy reacted different in everyone and at every age. He hadn't been this physically exhausted since he studied and crammed for his exams. He had collapsed and he recuperated at mother's house for a month. He couldn't allow that to happen now.

The latest news reports told of Rockwell's temporarily halting construction. He knew that meant that there would be a skeleton crew on for security and everyone else would get their temporary lay-off papers. Could it have only been the other night since he watched Tiffany maneuver hoses as experienced as any other volunteer firefighter? Then the missing dogs. Then the discovery of the injured Tony and Cleo.

He did drive Tiffany to the hotel. They did share a bed.

He bent in half and let the water pulse down his spine, hoping for some stimulation that would send the right messages to his body. Turning off the water, he reached for a towel. Morning shadow be damned. He needed sleep or he wouldn't do anyone any good.

"Paula," he called from the door.

"Yes?"

He tried to smile. "I need at least two hours of sleep. I know there are people who want to speak with me but if I don't sleep, I'll collapse."

"I know what exhaustion and collapse looks like." Paula wound her arm around his waist, led him to the side of the bed, then turned down his covers. "In you get. I'll field calls until I have to leave at one."

Only by leaning heavily on her support could he have made it to the side of the bed.

"Turn around. A man needs some mystery."

"Done." She walked over to the windows and drew the drapes tight, closing out any sunlight.

"Call Lacy and ask her if she can drive you to the interview." Will folded the sheet across his chest and closed his eyes. "If she's busy, just take my car."

"Sleep tight," his friend said.

He dreamt of wild boars chasing Tiffany. He tried to deflect them with his crutches. One of them gorged his leg. He cried out in pain. Tiffany massaged his calf, while Cleo and Tony formed a circle to keep the boars at bay.

He woke to the telephone ringing. Groping for it, he answered, "Hello."

"Will. I've had a call from the animal hospital and we need to pick up Tony and Cleo. Jim's had another emergency and he needs the kennels."

"Who is calling?" Will didn't recognize the husky voice.

"It's Pat."

Will heard the hospital intercom system announcing something or other in the background. "When does he need this to happen?" Will dangled his legs over the side of the bed.

"As soon as possible. And I don't want Tiffany to be there. She has done enough."

"I understand. Yes, she has," he said, remembering Tiffany's determination to return to the field even though the police were waiting for daybreak. If Tiffany hadn't been insistent, there might have been a different outcome.

"Will, are you still there?"

"I'll pick up Tony and Cleo." He stifled a yawn. "You take care of you."

"Thank you. I'm glad we met." The phone line went silent.

Will checked his watch, then hit the speed dial for Lacy. "Lacy, I need you to drive me to pick up Tony and Cleo."

"I thought they were staying another night. That's the word at the coffee shop."

"Something's changed. How soon can you be here?"

"I'm just hanging out, waiting for Paula."

He heard someone shouting in the background, "Ask him what his plans are now that the mine is on hold?"

"I'll be right there, boss," Lacy said. "I'll text Paula and tell her I had to leave. She's in her interview with Mrs. Leman. I sure hope she gets the job, she's real nice."

"Thanks. If I'm not at the front door, just give me a minute." He clicked off the phone. He could speak with Nikki on his way to Pleasant Ville.

Finally, his pants were straight, his shirt tucked in. An ultra-suede jacket added to the business-casual look. He needed to appear confident and at ease.

Paula had set up the one-cup coffee maker with a disposable cup and wrapped a peanut butter and banana sandwich, which he quickly stashed in his messenger bag. He could get used to having an extra pair of hands in the house. Locking the door, he knew he didn't just want hands. He wanted a lover, a forever friend. His heart beat double-time just thinking about Tiffany's blue eyes staring deeply into his last night, telling him he had to come with her. He had felt invincible. He had witnessed her strength and also her need for him. He leaned his shoulder against the heavy glass door.

A huge cloud floated over the sun, blocking the light, but it would pass. No one had the power to turn off the sun, not even Rockwell Mines.

Lacy parked the SUV close to the front doors. After he passed his crutches into the front seat and settled in, he said, "Where is everyone?"

"Not sure. Crying in their soup because their dreams aren't going to come true?"

"There's still time for dreams." He tapped his security password into his phone. "I'm going to work while you drive, so excuse me."

He scanned his messages then returned a call to Nosh, Nosh, and Crane. "Will here."

"I've heard bits and pieces, Mr. Nosh. Can you give me the company position?" Will listened.

"I understand, for now there will be no change. I'll be at the meeting in Toronto. Please have my travel documents sent by email. I'll make it." Will leaned his head against the closed window.

"Lacy, what you overhear today needs to be confidential."

"Everything I overhear is confidential, Will. I don't repeat anything, even to my mom."

"Thank you."

Will sat upright and dialed Nikki. "Hello, Will here."

"Slow down, Nikki. I was helping a friend with an emergency."

"What time and where?" It was easier to be direct than be caught up in her fury.

"Community Hall. Seven. Got it. Thanks. Nikki."

Lacy adjusted her speed behind a mobile home slowing down the traffic along the two-way highway.

Will's phone vibrated in his hand. He answered the call from Mayor Robert. "Good afternoon, Will here."

"On the highway to Pleasant Ville to pick up Pat's dogs from the Animal Hospital, then I'll be back in town."

Phones rang in the background and Mayor Robert told him about the town meeting tonight.

"I will be there."

The Mayor informed him about a special meeting of available councillors before the community meeting.

Will did a quick calculation of time. "An hour and a half." He glanced at Lacy, who nodded. "See you then."

"We're here."

He didn't argue when Lacy parked beside the animal hospital door in a handicap stall. Nor when she opened his door, helped him onto the ground, and handed him his crutches. He legs protested and he knew he was scuffing the toes of his shoes but he needed to push forward through the doors. There would be time for massages and rest after this crisis.

At the reception desk, Will handed over his debit card and paid the bill in full. An assistant brought Tony who nuzzled Will's leg and Cleo who lapped his fingers. They each had a different array of shaved fur and sutures. Tony's leg was wrapped in the white gauze.

"Lacy, can you put down the back seat and they will have lots of space to rest while we drive home."

"Right away."

"We'll wait here until you come back in. I'll need you to hold the leads."

She nodded. Lacy had all the qualities of a good childcare provider. She understood when to assist and when to stand by without hovering. Something his mother had always understood but the women his father dated never did. They were there doing things for him or rather to him, as if by being kind to him they would win his father's affection. It had taken Will a while to catch on. He had grown to dread those weekends but his mother had insisted that he needed to know his father's many good qualities. Will now understood that his mother also needed a break from being a single parent.

Tiffany hadn't expected less from him because of his challenges. She accepted what he could do and asked him to use the talents he had.

Lacy led both dogs into the back of the SUV. They laid down with their heads close to the front seat. Will thanked the staff, pressed the automatic door opener, and was grateful for the small concessions made by businesses who made access easier for persons with disabilities. His progress was slow toward the passenger door of his SUV.

Lacy waited in the driver's seat while he clambered onto the front seat and buckled his seatbelt. Then he turned and put his hand onto the back seat. Both dogs took turns licking his fingers.

"You're safe now," he said. "You need to thank Tiffany. If not for her, who knows what would have happened to you both?"

Lacy turned toward him, wide-eyed. "I thought *you* saved the dogs, calling the RCMP and everything."

"Tiffany and I searched together. More than anyone else's, her determination led us to these two."

"Wow. That's not what the coffee row is saying."

"You know better than to listen to the coffee-shop talk."

"Sometimes it's true."

"If they aren't giving Tiffany ninety-nine percent of the credit, they are wrong. Believe me."

Will's stomach rumbled, and he reached for the sandwich from his bag. After a quick bite, he said, "Lacy, can you drop me at the town office please and then take Tony and Cleo to Pat's? The neighbor has the key to the house."

"Sure, but who is going to help me lift the dogs out of the car? They don't look as if they are in shape to jump."

"Do you have any ideas?"

"Can't ask Tiffany. Pat said she didn't want Tiffany near the dogs again," Lacy said.

Will shook his head. "There's a miscommunication somewhere." He felt exhausted. "What about Andrew, the skateboarder? I'll pay." Reaching into his messenger bag, he brought out his wallet. "Twenty enough?"

"I'll find someone. I'll take the money but perhaps I'll find someone who will help for free."

"Can you stay with them or call someone else, just until

the meeting is over?"

"I'll check with Mom."

"What about Aussie? She'd looking for extra money for her trip to Australia."

"She's probably working at the hotel. That's all she ever does."

"Right. Paula's interview. Perhaps Mrs. Leman will hire Paula even if there isn't the kind of boom that we all anticipated."

"You just go and figure this all out so our town does get better, Will. You promised." Lacy patted his arm.

His mind raced but his body slowed him down. When tension increased, so did his symptoms. He walked on his toes, scuffing his shoes along the pavement. He leaned heavily on his crutches on his way up the ramp to the town office.

"Hi, Sylvia," Will called to the town administrator.

She didn't look into his eyes. "Go straight into the chambers. Most everyone is there."

When he entered the room, Rosie, one of the most astute councillors, stepped forward and turned a chair so he would have for easier access. "Glad you're here, Will." She bent and whispered in his ear, "You don't look well."

"Nothing I haven't dealt with before. I'll work through it."

"Will, glad you could make it. We've had quite the surprise this morning," Mayor Robert said.

Will's hands rested on the council table. It had been built in a U-shape, allowing all the members of council to see and hear each other clearly. "Thank you for inviting me, Mayor Robert, and councillors. I'm going to the community meeting tonight. I've been in touch with Nosh, Nosh, and Crane. Their position at this time is that the development is on track. I've been called to a meeting in Toronto. I want you to know that I'll fight for every nail and stud to keep this neighborhood. Do I have your support?"

Papers shuffled and shoes scraped across the carpet.

"Will," Mayor Robert said, "we know this is your baby, but we don't want any unfinished projects. We'll be behind you if you can guarantee that everything will go according to plan."

"I can't guarantee anything right now, but I give you my word, I will do everything in my power to make this happen."

"But I thought the whole plan was that there were jobs in the area."

"That was the easy part, when we were riding on the potash mine boom. Now we'll have to think of something different."

The overhead lights flickered. "I will update you on any information as soon as I receive it. This is a progressive barrier-free housing project with a purpose."

One by one, the councillors nodded.

"Not much else we can do for now. I'm so tired of being tied to someone else's kite. Make this happen," Mayor Robert said.

"I'll do what I can. I know I have your support." Will looked around. "Now I need a ride back to the lodge."

Rosie jumped up. "I'll do it."

"See everyone at six-fifty at the community meeting," Mayor Robert said. "We'll sit together to show a solid front no matter what Rockwell Mines throws at us. We need something to give to the folks."

"See you all there." Will slowly placed each foot on the floor while he walked out of the council chambers. He needed to appear strong.

"My car's in the parking lot." Rosie held open the council chamber door.

"Lead the way."

Once in the parking lot, Will slid easily into Rosie's full-sized sedan. She was a tall, stately woman and drove a car that reflected her personality. The interior held her favorite scent. "Will, why is Pat upset with Tiffany?" Rosie asked while they drove past the grocery store.

"I don't know. Tiffany is responsible for saving her pets' lives. She assisted Dr. Thienes while he operated on Cleo. I don't know all the details." Will reached down and rubbed his calf muscle. "Someone has the wrong end of what's happened."

"The truth will come out. It always does. Poor Tiffany. She's in more trouble because she helped out rather than if she hadn't. She has a big heart."

"People should be thankful that she has," Will said. "If she hadn't followed through, there would be a much different outcome today."

"In the past I've wanted to smack my brother upside the head. The more accomplished plumber Tiffany became, Fred started planning that she'd take over the business when he believed Eric never could." Rosie stopped close to the front doors. "See you later."

While his neighbors of Willow Lodge watched from the common room windows, the large slippery leather seat allowed him to exit with dignity. "Thanks for the ride. I'll see you at the meeting."

When the door swung open into the lodge, Will saw that most of the chairs in the common room were occupied.

"The more things change, the more they stay the same," Alfred said from a rocking chair facing the large windows.

Will sat down with his neighbors. They deserved at least this much from him. "What do you mean?"

"It's always been this way. Some big shots come to Apex with a plan. We get all excited and then it falls through." Alfred rocked the chair back and forth. "Same old. Same old."

"Yeah, remember the money we were going to make from cleaning grain?" Dorothy, his beer-sharing neighbor, said.

"Or what about the trucking hub?" Lorraine, who seemed to have everything that was necessary in an emergency, added.

"Apex deserves to have this project finished," Will said. "I'll try my best. I may need your help."

"As long as it isn't money, we're here," Dorothy said. "We've been scammed before."

"I'm going to the community meeting tonight. Then I'll be flying out to meet with Nosh, Nosh, and Crane in Toronto about the subdivision. After that, I'll know what can be saved and done. I'll keep you informed." He covered his eyes with his hand. "But right now I need to sleep if I'm going to retain anything."

"Good luck." Dorothy straightened the edge of her cardigan.

"Any of you need a ride to the meeting tonight? I have room for three in my car."

"We're coming but we'll ride with Alfred, he has a regular car we all can get into."

"Regular cars are good," Will said. Walking back to his apartment he wished he was cocooned inside another car with Tiffany. The stars in his life had aligned perfectly the night his rental quit on the side of a highway and held him captive until Tiffany walked across the road and into his life. He'd find a way to keep her.

Chapter 25

The car's daytime running lights flashed on Tiffany's bedroom window when Eric and Rebecca drove up to the house. There were hours of light before darkness. She closed the zipper on her suitcase.

"Tiff, we're home," Eric called. "Where are you?"

"Right here." Tiffany wheeled her suitcase down the hallway.

"You're leaving?" Eric frowned.

"Yes." She stretched her lips across her teeth. "My contract begins in a couple of days. You and dad have everything under control."

"But, sis, have you heard about the mine halting development?" He put a hand on her arm.

"Yes. I'm sure it will all work out though." She glanced at Eric and Rebecca. "I was only coming back for a few days and it's time for me to leave."

Eric wanted to argue. She recognized the signs. He stood firm. Rebecca put her hand in his and urged him out of Tiffany's way.

"Eric, if you need me, really need me, I'll come back. I don't understand what is going on with Mom and Dad and me right now, but it isn't healthy. Maybe I've misunderstood all these years. I'm not sure what it is." Tiffany gave him a quick hug. "Look after them." She bit her lip and stepped toward Rebecca. "Take care of my little brother."

Rebecca wrapped Tiffany in a bear hug. "We're only a text away."

"I've said goodbye to Mom and Dad. Remember, this was a break for me before I began the commission."

Eric nodded and reached for Rebecca's hand.

Once outside, she loaded her suitcase and laptop, then she slammed the trunk on Tony and Cleo's dry bloodstains on the carpet. She tossed her backpack with her drawing supplies onto the front passenger seat.

Her parents didn't understand her, but Will did. He had reached across the console and had supported her throughout the scary time of locating and rescuing Tony and Cleo.

Tiffany backed her car out of the driveway, and the disappointment, sadness, and anger she'd been swallowing brimmed over. Tears pooled in her eyes, but she blinked hard. She couldn't let them flow until she was out of sight. She raised her hand to Eric and Rebecca on the deck.

Winnipeg was nine hours away. She could cry for all that time if she needed to but not until her speedometer climbed to sixty-five miles per hour on the highway.

Tiffany drove past Aunt Pat's house. Will's SUV was in the driveway. The dogs were safely home. Others would set up a care schedule for them because Tony and Cleo were part of the community and apparently she wasn't. Stopping briefly, she knocked on Aunt Pat's door. She could at least say goodbye to Will.

Lacy answered the door. "Is Will here?"

"No, Tiffany." Lacy put her fingers to her lips. "Shhh, Tony and Cleo are asleep."

"Okay. See you," Tiffany said. Turning, she swiped her hand across her eyes on the way to her car.

When she drove past the sign that thanked her for visiting Apex, she wondered why she ever thought leaving would be too hard. She had until the outskirts of Winnipeg to gather her wits and then she would be back to her life as an urban artist. Apex was over for her.

It seemed as if she was the only car on the road, with the occasional semi passing her, but of course that wasn't true. She knew she wasn't paying attention to anything. She had the music blaring and her phone turned off. She was invisible to anyone from Apex. That is what she seemed to be to her parents and to Aunt Pat. It was as if someone had placed a spell on them, causing them to forget the good things she had done for everyone. No, she was not going to try and sort it out. Instead, she would stop at the next service station with a car wash and clean her car, inside and out. She would wash away traces of the nightmare.

The Esso station advertised a car wash. She borrowed a bucket and purchased cloths and soap. She stood her suitcase on the ground and vacuumed the interior, and then bit her cheek to keep from crying when she scrubbed at the bloodstains. If anyone came upon her now they'd think she had had a body in her trunk. She recalled Will stretched out beside Tony and then helping lift Cleo into the back. He was strong in so many ways. He'd slept with Tony's head next to his foot while she assisted Dr. Jim with Cleo. Even though he'd been exhausted, he drove them to the motel. When she had wakened during the night, she was curled into his back and felt safe. With the water beating against her car, she wished they'd have stayed that way. But they hadn't. It was as if the earth's axis changed and nothing was ever going to be the same again.

The dawn rays peeked over the horizon when she drove onto her street and the safety of the underground garage. Slinging her art backpack over her shoulder, she rolled her suitcase and laptop to the elevator.

When she opened the door and turned on the light in her apartment, nothing had changed. Other than her plant leaves drooping and a hint of dust on the surfaces, everything remained untouched by the days she was gone.

Without unpacking, she stepped out of her clothes, washed her face, and then got into bed and slid under the covers. Perhaps she'd wake up and find out this was part dream and part nightmare. How could she fall so far from dedicated daughter and friend to someone who could be discarded without thoughts for her? Crushing the pillow to her chest, she couldn't hold her eyelids open another second.

When she woke, she checked her text messages. She smiled at a text from Dog Whisperer. *Missed you at the meeting last night. Heard you've left town. I'll miss being your shotgun rider.*

She replied with an emoticon blowing a kiss.

A message from Eric said there was a chance the neighborhood would go ahead. She replied with a happy-faced wink.

A message from Owen, happy she was back and information about a meeting time for one o'clock at the business center. She replied with a thumbs-up symbol. This shorthand texting was quick. No emotions, even though she brushed random tears from her cheeks. A quick shower, gelled spikes, a professional outfit, and she'd be ready for her day.

If launching fearlessly back into her life was that easy, then why were her blond roots showing? Whipping out her mascara wand, she did a quick touch up and then called her stylist for an appointment.

Her clothes seemed to hang from her shoulder blades as if they were still on the hanger in the department store. Belting the sweater around her waist reminded her of her tool belt back in Apex. But her leggings and open-toed sandals quickly dispensed with the association to the past.

Her freezer contained a frozen breakfast sandwich. After heating it in the microwave and forcing herself to eat, she studied her design again. It resembled an imagined underwater scene with coppery fishes shimmering in the sunlight. The undersea would be created in sections by a fresco technique and her fish and plant life would be anchored to the wall, providing a three-dimensional scene.

Fresco had been a course offered at art school, and because she had worked with different materials, the idea of mixing sand and lime and then spreading it on a wall and later painting with natural pigment appealed to her sense of adventure. Her copper fish sculpture techniques grew out of all of the pounding in the garage in Apex. A tear slid down her cheek when she thought about Will's positive principle. She missed her Soul Whisperer reminding her she made the choices which moved her toward her destiny.

Tiffany was finally going to make her art come to life. Her heart leapt and slid around in her chest like a jumping bean. Before, she had busied herself creating, healing, thinking, and had come out wiser. She would again. But this time she chose her path.

Her mentor, Owen waited for her in the vestibule of the new office tower. "I can't believe the mural is really happening." She held on to herself to keep from dancing and ran her hand along the wall, stroking the smooth clean surface. A coffee-shop with windows gave a clear view of the wall she would be working on. She sighed. Espresso would be her coffee of choice.

"You have a lot of work ahead of you. I've lined up Scott as the foreman of the work crew. He's helped me prepare walls with the plaster for our class exercises. He'll help you put the first layers on the wall, and then anything else you need," Owen said.

"You'll come by and check on me?"

"Of course. Here's Mr. Parker." Owen shook hands with a businessman with red-framed glasses.

Tiffany straightened her shoulders, ready to meet the interior designer of Fairview Mall. He was dressed in a sports coat, dress pants and loafers.

"You remember Tiffany George?" Owen asked.

"How could I forget?" Mr. Parker extended his hand to her. "Welcome."

Tiffany gripped his hand firmly, just as her father had taught her. "Yes, thank you." She turned toward the windows and blinked quickly. "The area is flooded with fabulous light. You won't be disappointed."

"Owen assures me you are up for the job." Mr. Parker nodded toward her mentor.

"She's taken to this method as if it's in her genes." Owen put his arm around Tiffany.

"There is a complication we hadn't anticipated." Mr. Parker indicated the coffee shop and then the elevator doors. "We've moved some of our tenants in earlier than expected due to a flood in their previous office space." He faced Tiffany. "I'm afraid you'll have to work with people moving in and out of your space. Will that be a problem?"

"I'll make it work. We'll need caution tape to keep everyone safe."

"I told you it wouldn't be a problem. Tiffany is very accommodating." Owen's smile was wide and he seemed to be excited when he shook Mr. Parker's hand.

"Glad to hear." He glanced at his wristwatch. "I have a meeting right now, but I'll check on your progress, Tiffany."

Mr. Parker sauntered down the expansive office corridor while Owen and Tiffany entered the coffee shop, placed their order at the counter and sat at a table with a clear view of the future work of art.

Tiffany sipped her coffee from the tiny cup. "I'll need

help to make sure we all stay safe, especially when we're on the scaffold."

"I'll encourage other students to volunteer as your assistants." Owen sipped his café au lait.

"You'll supervise and tell me if my plaster isn't working or my pigments are off."

"This is a feather in the academy's cap. Of course I'll supervise."

Tiffany stretched her hand across the table. "Thank you for being accommodating." Her smile felt tight. "I'll go to the shop and touch up the fish I was working on."

"Tiffany, you look like a light has been blown out." Owen had both his elbows on the table and scrutinized her face and posture. "This is a fanciful piece. A fun piece."

"I know. I'll get there again. Don't they say each hurt takes less time to grieve over?" Tiffany wiped the table with her napkin for something to do rather than look at him.

Owen covered her hand with his. "I have faith in you as an artist to bring everything you have to this piece."

Tiffany stood. "I'm off to pound metal. Good therapy for what ails me."

"Meet us here tomorrow bright and early and we'll begin this fabulous mural. Businesses and towns will be asking for you after this. You will be famous."

"Thanks, Owen, for your confidence." Her voice wobbled. With her shoulders back, she thrust her chin forward. *I cannot do anything about others' feelings toward me. I can only do something about my own feelings.*

"You're good. Fresco is a tricky process, but your ability is the necessary ingredient." He stood.

"Come on, I'll show you where we stored the supplies and where you can clean your equipment."

The room they had been given was huge. The scaffold frame leaned against one wall. A utility sink was on the other wall next to floor-to-ceiling locked cupboards.

"I'm in heaven." Tiffany spun around, taking it all in.

"Scott and his crew will set up the scaffold, and we'll be ready to go in the morning," Owen said. "I won't have to bring coffee since this place will be open." He checked his watch. "Time to run. I have a class to teach."

Tiffany reached her workshop located in the industrial part of Winnipeg and upon opening the door, she found the odors of metal and heat mixed with shellac a welcome comfort. She lifted brown bib overalls from the hook, put them on, then covered her hair with a baseball cap. She was home. Looking at the glimmering copper fins, gills and eyes, at fish with their mouths open and exposing jagged teeth, some with their tails curled around, and others jumping, she realized she was a good metal sculptor.

Tiffany sat at her drafting table and designed an additional fish. She knew just the materials she would use to bring it to life. Unlocking her back door, she searched through the pile of metal next to the building and chose a scrap piece of mild steel. She traced her design on the steel, and while heating up her cutting torch, she exchanged her hat for a helmet. The sparks flashed while she cut. Her ear protection muffled the noise while the grinder smoothed the edges. Her special fish was taking shape.

Her stomach growled. Looking up and out the window, she realized that the sun had set and the alley was in darkness. She checked the time on her phone. Eleven o'clock.

Switching off the lights and locking the door, she drove to a deli on her way home and picked up lasagna and a Greek salad. She was starved. When she arrived home, she ate quickly while watching something mindless on TV. She crashed onto her bed and slept. The dreams were slow and easy about a man with his hand over his heart, ahead of her, setting a pace she couldn't match.

At the meeting, Will sat next to Sylvia, the town administrator, and listened to the Rockwell Mines official explaining that they would not stop work on the mine.

"This is the largest potash find, the prices are low but we are committed, even though we will slow down the pace." Cheers rose from the room.

Will felt his shoulders relax. He wouldn't have to carry this project all alone.

The official fingered the pages of his report. "We're cooperating with the RCMP during their investigation of the fire and, if you haven't heard, we're dealing with a wild boar problem in the area that is causing havoc for some of our plans."

Mosquitoes buzzed against the screens of the open windows. Occasionally, Will heard a slap and another mosquito died.

Will scanned the crowd, hoping to see Tiffany, but only Eric and Rebecca sat together.

Nikki rose to speak. "Only a few days ago, our dreams were large, and now they will be slower but manageable." Will recognized her game face. She balanced her hands on the podium and spoke directly to the audience. "Rockwell Mining will honor their commitments to the town for the new waterlines as well as the expansion of the water treatment plant on schedule. Therefore, a smaller contingent of Rockwell employees will remain in the area, continuing to build the main plant, and gradually more will arrive as the world prices improve."

There was a visible sound of relief and then people applauded.

Paula sat beside Mrs. Leman, who stood up and announced, "I've hired a qualified chef for the hotel. I have faith we will grow." She turned toward Paula. "Paula Day, meet the residents of Apex who will be flocking to taste your new menu."

"What a relief," Dorothy said, leaning on her three-pronged cane. "I'll share my recipes."

The crowd applauded then Mayor Robert stood and explained that they were ready to proceed with the infrastructure plans. He thanked Rockwell Mining for honoring their commitment.

Someone called from the back of the hall, "What about the new neighborhood? The pool and library?"

Will braced his crutches on the floor and stood. "I'm meeting with Nosh, Nosh, and Crane, I am hopeful for a positive outcome for jobs and for new members of your community. I will make the announcement as soon as possible." Will sank to his chair accompanied by a spattering of applause.

A man in a cowboy hat called out, "The apartment in my house is ready for occupancy."

Nikki stood. "Thank you. We'll need accommodations until the camp is up and running. Please help yourself to coffee and tea."

Chairs scraped along the floor. People mumbled. A child cried. Will texted Lacy that he was ready to leave. She waved from the back of the hall.

The Mayor patted Will's shoulder. "I know you'll do your best. You have passion, and sometimes it works where logic doesn't."

"I have to rest, then pack, and prepare for my meeting. If you think of anything you want me to stress, please email me," Will said.

Nikki rounded the last row of chairs. "Will, you're not leaving."

"Yes. I'm going to Toronto for a meeting." Will could feel the exhaustion throughout his body. He kept moving forward at a slow pace. "You were wonderful tonight. You were forthright and honest to the residents of Apex."

"This situation isn't exactly what Rockwell Mines planned but we are committed to prepare for the future." She struck a pose, head held high.

"We'll talk when I return."

"Will, you're exhausted. I know you all too well." Nikki draped her arm around him. "Take care of yourself."

Will leaned into her shoulder. He had been here before. The past was as comforting as an old security blanket. He couldn't tell her that of course. Nikki needed to be associated with everything new and exciting. He could feel each of his thirty-six years jamming in his muscles. "Thanks, Nikki, I'm fine."

"I envy you. Back in the big city." Little lines between her eyebrows deepened, "Did you know something some of us didn't?"

He paused. "What do you mean?"

"You tell me. You're the one who didn't bring any personal property here." She glared at him with her hands on her hips. "You could have told me what you suspected."

"I'm coming back from Toronto. My future is here." There was a time to repeat that he didn't bring his personal property because there wasn't room, but this definitely wasn't it.

"Will." She stomped her foot.

"Goodnight, Nikki."

Lacy strode next to him and whispered, "Give me your bag before it throws you off balance."

He ducked his head out from under the strap. Another battle not worth expending energy for. She kept pace with him and held the door open for him, until he was seated and his seatbelt was in place.

Dusk had settled around the town. Tonight there weren't

any kids riding bicycles or skateboards on Elm Street. There weren't couples strolling in the early summer air. The night was quiet.

"What time is your flight, Will?" she asked.

"I have to be at the airport by six." He yawned. "I should go to Regina this evening."

"It'll be my honor to drive you in the morning." She stopped close to the lodge's front doors.

"Why don't you take my car home?"

"Good idea. I'll be here at four sharp. There won't be much traffic so we'll make it in under an hour and that will give you time to board."

"Thanks, Lacy. Who was it that recommended you for this job again?"

The interior light accentuated the freckles scattered across both her cheeks then met on the bridge of her nose.

"I had three references, remember?" Then she smiled. "I was the only applicant."

"I must have had a lucky star that day."

"Four sharp."

He closed the passenger door, and she waited until he opened the security doors. Once inside, he found the common room was empty. As if everyone had gone into their shelter to regroup. He knew about this. He had done it himself after setbacks. But it was up to him to keep his promise to these people. Will checked his phone one last time for a message from Tiffany. She certainly was living up to his image of a solitary person. Tomorrow he'd travel light. His meds, his tablet, his phone, because everything else he'd need was in his condo in Toronto.

He reached out to Tiffany with one text. He wanted her to know he understood her choice, he had fought all his life for people to accept him for who he was rather than a preconceived notion of who he should be.

Once inside the apartment, he switched the alarm on his clock radio, set his phone as a backup, then turned off the light. A *bing* indicated a new text. His heart skipped and he felt a longing for his sprite. Picking up his phone, he closed his eyes when he saw the text from his mother not Tiffany. Will's mother texted that she would meet his plane. He quickly replied, *Thx*, then he rolled over. If only fantasy could meld with reality, and his sprite could join him on his rescue mission. But he'd never ask because she needed to make her own choices.

Chapter 26

Tiffany arrived at the mall just when the sun crested the horizon. Sitting and staring at the erected scaffold, she tried to imagine working in the hustle and bustle of office personnel and shoppers. What had she been thinking? A rumble of buckets and metal tubs moving across the floor brought her back to the reality of her situation. The men dragged dollies stacked with the equipment from the storage room Owen had shown Tiffany yesterday. They began measuring the sand and lime, the mixing and then scraping along the sides of the tub reminded her of the wild boars moving through the darkness and rubbing against her fender. She thought of Tony and Cleo, missing them, *No wallowing allowed*. Will, her shotgun rider for a night, her friend, had been beside her. She pressed her fingers to her lips recalling his hip against the car, his arms outstretched, ready to toss her tire toward the enemy in the darkness. Her breathing relaxed. He had also been beside here while she slept. With her palm on her heart, he was still here in her memory.

Tiffany slapped her hands down on the table, strode toward the team of apprentice artists where they scooped the mixture into buckets and were carrying them toward the scaffold. The past events were not going to spoil this day.

She picked up the trowel. "Hi, I'm Tiffany. I'll begin the skim coat in the far corner."

A tall, lanky man with blond hair and blue eyes extended a hand covered with leather work gloves. "Pleased to meet you. I'm Scott, your assistant for the mural."

"Owen Marshal spoke highly of you. I'm looking

forward to working together."

Scott indicated the other men, "They helped me set up the scaffold and will hang around in case we need them today."

"Thanks guys. This looks great." Tiffany climbed onto the scaffold and one of the men passed her a bucket of plaster. She began the methodical motion of skimming the base coat of plaster onto the wall. When her bucket was empty, another student with a tattoo sleeve on his left arm hoisted up another fresh bucket of plaster. As she worked, her shoulders loosened and her mind emptied of everything other than preparing a smooth wall for her layered mural. Creating art was her passion, and she'd landed in a pretty sweet spot. She'd created before, sometimes out of need and sometimes out of anger, but this time it was her choice, her decision to fulfill her destiny. Survival was limiting and small. She'd do more. She'd live.

"Hold on a minute," Tiffany called down to Scott. "I'm coming down."

Tiffany advanced on her purse like a dog on a scent. She fumbled for her earbuds and her music. Now she was ready. Everything else would take care of itself. Nodding at Scott, who was scrapping and shoveling plaster into another bucket, she climbed back up to the top, scooped plaster onto her board, and skimmed the surface smooth in rhythm along with the music.

When Owen touched her shoulder, she almost committed a first-year apprentice mistake. She swung around but she remembered to guard her trowel tip from nicking the wall. Ripping her earbuds free, she said, "What are you doing up here?"

"You were supposed to meet me in the shop." Owen held out his arm to steady her.

"What time is it?" She shook her head, clearing away the peace of repetitive motion.

"Past that time." Owen took the trowel from her hand and

scraped the remnants of dried plaster into the waste bucket.

Pushing her hands down her jeans, she glanced at her watch. She had missed the appointment by an hour. "How did you know I'd be here?"

"I know emerging artists. They want to be involved at every stage. When you are mature, you'll allow those whose job it is to prepare a surface to do that job, and you will trust them. Besides, since you didn't turn up, I came here to check on this." His arms encompassed the wall, the busy hallway with office staff standing around and watching the process, a group of older women who sat at a table behind the glass wall of the coffee shop and pointed when she turned around.

"I wondered if I could work in this environment." Tiffany smiled to herself. "I can."

"I never doubted it." Owen turned to climb down the ladder. "Coming?"

Tiffany brushed her hands together. "I'm maintaining control over the final outcome. Every layer is important to the finished piece."

"Give these guys a break. They need experience too."

She tucked her hands into her pockets and shrugged. He had a point.

Owen took her arm and led her out of the mall and stood beside her car. "I'll meet you at the shop."

"Yes." She was in that pleasant place where her mind was at peace and her body was tired from exertion. She sat behind the wheel and gulped the bottle of cold water Owen passed to her.

"Are you ready to drive, or do you want to ride with me?"

"I'll drive." Her favorite music pounded out of the speakers, while she followed Owen's rear lights through the Winnipeg streets to the studio.

He brought two cups of coffee and submarine sandwiches into the shop. "Did you sleep at all last night?"

He surveyed the sculptures she had completed.

"Sure did." Tiffany slipped down onto the sofa, and the worn cushions cradled her back.

"These are good." He traced his finger along a brass fish, then an underwater plant with leaves furrowing as if in a current of water, and lifted a frog from the table and held it toward the light. "But you need to eat. Then we'll discuss what needs to be done."

Owen passed her a sub.

She held it to her forehead. "Let me conjure up the image of my treat." She breathed in the spicy aroma.

"Just eat."

While biting into the meatball sandwich she heard Owen banging cupboard doors, running the tap, and opening the fridge. "I don't miss these studio days," he called above the din.

"I love the smell of solder lingering in the air." Tiffany leaned her head back.

"What are you doing here?" Owen asked, picking up a piece of discarded steel lying next to a crudely fashioned fish.

"I found that piece out back. I thought it would be a good idea to mix metals and . . ." She shrugged. ". . . recycle?"

"This doesn't look like a whole fish?"

"It isn't. I'm thinking about inclusion." Her heart banged against her ribcage.

Owen held the welded pieces up toward the light. "It's going to take a lot of grinding to make this pretty."

"Not everything is pretty." Tiffany stood and moved toward the sculpture. "He'll be fine, you wait and see. If anyone notices he's different, they won't care or even they could be surprised and pleased."

Owen surveyed the diagram of the underwater scape. "Where are you going to put this guy so he'll survive?"

Tiffany chuckled. "You do know it isn't real?"

Owen held the metal sculpture and tried it in one corner, then on the top of the seascape, finally on the bottom. "I give up. Where will you place this one?"

Tiffany took the sculpture from him. "Right here on top, watching over everyone."

Owen took a few steps backward and surveyed the positioning on the mural. "A little to your left and up four inches and you've done it."

"Bring me the marker, please." Tiffany wrote four letters on the wall. *Will.*

Owen entered the new addition into the computer. "After we go over the paint list, you should get some sleep. You look exhausted. You know this is going to be demanding over the next while."

Tiffany ran her hand through her hair. "I'm ready, thanks to you." She flexed her biceps.

Owen looked up from the inventory list. "I've been in this business long enough to know an old technique brought back and a new company ready to accept the old with a new twist are going to be in demand." Owen chuckled. "You will also need to use that big heart of yours and nurture the plaster."

Tiffany put her hand on her heart. "It's thumping." She didn't have anyone else calling on her heart, except this piece of art. Everyone else was busy with their own lives.

The airline check-in clerk took one look at Will and said, "For a minimal fee you can upgrade to business class. We have seats that haven't been sold."

Will drew his credit card from his wallet. "Thank you." There were times when comfort was more important than making a point that he was just like everyone else.

"You look as if you could use some down time." Her courtesy smile actually reached her eyes. "Any baggage?"

"Just carry-on." He collected his boarding pass and spoke to Lacy. "I'll email or text you when I know I'm coming back."

"You'll come back?" She seemed unsure.

"Of course. I promised the residents of Apex. My plan is to carry it through." He coughed into his elbow.

Other travellers hurried past him to the escalators and toward security.

"I could have gone with you. Driven you around." Lacy covered her mouth as she yawned. "Is someone meeting you at the airport? Perhaps next time I can experience big city driving."

Will smiled, thinking of Lacy driving in the heavy Toronto traffic. "My mom's meeting me."

Lacy's forehead crinkled under her hat. "You're a little old to have a mom picking you up, aren't you?"

"Moms are moms. See you later. And tell everyone I'm coming back." Taking a deep breath, he propelled himself toward the elevator. He turned toward Lacy, "Don't let them rent out my apartment."

Lacy saluted against the brim of her baseball hat. "As if."

Today, Will took advantage of every perk given to someone who needed more time to board the plane. Settling in next to the window, he tightened his seatbelt across his hips, made sure it was visible, popped a cough drop into his mouth and closed his eyes. The next thing he knew, he heard the announcement that they were descending into Toronto. He scrubbed his eyes and looked around him. "I hope I didn't snore," he said to the woman next to him.

"Pardon?" She cupped her hand around her ear. "My ears always stop up during a flight."

He coughed into his sleeve again. His chest was tightening up by the hour. As soon as he could use his phone he'd message Anthony, his physiotherapist. He needed to get a quick and good hold on this chest cold. Nothing must slow him down.

When leaving the plane he looked longingly at the wheelchair waiting for someone else. His bag felt heavy. He gave in to pride and waved down one of the trolleys that transported passengers from place to place.

At the arrival area, his mother took one look at him and shook her head. "What have you done to yourself?"

He attempted a smile. "Not much."

She reached toward him. "Your bag."

He surrendered his precious possessions to one of the few people he trusted to hold his electronic equipment and medications. "You sit here, and I'll get a wheelchair. This airport is too big and I couldn't park close."

"Thanks, Mom." He slid onto a bench. "It's been a hectic few days and a very early morning." He didn't have to explain his exhaustion to her. She'd seen him in this state too many times, but he was a grown man now and should have learned all the lessons. While his mother searched for a wheelchair he thought about Tony crawling to gain attention for Cleo. Could he ever be physically strong enough to save someone he loved?

"Why the sad face, mister?" His mother held the chair stable.

An incoming text saved him from answering. His heart skipped a beat every time a new message came in. He hoped his sprite had come to his rescue again. Not to be, but Anthony would make room for him early that evening. "Good news, Mom. Anthony can see me. He'll help bring me back to life."

"And so will my chicken soup."

In a large city, people have a way of not seeing individuals the way they did in a smaller community. That wasn't true this time though. Here he was, a thirty-six-year-old man being pushed around by his sixty-nine-year-old mother. This was hard to take, but necessary. His mother almost dumped him from his seat. "Wake up. I can't lift you into the car anymore."

Will lifted himself and slid his butt onto the seat. His mother had a sixth sense about him. "I'm ready." Will buckled up in the front seat while his mother parked the wheelchair in the retrieval space for luggage carts. The driver door opened and his mother, with her brand-named sunglasses in place and leather jacket on, slipped into her seat. "Where are we going, Will?"

"Ummm, you brought soup in the car? It smells delicious. I can't recall the last time I ate," he said. "My place."

"You got it."

His phone binged.

"Will, turn that thing off and rest."

Checking his phone, he said, "It was off throughout the whole plane trip. I'm important."

He was familiar with his mother's sighs and what they meant. When he opened his message, he saw a photo of Tiffany on a scaffold spreading gray plaster on a wall. Will placed his hand over his tightening chest. His mother's quick turn of her head indicated that she noticed him rubbing his chest.

"Must be my cold."

"Don't try to kid your mother." She expertly merged the car in and out of traffic.

"You're right. A special woman, Mom."

"Where is she?"

"Don't know exactly." He spread his fingers apart on the photo and shifted the image around. "She's on a scaffold, working with plaster. Indoors, I think."

"Shouldn't be hard to investigate and gain the details." She looked at him pointedly while they were stopped at a red light.

He placed the phone in his breast pocket. It felt right to have the photo close to his heart while he thought of an appropriate reply. "True. But I want her to tell me, rather than me finding out by Googling."

Reaching across the counsel, his mother patted his knee. "You're such a romantic."

"I've learned from the best." He framed his hands, as if he were making a movie. "Not many sons can say they have a famous romance author as a mother."

She concentrated on the traffic, switching lanes, and drove into the underground parking at his condo. "There aren't any secrets if someone wants to find out."

"Home sweet home." Will dug into his pocket for keys. "How is the writing going?"

"I'm researching, therefore the soup. My best thinking happens when I'm tending something on the stove."

Will turned and took in his mother's chin-length hairstyle. She had been a deep brunette, but now her hair was pure white. "Have you met anyone who meets your romantic expectations while I was away?"

His mother removed her sunglasses and winked. "You mean research?"

Opening the car door, Will laughed. "Whatever you'd like to label it, it is still meeting someone."

"That's for me to know." She opened her door. "I'm grabbing a cart. Your bag is heavy and so is the soup." She unloaded soup containers and grocery bags from the trunk.

"I'm curious about the contents of those bags." Will hit the automatic door open button.

"Soon enough." The elevator rose quickly and the doors opened into the hallway leading to his Toronto home.

Inside, Will sunk into his recliner, which gave him a view of Toronto's downtown high-rises. "It's good to be back."

His mother busied herself in the kitchen. He heard his refrigerator door open, his cupboard doors thud against their frames, the taps running, and soon the aroma of coffee greeted him.

"Hot soup first to loosen your chest," she said, setting up a TV tray.

Will leaned forward in his chair. "The onions and chives bring back so many memories." He blew against the steam rising from his spoon.

"Tell me one thing about this woman and then I'll wait for more after you've rested," she said, sipping the coffee from her mug.

"She's got a strong and caring spirit." Will felt his mood lighten when he recalled her at his door ready to save him, lifting him, a heavy water bottle, and a big injured dog.

His mother sighed.

His phone rang, but he allowed his voicemail to answer. "Mom, I'd like to reply to her text. Before you go, will you take a picture of me? She's creative and I want to accept what she gives me."

It was midnight when Tiffany submerged into her bath. One day had blurred into the next. While she carefully added layers of plaster. Her body ached from the demands of her fresco. She smiled, thinking about rubbing Will's calf on a highway. Too bad he wasn't here to return the favor. She pushed the sponge down her legs and massaged her calves and ankles. Everything hurt, even her toes.

Applying the plaster was dirty, hard, physical work but a labor of love. An outlet for her nurturing. Each application of plaster had to be smoother than the one before.

She missed her soul whisperer. Her champion. Will encouraged her to follow her passion. It was hard to explain, but she felt a kinship toward this old method of creating art that would be shared by many. Will had built his own life and, layered by experiences, he now wanted others to gain from his expertise.

While she towelled off, she noticed that her blond roots grew against the black. She'd have to wear hats until both she and her stylist had time to color it again. She wrapped her towel and arms around her body in a self-hug.

Tiffany was fortunate that her mural wall was in a climate-controlled atmosphere. She didn't have to be concerned about rain or wind, just an audience that grew every day. Burrowing under the covers, Tiffany closed her eyes.

In the morning, she checked her phone. Dead. No time to charge it. Besides, she didn't want anything to disturb her concentration. A whisper of guilt nudged her to email Eric. *Tell him you don't have a phone, in case he needs you.*

"No," she said aloud, "I gave him Owen's cell phone number in case of an emergency and I couldn't be reached."

With coffee, fruit, and a bag of mini carrots tucked in a lunch bag, she drove to the studio and picked up her sketches. The rising sun outlined the city's office towers.

After passing through security, she sat in one of the plastic chairs and studied her wall canvas for today. Soon she heard whistling and the sounds of trolley wheels groaning under the weight of tubs, sand, water, and tools. The day was about to begin. Her heart beat with excitement. When she used earth colors extracted from dirt, she would be part of a continuous line from the ancient cave dwellers who painted on rock walls.

"Morning, Tiffany." Scott, her assistant and talented man behind the careful mixing of sand and lime, called.

The wall was smooth and dried to the right texture.

"Hello, Scott. We're in for a wonderful day. I'm glad we

can begin before the audience arrives," Tiffany said, closing the distance between them.

He turned his head over his shoulder.

Tiffany followed his gaze and saw two security guards with coffee in disposable cups settling around a plastic table. "Ah, good morning, gentlemen."

"This is the first time I've seen plaster used for art." A young guard with a tiny stud in his ear furrowed his brow.

"It has a long history but it isn't common today." Tiffany buckled her apron across her hips. "It takes a team to complete a fresco."

"I've seen that type of art in churches when I travelled." The other guard lifted his chest and sucked in his belly, proud of his experience.

"This isn't a church," the first guard replied, twisting his earring.

"But a lot more visitors come through here than some churches these days, so it is as good a place as any to bring back the old ways in a new space," the older, world-traveled guard added when the younger one finished talking.

"Thanks for following our progress, but I hear the plaster calling me." Tiffany climbed the scaffold. She spread the final thin layer along the edge and dipped her trowel into water, spreading an even thickness. Speed and concentration were necessary to avoid dryness. Tiffany incised the contours of the boat into the wet plaster. Next, she poked small holes into the paper design outlining the noses, mouths, and eyes looking out from the boat into the sea. Pounding bits of charcoal dust over the drawing filled up the holes and provided an outline for her to paint with pure pigments onto the moist plaster.

When the plaster dried, it entered its golden hour, the time just before the plaster was too dry. Then she added shading and contours to the faces gazing into the sea. She worked quickly before the lime, water, and air chemically changed and her paint became locked underneath a lime-skin, like millions of tiny pieces of mosaic. Hours had passed before she tipped her head from one side to another, and laid her brushes in the tray.

Owen touched her gently and then passed her a bottle of cold water. Condensation made it slippery to hold on to, and her fingers and wrists were limp with exhaustion.

"Tiffany, you are something else."

She shook her head. Her lip quivered.

Owen took her by her arm. "You've got to come down and look at this from farther away."

She leaned against him, suddenly weak.

The office corridor was quiet, and the coffee shop lights were off. "What time is it?"

"Shh. Just wait." He guided her off of the scaffold. "Sit." She slid onto the chair he held, and then stepped out of her view. "Look."

Tiffany scanned the top portion of the wall that was finished. The lights were angled to pick up the subtly of color. "It's beautiful." Her chin wobbled, then she covered her face with her hands and sobbed.

"Yes, it is, and you're exhausted." He passed her another bottle of water. "Drink. I'll get Scott to drive your car. I'll bring him back and he can pick up his truck."

Tiffany buckled her seatbelt in the passenger seat. While Scott drove, she closed her eyes, and felt comforted knowing her shotgun rider, her dog whisperer, her soul whisperer, and her friend had been in this very place, in her car.

After they parked her car in the underground garage, Owen accompanied her to the elevator. "You're sure you'll be okay?"

"Yes." Tiffany leaned her head against the wall of the elevator. She understood that this would be difficult. The fresco lived and changed chemically. Every stroke of the brush had to be done when the plaster was just right. Her cell phone signaled a text message had arrived. She'd forgotten she had charged it at the mall.

Checking the icon, she saw she had two messages. The elevator doors opened. She unlocked the door to her home then searched the fridge for food, anything that was edible. Apples, cheese, and crackers would do after her shower. She rubbed a numbing cream over her arms, her shoulders, and the backs of her legs. With her snacks piled on a tray, she carried them into her bedroom. Her phone blinked at her, demanding attention. Finally, she had enough strength to slide the screen and tap in her password. One message from Eric. *Setting the day. Will you be my best woman?*

Her eyes filled with tears. *Of course. I need a solid week or more here.*

The next was from Dog Whisperer. A photograph of Will standing with his back to a city skyline seen through large windows. Will was a living, breathing gift. She couldn't see his face because his body was outlined by light and office towers or apartment complex windows in the background. His hands were positioned so he was supported by the window frame. Who was the photographer? She expanded the photo and scanned the shelves with books and small sculptures she could see then pinched it back. Her fingers hovered over the keypad. A reply required more than two active brain cells. She turned her left palm up and angled the camera lens to include her calloused palm, lifeline, and the stubborn paint that lingered on her fingers. She clicked. She pressed 'send.' They were building a relationship in the modern world.

When the alarm rang, she flung back her covers, glanced out the window and saw the sun cresting over the horizon.

Another clear day was promised by the female weather reporter on the radio.

Tiffany smiled when she noticed a message had been delivered while she slept. When she thumbed to read it, a nanosecond of disappointment skimmed over her when Eric's name was in bold print.

Fantastic. Let you know as soon as possible. BTW, M&D better. Everything slow here.

It isn't slow here, she replied in the message bubble.

Tossing the last couple of apples and a chunk of cheese along with some snow peas into her lunch bag, she was out the door. "Groceries, remember groceries."

Tiffany climbed the scaffold and searched the finished product for signs that the plaster had lifted or cracked. The wheels of the trolley carrying the tools brought her out of her concentrated inspection. Climbing down the scaffold, she called, "Hey, Scott."

"Morning, Tiffany. You'll have to share your secret. You don't look stiff." He uncovered the tub.

"I have a special cream that does the work. You look in fine form too."

"I'm used to labor."

Tiffany gathered her paints and her trowel. "So am I." Speed was important to prevent dryness at the joint from yesterday to today's painted surface. Scott helped her trace today's design portion. Because they outlined plants and small sea creatures, it allowed for more creativity with the paint. She screwed anchors where the sculptured sea life would be placed.

With music shuffling through her earbuds, she worked at a slow and precise rhythm. Occasionally sounds from the mall interrupted her or when Scott brought her water, or her lunch bag. But she was in her place. Just her and her creation. She snapped a close up of an underwater plant leaf, just in case Will replied with a photo again.

Her stomach growled. The corridor was quiet. The office workers had left for the day and the coffee house staff were washing the floors. She, too, had completed her day's work. Calling down to Scott, she gave him a sign that suggested he ask the coffee staff if they had any leftover coffee. He immediately opened the glass door and entered. "Sorry," he called up when he returned.

Tiffany scanned her work and the bare edge ready for tomorrow's plaster join. She climbed down and stretched her arms and back. Today she wasn't a bundle of exhaustion, she was alive. She snapped two pictures, one of the scaffold pipe support and the other a close up of the grains of sand and lime.

Packing up her paint, she said, "Scott, I need to leave, are you all right on your own?"

"Sure, Tiffany." He was loading the tub onto the trolley. "See you in the morning."

Tiffany locked the cupboard that held her paints and brushes. She had to buy groceries. Her cupboards and refrigerator was bare. The parking lot at the supermarket was busy. Pushing the grocery cart past the cooler containing steaks, she thought about Will's precise movements while cutting his steak, his perfect teeth when he smiled during the dinner conversation, then his keen observation while she thought she had covertly glanced at her phone, hoping for a call from Pearson or Nikki about Tony and Cleo. When he knew the problem, he hadn't ordered a course of action, he joined her as a team, to solve the mystery together.

Chapter 27

After breakfast, Will opened the text photo from Tiffany. He scanned her calloused laborer's palm, embedded paint in her lifeline. The bits of visible nails were chipped, uneven, and dyed with blue paint. Behind her palm, he saw a quilt of many colors and a room outlined in soft lamplight with sheer drapes closed across the window. A cozy feeling seeped through him. This certainly wasn't sexting. It was the distant brought close. The invisible made visible. A gift exchange.

He'd have to think about what he'd send her next, but right now he had to convince Nosh, Nosh, and Crane to continue their support of the Apex development. The potash prices would come back. This setback could be used to their advantage. The community would be well established before the return of the miners. There would be a secure atmosphere in which employees would want to stay.

The doorman called up, informing Will that his car had arrived. Will straightened his tie, checked his slicked back hair, the leather briefcase and highly polished shoes. The knife crease in his gray business suit broke across his knees as he moved slowly down the hall to the elevator.

"Good morning, Alvin. Nice to see you. How's Rocky?" Will extended his hand to the man who held the post as security and concierge for the years he had lived in his condo.

"Getting long in the tooth, just like me, Will." Alvin gripped Will's hand. "Welcome home. Rocky has missed all the treats you used to give him."

"I'll have to rectify that soon," Will said, while Alvin held opened the door to the street.

"It promises to be a hot day. Take care, now." Alvin closed the security door with a thud.

The man in the driver's hat turned. "The dispatcher noted you wanted to go to First Canadian Place."

"Yes, thank you." Will slid onto the seat while the driver held the door.

Will knew he was on his way to a morning that could change the trajectory of his life. The odor of exhaust wafted into the interior of the car. He longed for the breeze in his face or the sound of frogs at sunset in his soon-to-be new home and community, Apex. He wouldn't allow this project to get sidelined. Inclusive opportunities in a smaller community like Apex were more important than ever.

Will reached into his breast pocket for his phone. He snapped a picture of the crease in his pant leg, the bend of his knee, the space to the back of the driver's seat, the skipping shadow from passing vehicles. Why this photo, and why now? He was trying to carve out a new place for himself, and his future, and if a thousand-dollar suit and a good press would do it, then that was who he would be right now. He attached it to Tiffany's name and tapped 'send.'

"We're here, sir." The driver parked in front of the glass business tower.

"I missed your name," Will said, while he gripped the armrest on the door and stood.

The driver shook his hand. "Bob Lawton."

Will straightened, pushing his arms through the cuffs of his crutches. "This meeting is scheduled to last approximately two hours. Would you come back and pick me up, please?"

"Absolutely, sir. I'm your driver for the duration." He waited for Will to step away before he closed the door.

Will slung his leather briefcase strap across his chest and moved straight and tall into the building. On his way to the seventieth floor, Will thought of Apex's community leaders who had kept the town alive, waiting for the moment when it could move forward again. The fire department that embraced his involvement, the community that supported one woman and her dogs, Tony and Cleo, which led him right back to his sprite, Tiffany, one of a kind.

When the doors swept open, he was ready to make this growth happen for them. In the rotunda of Nosh, Nosh, and Crane the wood shone deep and warm. The walls were lined with framed photographs of the heads of departments. The oak boardroom doors were open. Murmurs, creaking leather seats, and coffee cups placed in saucers indicated that the principals were organizing for the meeting. Will strode into the room. "Good morning. Nice to see you Jim, Stan, Aaron."

"Hey there, Will, welcome back to the land of the sophisticated," Jim said. He had a diamond stud in his ear. He shuffled papers with a new vice-presidency confidence.

"What took you so long to get back from the out and beyond?" Stan, head of their legal department, asked while reaching for a doughnut.

Aaron, from Accounts, moved his chair as close to the table as his abdomen would allow, creating space for Will to move between the chairs and the wall. "I think the guy has developed muscles. They making you work in the hinterland?"

Will slid his chair up to the table, and reached for a glass of ice water. "I'm hoping you will all come out and see for yourselves that a small town does not have to be a dull town."

Mr. Crane, one of the partners, walked in and closed the door. "Glad to see we are all here." Sitting at the head of the table, he said, "Let's get started. Jim, would you begin?"

"We're here to discuss our involvement in Apex, Saskatchewan, under new circumstances because Rockwell Mining has slowed their involvement in the mine at this time. You can see from the figures in your package that we're heavily invested to date and we need to decide if it is worth going forward or if the first loss is the least lost."

The men around the table shuffled the papers and glanced at the figures in front of them. Will thought his heartbeat seemed to be adding up the columns and coming up to a marathon runners beat. He concentrated on quieting his breathing and keeping his game face on.

Mr. Crane nodded toward Aaron. "What's your opinion?"

Aaron rubbed the icing off his fingertips, then lifted his coffee mug to his lips. Will recognized his corporate stance. He'd been around this table often.

"We own the land," Aaron said. "The surveys and blueprints are completed. Nothing will change for a couple of years. I say we halt the development at this stage. We watch what happens. We can resell the land if necessary and perhaps use the blueprints in another development."

Mr. Crane jotted a few notes and turned toward Stan. "As your legal adviser," Stan said, "I've looked over the contracts and I believe we can delay this development without any legal difficulties. We had every form of contingency in the contract." Stan twirled his pen.

Will looked down at his palm. His lifeline wasn't as long as Tiffany's but his hand was smooth. He had used his brain and mediation skills to find his way around obstacles. This was a disruption. Mr. Crane's famous throat clearing interrupted his thoughts. "Will?"

He looked up into Mr. Crane's face.

Will pushed his hands on the table and stood. "The numbers and the contracts may say we can drop this project without any consequences, but the people who have their hopes and plans for a different future are our moral responsibility."

"Morals won't make us any money." Jim twisted the diamond stud in his ear.

"Of course they don't appear to, but we all know that when we uphold our end of the bargain, it has rippling effects for our future. Isn't that what Mr. Nosh, Senior, says? That's how he started this business." Will paused for effect. "This time lapse can benefit us. Continuing to move forward, we will be in a better place when the mine ramps up production, and we know that it will. Rockwell Mines will not sit on the largest potash find when there are people starving in the world. Besides, Rockwell isn't moving everyone out, they are going to upgrade the water and lagoon to accommodate their future needs, complete the contracted roadwork, and continue to build the main plant. There will be a couple of hundred extra men around. They may even stay behind and help us build our complex."

"They might work for less," Jim said.

Will turned toward Jim. "We honor our contracts."

"Just trying to give you some help here, buddy. I can tell you want to go through with this."

"I do. But not at the cost of labor." Will shifted his weight. "We've always been fair to our employees."

Mr. Crane nodded. "Tell us more of your thoughts, Will."

"I believe we can move forward with our plans. Rockwell wouldn't keep their commitments if they didn't believe in the resource and its potential."

"Will, sit down. We're listening," Mr. Crane said calmly.

"Thank you." Will snagged his leather boardroom chair with his hand and settled himself onto the seat. "I've made up a time table and a cost analysis." Will passed copies down the table. "As you can see, it is cost effective to continue. And in addition to highlighting our new model, I believe that we will garner a lot of press and have more companies asking for our assistance. Gentlemen, I believe so strongly in this project that I'm willing to forgo my salary and oversee this development on my own resources." Will drank water from his glass.

The shuffling papers and wheeled motion of chairs on the carpet indicated that the other men around the table were considering his offer.

"That is honorable of you, Will. But if we are going to continue with our plans we will honor your contract as well." Mr. Crane glanced at the clock on the wall. "I need to contact Mr. Nosh, Senior, and Mr. Nosh, Junior, with the information you have all provided today. I suggest we meet back here on Monday for further discussions." Mr. Crane stacked his papers and rose from his seat. "Monday at ten then, gentlemen."

Everyone around the table murmured their assent.

Will reached for his crutches. Monday was four days away. What was he going to do for four days?

Stan held the door for Will. "As the legal advisor, we planned for all contingencies in our contracts."

"I know. You're good at what you do Stan, but this idea is a great one," he said. "We aren't part of Rockwell mining operation. I know this will make it on its own." Will slung his bag across his chest. "I need to find a way to keep the shareholders happy and the future residents of the neighborhood hopeful."

"Good luck." Stan closed the door behind Will.

The meeting had been shorter than he calculated. Walking toward his office, he noted the art by renowned Canadian artists had been changed, the thick carpet muffled the sounds of the busy office, and his office was as large as the Apex council chambers. Sinking into his ergonomically correct chair and scanning the citations of excellence on the wall, he realized the advantages he had. His in-basket was empty as was his out-basket. Nosh, Nosh, and Crane had done very well without him here at the head office. The partners had provided the opportunities, and over the years Will had worked hard to honor the faith placed in him. Nosh, Sr., might support Will's efforts to continue with the program. Nosh Jr.'s expertise lay in the mining camp sector.

Turning his chair to the skyline gave him a point of focus. Who did he know who would believe in him enough to finance the completion of the inclusive neighborhood, if it came to that?

At the mall, Tiffany and her assistant extraordinaire Scott ate the hamburgers and fries Owen had brought. They were all quiet, just staring at the mural.

"Tiffany, you have made fantastic progress. I wouldn't have believed it if I hadn't seen it myself. We are ahead of schedule." Owen sidestepped slowly and carefully scrutinized the underwater mural. The giant clams were embedded in the sand in one corner, the cabbage coral shimmered, and sea plants' leaves appeared to sway in the light. "The passengers on the glass-bottom boat look like they are having a great time." Turning back toward Tiffany and Scott, Owen said, "When your sculptures are anchored, this mural will provide so much pleasure to those who stop and stare."

Tiffany's hand shook when she pushed it through her hair. "Credit goes to Scott. If he hadn't kept the materials ready each day and at just the right moisture level we could have been in big trouble. He is a wonderful assistant all around."

"The climate control in here helps as well." Scott chugged a soda. "I was concerned the foot traffic would cause a problem, but everyone has been respectful."

"Research indicates that murals become community property," Owen said.

"Although I'm bringing it to life, it doesn't belong to me. It will belong to everyone who experiences the beauty of the mural," Tiffany said, while they watched the play of light against the paint, the delicate balance of materials which would continue to harden over time, drawing more of the color into it and turning into rock. The multicolored coral reef with its gleaming pinks, corals, and reds would glitter forever.

Scott stood and gathered up the tools. "There are many hours left before we can wax on about beauty and ownership."

The security guard strolled past doing his rounds. The June sun bathed the corridor in a golden orange-yellow glow. Tiffany stood, then bent and touched the floor, rounding her back and shoulders. "Tomorrow will be our last day of painting, then Saturday for the wall to harden, and then we can attach the sea creatures on Sunday."

"The company would like you to cover the wall after you have completed the work so they can have a grand unveiling on Wednesday," Owen said.

"Perfect. We'll drape it before the majority of office staff return."

"I can help on Sunday," Owen said.

Tiffany threw her arm around Owen's shoulder, "Yes, I'd like that. I have the design, the anchors are in place, but your expert eye will help tilt the sculptures to receive the best light."

"I'll meet you at the shop on Saturday morning and we can pick up your fishes and bring them here. Then on Sunday when the plaster is hardened, your sculptures will be in their new home. You both deserve some time off." Owen wrapped his arms around Scott and Tiffany for a group hug. "Now go home." Owen tapped Tiffany on the shoulder. "Turn on your phone, you have messages. Your brother called."

"Oh, he called you, did he?" She reached for her phone. Her stomach sank. "An emergency?"

"No. He knows how you get lost in your work." Owen put his hand over hers. "No hurry, he wanted to check on you."

"Okay, I'll reply when we're done. I don't want disturbances during the work." Tiffany helped Scott place the tarp that kept the sand clean and moist over the tub before locking up her pure pigment jars and brushes. "See you tomorrow."

Still high on adrenalin, Tiffany found she wasn't ready to go home. She drove to and parked next to the Assiniboine River, which flowed between banks with overhanging trees and places for families to picnic. She turned on her phone. Her messages binged like an alarm clock. Her brother gave her two possible dates to check against her schedule for their wedding. Her stylist reminded her she had an appointment on Monday, her dental hygienist told her it was time for her cleaning, and her dog whisperer sent a photo.

Tiffany opened the photo, then spread it with her fingers searching for clues. Obviously, a pressed suit pant leg broken by a knee resting against a leather seat.

"Where are you, Will?"

She noticed the edge of a briefcase and a railing usually found on a busy thoroughfare. It appeared as if Will had abandoned Apex, too. Watching a sea gull fly across the sky with its wings spread, opened her soul. Sometimes you just had to soar alone. But then there were other gulls and ducks floating on the river's surface. She focused on a sea gull against a clear mauve sky. Tiffany attached the photo to a message for Will and pressed the send icon.

Leaning her head back, she noticed the area filling up with cars. Music filtered into the air through open windows, couples strolled the boardwalk. A make-out spot. Time to leave. Tiffany turned her key and the car engine purred. Her mobile rang. Before driving, she checked the number and smiled. "Hello, Shotgun Rider."

"Hello, Sprite. Great picture. Where are you?"

"At a make-out spot." She laughed, and it felt good.

"That gull looks lonely soaring in the dusk."

Tiffany heard leather creak. "Sometimes everyone needs a bird's eye view of their community." She turned off the engine. "There are many other ducks and gulls on the river."

"Is that what you're doing?"

"Soaring?" *Yes.* "I was pretty high a couple of hours ago."

"Tell your shotgun rider all about it."

She heard ice cubes clink against glass.

"Since I'm parked in a lover's lane, I'd rather share sweet whispers." Tiffany smiled. Will definitely brought out the fun, sexy side of her.

"I'm sitting in my recliner after a hard day, wishing it was a compact car at the side of the road waiting for my rescuer." A husky whisper flowed into her ear, "A beautiful, common-sense sprite arrived, so much better looking than the burly tow-truck driver."

"That night, I almost drove past. I had been secure in my urban attitude, but small-town neighborliness nudged me to investigate."

"It was destiny reeling us together."

"Oh yes, especially when you were so happy to see the flashing saviour lights cresting the hill."

"I was scared."

"Of me?"

"Of the way you fit into to me like a piece of my puzzle of life."

"How's the empty space doing?"

"Empty."

"Mine too."

"Want to get together and complete each other?"

"Sure. I'm in Winnipeg. You?"

"Toronto."

"I can't come your way. I have time-sensitive work to finish."

"I don't mind coming to you, but I have to be back by Monday."

Car lights flashed across her dark interior. "I'm working hard tomorrow but if all goes according to plan, I'm free for a while on Saturday."

"I can watch you work."

"Hmmm, I think we've been here before." She recalled him slouched in a chair, asleep with Tony's head resting on his foot. She sighed.

"I won't fall asleep this time." He seemed to read her thoughts.

"It is a nice dream, thinking that your Pollyanna might see what I'm doing."

"I'm good at making dreams come true."

"Okay, dream maker, call when you arrive in town and I'll tell you where I am." She chuckled. "Oh-oh."

"What?"

"The security man is out with his flashlight, telling people to move on."

"Good night, Sprite. See you soon."

"Good night, dog whisperer, shotgun rider, dream-maker." The screen went black.

Tiffany shielded her eyes from the flashlight, turned on the ignition, and rolled down the window. "I'm leaving."

Tiffany giggled all the way back to her apartment. The memory of Will's husky voice whispering in her ear sent little thrills through her.

Chapter 28

Will disconnected the call. Tiffany was one plane ticket away. He could be there in two hours and thirty minutes airtime, but of course, there was travel to and from airports and waiting time. In six hours, he could be with Tiffany. Taking a deep breath his lungs felt clearer. His therapist and his mother's chicken soup had worked wonders. He could go to his office bright and early and pick up the papers he needed, and fly into Winnipeg by midafternoon. How would he find Tiffany? She called him her shotgun rider, dog whisperer, and dream maker. She was reaching out to him. He checked on the availability of a round trip to Winnipeg.

What were his plans for the weekend? He had promised to have dinner with his mother, research, and rest. When he clicked on the after-lunch flight, two seats were available. He picked up the phone and called his mother. She was excited to accompany him to Winnipeg for the weekend. He purchased the seats. He had cast his dice. If Tiffany didn't make time for him, he'd have a weekend in another city.

Should he tell Tiffany or surprise her? Almost every meeting between them had been a surprise. Even though he had suggested he may visit her, they hadn't made definite plans. Surprise it would be.

His mother's text requested the special woman's name. He replied, *Tiffany George*. He knew his mother. Research was the nature of her writing and his mom wouldn't be able to help herself find out as much as she possibly could about Tiffany George.

The next morning, he packed for the weekend, had the driver take him to the office, and then to the airport. His mother was waiting for him. This time they walked together, rather than her pushing him in a wheelchair as she had when he had first arrived back in Toronto.

"Do you want to know what I discovered about Tiffany?" his mother asked when they had passed through security and were seated at the gate waiting for the boarding to be called.

"No thank you. Not now," he said. "But if I need to find her, I will ask."

"Fine. I think you should see the spectacular project she is doing."

"Thanks, Mom, but I want her to tell me."

The pre-boarding began.

During the flight, Will brought his mother up to date with his hopes and concerns about the future of his project in Apex.

"Do you have a list of investors if the company decides not to follow through?" his mother asked.

"I'm doing that now."

"I'd certainly like to be a partner if it came to that. I know how important this is to everyone, including you."

"Thanks, Mom. I have savings, and my condo that I'm prepared to use. I'll contact other corporations. But I have been thinking, I may offer the residents of Apex an opportunity to be financially involved, perhaps by purchasing shares."

"Don't get ahead of yourself, son. Both Mr. Noshes have a personal interest and it will be fabulous promotion for them. Inclusion today is a wonderful opportunity to make communities better and that has a rippling effect." She changed the channels on the TV.

"I shared my positive Pollyanna principle with Tiffany."

His mother put her hand on his cheek. "She must be special."

The attendants' cart filled the aisle and passengers seemed content eating their cookies or pretzels and drinking their choice of beverage.

"Mom, I've been thinking, how about one morsel of information about Tiffany?" Will wanted to know but felt as if he shouldn't be gaining information when Tiffany hadn't shared it.

"Sorry, I always believe you the first time. Besides, if you wanted information you would have been all over this the hours after you met." His mother sipped her coffee.

Will stretched his legs, which were a normal size for a man his height and weight and for that he had to thank his strong-minded mother, connected father, and the surgeon who had been making research strides with Cerebral Palsy children when he was born. Even though both of them had to move to the other side of the country for almost a year, they did. And because of them he walked today. "Thanks, Mom, for my legs."

"I noticed you're starting to walk on your toes again. You really need to keep up those stretches."

"I know, but I didn't find a physiotherapist in Apex and going to Regina was complicated because of the distance."

"You're past the age of my influence, but I'm still your mom. Promise me you'll look after this soon."

"Yes, Mother." He smiled. They'd had this conversation thousands of times during his lifetime. "Do you ever wish Dad had stayed?" His mother wrote romance novels but her marriage had disintegrated because his father looked further afield.

"Sometimes. We had a lot of fun over the years. But that is over and done with now. I hope he is happier." Reaching for Will's empty cup and snack wrapper, she passed them to the attendant collecting garbage.

"I know I've told you often and I'm not too old to say it again, thank you for staying." Will swallowed the familiar lump in his throat when he thought about his mother's sadness. He had one moment that appeared in his mind, every time he thought about those days immediately after the separation. He'd read that sadness was etched on a face but until that day, he hadn't been able to imagine it.

"You're my son. Of course I stayed." She clicked her table into the seat in front of her, then pushed her purse securely under the seat and reached for his hand. "I love you."

The pilot announced the weather in Winnipeg, while the plane descended onto the runway.

Will was anxious to leave the airplane and let the adventure begin, but he waited for those anxious to disembark. His mother freshened her lipstick and checked her hair.

"You're beautiful, Mom."

"What's your plan?"

"We go to the hotel. I send Tiffany a message photo of the sign outside our hotel and wait." He shrugged.

"Good for you. But what about coming to the Canadian Museum for Human Rights with me? You'll wait a whole lot easier."

"Great idea. We can have a snack there."

"From my research, I'll tell you that Tiffany can't leave until the day's work is completed." She pointed toward the sign that indicated the baggage pickup area.

"Bags, hotel, and then the museum. Got it." Will snapped photos at every stop, clicked the send icon and the photo whooshed to Tiffany.

Chapter 29

Tiffany's early morning coffee was accompanied by wonder and hope that her dream maker might appear. She swallowed hard. She couldn't think about Will. She had to stay focused today, or she could ruin all of her work. Her last corner had to be painted on the wet plaster before it cured. There would be no dreaming allowed today. Reluctantly, she set her phone to airplane mode. She would not send or receive any messages or calls. She'd listen to music while she worked until her day was done.

Scott was onsite when she brought her paints and brushes into the mall area. "Morning, Scott. Can you believe today the plaster and painting will be done?"

"That's why I'm here early. I couldn't sleep." He pulled his hoe through the lime and sand mixture.

"I almost had a heart attack. I thought I was out of the pigment needed for the sea." She held the container close to her chest. "But the label was turned backward."

They worked in unison, putting on the final coat, preparing the cartoon with the sea plants and anchors ready to receive the sculptures. She painted the darker green pigment shading against the leaves of the waving plants and rocks for sea life habitat. When the wall dried, the paint became part of the stone, an integral part of the wall. While she worked on detail, her thoughts followed the process: Getting to really know someone went down into the layers and came back up again more brilliant and solid.

When she removed her earbuds, she noticed the day's hustle and bustle had disappeared.

The sun glowed against the sea. Her legs wobbled, but the mural was finished and ready for the sculptures.

By six p.m., all that was left now was to cover and lock up their supplies in case there was a problem when they returned on Saturday to bring in the sea life. Then on Sunday they would complete the mounting and cover the mural until the grand unveiling on Wednesday. She thought about the new fish she had created when she had returned from Apex. It would float among the other fish. Initially, she had thought he would be above everyone but the more she had thought of inclusion she knew this special fish needed to be in the center of the mural. She'd worked out the design as she painted.

With her arm around Scott, she said, "You are the best assistant. You will go far. Perhaps you'll design and create your own fresco one day soon."

"I'll have to improve my painting skills first, but this is a wonderful medium. I can't believe how patient you have been. Another skill I'll need to nurture." He wrapped his arm around her waist. "Promise me, when you receive another commission you'll think of me as your helper."

Tiffany reached around and hugged the rock-solid man. "You've got it."

Just then, a banging on the glass door echoed from the floor to the ceiling. "Tiffany."

They both turned.

Will pounded at the locked doors.

Tiffany ran. She placed her hand on the glass as if to touch him. "I don't have the key." She turned around to see Scott pointing toward the back door. "Wait there. I'll come and get you."

Tiffany sprinted past the scaffold, through an open door, down a hallway, out the backdoor and through an alley, past dumpsters, and then out onto the street.

"You came." Tiffany flung her arms around Will's neck. He was the very person she wanted to share this time with.

The ending stage of the mural, waiting for the pigment to deepen and the plaster to harden.

"I've been picture-messaging you all day." His crutch clattered to the ground, and she moved to retrieve it. "Let it be." He wrapped his arms around her. She had the stabilizing strength for both of them.

She felt his heart beat pulse in his neck against her lips when she planted a kiss on his skin. She breathed in his aftershave, slid her hand across his stubble beard, and tugged on his earlobe.

"I turn off my phone when I'm working." She wanted to melt into him. Will, her soul whisperer, understood that she needed to leave other's expectations of who she should be in order to become the woman she didn't know she could be.

He wobbled and flung his hand out toward the glass tower. Tiffany's feet slid to the walkway. She slipped under his arm and stabilized his stance. "I've really bowled you over."

"You're full of surprises, Miss George." His brown eyes were wide and the skin on the side of his mouth furrowed when he smiled. His focus was drawn toward the window.

"No." Turning his face with her palm, she said, "Wait, it's not done. Please." Tiffany wanted to feel his lips on her lips, his breath against her skin, his hand cradling her butt. "Kiss me."

"I thought you'd never ask." Leaning down and tilting his head he pressed his lips to hers. Her eyes closed. When he drew his lips away their breath mingling, her breasts ached and she clasped her arms around his neck. "I missed you."

He slid his hand across the small of her back, "How's the butterfly?"

"Ready to fly." She sighed. "How long are you staying?"

"Sunday," he said.

"I know the synchronized steps. Let's walk to my car." She saw the fatigue in his eyes. "Or I could run and get it?"

"How far? I do need to rest for a few minutes."

"Just around the back. We can go down the alley as a short cut."

"Let's walk."

Tiffany rested her hand on his forearm and they moved slowly around the building. She watched him place each heel then toe. It didn't matter if they went at a snail's pace. This was Will. He'd come. Her eyes filled with tears. She blinked hard. She must be more exhausted than she thought. When they neared the back door of the building, Scott was locking up. "Tiffany, everything is sealed and put away."

"Thank you, Scott." She put pressure on Will's forearm, and he stopped. "Scott, I'd like you to meet Will Cleaver."

Scott nodded.

Will extended his hand. "Pleased to meet you, Scott." Will's voice was business-like.

Tiffany frowned. "Scott and I have been working together non-stop since I returned from Apex. He is an exemplary apprentice."

"It's easy to work with a talented artist. Wouldn't you agree, Will?"

"I haven't had the pleasure of seeing Tiffany in that capacity, but I will attest that she is a woman of many talents."

Tiffany felt Will's muscles tighten in his arm.

He straightened.

"See you Sunday, Scott," she said, "unless you want to move sculptures tomorrow."

"Yes, I was hoping you'd ask."

"I'll firm it up with Owen and then text you, if that works for you." Tiffany wanted Scott to have a look at the fish and plant life that would be added to the painting.

Scott held up his phone. "I'll turn it on."

Tiffany chuckled. "See, I'm not the only one." She put a little pressure on Will's arm and began to walk. "There's the car."

"That man has a crush on you." Will stumbled. "And I could crush you if I fall on you."

"Will Cleaver, you know how strong I am. You won't crash with me around." She held the car door open for him.

Will settled in the seat.

"If Scott does have a crush, it will pass. It is that bond between artists. The trick is not to act on it." She put her hands on Will's cheeks, drew his face to her, and kissed him. "Hmm." She nuzzled his neck.

A car horn honked, and a voice yelled, "Get a room."

"Mr. Cleaver, what's on your agenda, now that you're here?"

He shifted his weight and his brown eyes gazed deep into her eyes. "You know that I'm an architect?" She nodded. "Architects design for the future." He reached for her hand and folded his fingers through hers. "My agenda consists of spending as much time as I can to convince you that we'd be good together and design the foundation and walls so that you can love me and I'll love you."

"Anything else?" Tiffany stared back into his eyes and ran her fingers over his knuckles.

He cleared his throat. "Hmm, introduce you to my mother."

An astonished puff of air escaped Tiffany's lips. "Where is she?"

"Back at the hotel." He slipped his thumb onto her palm and stroked in a circular motion. "I promised I'd spend time with her while I was in Toronto, but when the opportunity to be a dream maker came up, and I couldn't refuse." He shook his head and a small smile played at the corners of his mouth. "I wanted her to meet you."

"They say a woman should see how a man treats his mother before a relationship progresses." She gave his hand a final squeeze then started the car. "I can either drive you to the hotel and go home and clean up." She felt the pressure of his hand on her thigh. "Or you could come with me, and then we can meet your mother after I've had a chance to shower."

"Sometimes the universe provides a perfect time for an adventure."

"I don't have a lot of energy for an adventure, Mr. Cleaver." Tiffany glanced at him at the red light.

"No, not even for falling in love?"

Tiffany reached across the console and felt his thigh under his navy khaki pants.

"I'll text Mom and tell her the plan." He looked at his watch. "An hour?"

His phone message binged. "She's excited to meet you." Will coughed into his elbow.

"Are you sure you don't want to rest?" Tiffany asked. "I could drop you at the hotel and meet you as soon as I'm ready."

"I'm right where I want to be. I don't want to miss a single moment in the time we have together."

Tiffany had stopped the car. "Wake up, mister," she said, stroking the back of his hand.

He turned toward her. "Not asleep, just luxuriating in being with you."

"We're here."

Will used his strength to push his way out of the car. She waited for him and then placed her hand on his arm. "This way."

They walked through an underground garage to an elevator and rode up to the third floor. Tiffany opened the door to 301 and stepped back for him to enter. "Leave your shoes on. Sorry, I haven't been home much." She led the way into the small living room. "Have a seat. Can I get you a juice, a glass of water, while I transform from artist to dinner guest?"

Will moved to the sofa. "I'd appreciate a glass of cold water. Would you mind if I stretch out while you change?"

Tiffany fluffed the cushions. He bent down to take off his shoes. She leaned over and removed his loafers. "Love those polka-dot socks."

"A man's got to add color to his world when he can." He settled himself into the cushions where she probably spent time watching TV or reading. "Don't hurry, I'm comfy right here."

He heard Tiffany cracking an ice cube tray and plopping them into a glass, then she ran the tap. Soon she was at his side. "Here you go." She watched him gulp his drink. "Don't be afraid to catch a few winks. After all, we've shared a bed." He reached out to her. She sidestepped his hand. "Don't tempt me, dream maker. I'm not going to be late for a meeting with your mother." Tiffany took off her hat then ran her fingers through her hair, "But I'm not sure you want her to meet me with two-toned hair."

"You're a natural blonde?"

"If you mean that blond is the color of hair I was born with, then yes. Is that a problem?"

"No. Many women try to be blond."

"As you know, I'm not like many women. Are you okay with that?"

"Yes." All he wanted was to have her close to him.

"I'll be back in a few." She bent down and kissed him. Then she broke off the kiss. "Here's the remote."

Soon he heard the shower running. Then it stopped. She called from behind him, "Where are we going?"

"The Steakhouse in the hotel."

"Good luck on a Friday evening."

"No problem, I made a reservation earlier with high hopes."

He heard her laugh and then the door swooshed closed.

Will dialed his phone and confirmed three for dinner. Then he closed his eyes for just a minute.

He woke when Tiffany touched his shoulder. "Wakey, wakey."

She stood before him as he had never seen her before, in a simple sleeveless black dress that clung to her every perfect curve, a cardigan draped over her arm, and flat espadrilles. "Ready when you are."

"Wow." He swung his legs onto the floor. She slid his loafers toward him. "No spikes?"

"I gave them up when I came home. Too hard to keep under a cap." She picked up a black-and-white-striped purse with a wrist strap. "Are we meeting your mom at the restaurant or the lobby?"

"The restaurant. I'm starved."

"Me, too. This is going to be my first good meal since the BBQ in Apex." Her smile faltered for a minute. "How are Tony and Cleo?" She opened and closed the zipper on her purse. "I haven't heard a word since Pat blamed me for what happened to them."

Will was confused too, since Tiffany had seemed an integral part of Pat and the dogs' lives when they first met.

"Pat and the dogs are recuperating together at home. The neighbors are dropping in and filling in the necessary care they all need. Lacy's been keeping me up to date."

"I don't understand what happened, Will." Tiffany turned toward him, and he saw tears in her eyes.

He drew her close. "I don't either. I left soon after the dogs returned. I only know that Lacy said the town thought I was the hero." He sighed. "I told her it was all you."

"It's as if a spell was cast on Apex and I became . . . unacceptable." Tiffany straightened and jingled her keys.

He gave her an extra squeeze. "We know the truth."

She put her hand on his arm. "Let's move."

Chapter 30

Tiffany pointed out landmarks along the way to the hotel. Will looked casual and relaxed in his khakis and navy-blue collar shirt. His tasselled loafers were scuffed on the toes, and he was struggling with his usual gait.

"Will?" How should she phrase her observation?

"Hmm." His head was back against the headrest, his body relaxed. He sat up. "You're not concerned about meeting my mother, are you?"

"Should I be?" Her heart skidded an extra beat. The car in front of her was in the wrong lane and prevented her from turning toward the hotel.

"I wouldn't think so." He cleared his throat. "She's skilled at asking questions, so if don't want to answer, be forthright."

"I repeat your advice many times a day, when I think I should be nice to people at the expense of my goals. I choose my priorities." Tiffany covered his hand, which rested on his thigh. "Thank you."

"You're welcome. Mom helped me master that advice, too." He looked around. "We're almost here."

"Would you like me to drop you at the door, then I'll park?"

"No way." He stretched his legs. "You've noticed my gait has changed."

"Yes."

"When I don't have enough rest, or don't use my time wisely and stretch or exercise, my muscles tend to contract. Then I'm up on my toes."

"I wondered. Thanks for telling me." Tiffany drove into a spot at the furthest edge of the parking lot. "Closest I can get."

"All the more time for us to walk together, my dear." Will chuckled while he opened the door.

Tiffany leaned in and kissed his cheek. "I like kissing you, Mr. Cleaver."

"I'm glad. Be my guest."

"Even in front of your mother?" She kept her pace matched to his.

"Of course. If the moment comes over you, just land one right here." He puckered his lips at her.

She kissed her fingertips and placed them on his lips without breaking stride.

Tiffany pushed the automatic door opener button with the standardized wheelchair symbol on the side of the restaurant door. The big oak door swung open and they walked in side-by-side. The interior had limited lighting and a gentle hum of voices rose and fell while the hostess approached them.

"We have a reservation. Will Cleaver."

"Welcome, Mr. Cleaver. One of your guests is seated at your table. Your server will show you the way."

Will dropped back and allowed Tiffany to proceed in front of him.

A stunning woman waved to them. "Will, Tiffany, over here."

"Tiffany George, Rhonda Carmichael, my mother."

Will's mother was tall and slim with a white, chin-length bob, piercing blue eyes, and ruby-red studs glittering in her ears. Tiffany marveled at the royal blue-and-black evening suit.

"Glad to meet you, Tiffany." Rhonda had a firm handshake.

"I can see where Will gets his height."

Mother and son also shared the same nose and jaw line.

"Let's sit down." Will held a chair for Tiffany.

Rhonda sat in her chair, and Will moved to his seat between the two women.

"This is one of the most popular steakhouses in the city." Tiffany felt Will's hand on her thigh. "I haven't had an opportunity to have dinner here before." Trays of food were delivered to surrounding tables. "I'm getting hungrier by the minute."

They opened their menus and discussed the merits of the specials. Will and Rhonda discussed the type of wine that would pair well with the meals.

The server took their order then poured the wine.

Will raised his glass. "To a wonderful meal."

Tiffany met Rhonda's eyes as they each tapped Will's glass with their own.

"Will, did you tell Tiffany how you found her?" Rhonda twirled the red wine in her glass.

"I've been wondering the same thing," Tiffany said, looking over at Will.

"I'm an intrepid kind of guy?" He placed his glass on the table and reached for her hand. "When you didn't respond to any of my texts today . . ." He swallowed. "I thought you might have changed your mind about seeing me."

Rhonda interrupted, "Instead of enjoying the museum and my witty comments he kept checking his phone. Finally, I put him out of his misery and provided the address to your mural site."

"But how?"

The serving staff continued to move through the crowded restaurant, and the conversations rose and fell.

"The Internet knows all," Rhonda said.

"Mom's a good researcher. She's known for a couple of days but I asked her not to tell me anything she learned." He leaned closer to Tiffany. "I didn't want to take a chance that technology might mess up my chance to be with you."

"You should have seen him banging on the glass door." Tiffany turned toward Rhonda.

"Yes, but you remember you were in an embrace with a big muscular man on the other side of that door." Will picked up a breadstick. "I wanted to get your attention."

"He got it, all right." Tiffany broke a warm bun and buttered it.

"I didn't have any idea what you were doing. Mom didn't give me any information other than the address."

"We were packing up. If you'd have been thirty minutes later, we would have been gone." Tiffany felt her eyes widen. Then she sighed. "But I would have opened my messages and texted you back." She chewed thoughtfully. "Thank you, Rhonda. Otherwise, I wouldn't be here for dinner."

"Will likes to keep his promises, even if it means he loses out."

Rhonda's plate arrived and then the servers brought Will and Tiffany's meals.

Rhonda talked about the museum, the hotel, and the trees along the boulevards. Will complimented the tenderness of the steak. Tiffany commented on the *al dente* vegetables.

When the servers had cleared the plates and filled their cups with coffee, Rhonda sat back and folded her hands into her lap. "I'd like to suggest an experiment for the rest of the evening."

Will moaned. "Mom."

"What is your experiment?" Tiffany folded her napkin in her lap.

"During my research I've come across a nineteen ninety-seven study by psychologist Arthur Aron and his team who questioned if the process of falling in love could be speeded up by asking thirty-six questions."

"Mom, that's almost two decades ago."

"Some things never go out of style." She went on. "These questions begin mild and become more intimate. They are meant to create a feeling of connection." She turned to Will. "I'd like you to download the app and then I'll leave and give you some privacy." She winked at Will. "I have my own reasons for asking you, as neither of you are young anymore. You seem as if you would be a good fit, but you never know it may be the discussions prompted by these questions that suggest a future." She looked at Tiffany. "My son thinks you are special and I observed that you reciprocate those feelings." She held her phone out to Will. "Here's the name of the app."

"What do you think?" Will asked.

"There's nothing to say we have to continue if we find we don't like the questions." She looked around. "There doesn't seem to be people waiting for our table."

"Okay, Mom." Will searched for the app. "While I'm doing this, Mom tell Tiffany what you do for a living so she doesn't think we're both bonkers."

Rhonda picked up her evening bag and opened it. She handed Tiffany a business card. "The fresco you are creating is similar to how I work. You start off with a rough foundation and gradually end up with a smooth surface and add color." Tiffany stared at the card. "I do the same with my characters. They usually rub against each other the wrong way because of misconceptions and then as they discover each other's qualities, love grows and deepens." She held her hands wide. "*Voila.*"

"You're a writer?" Tiffany asked, uncertain if she should acknowledge that she hadn't read any of Rhonda's novels.

Rhonda folded her napkin. "Don't worry if you haven't read any of my work before, I'll only hope you will read it in the future."

"Thank you. I'll do an Internet search for your novels after this mural is unveiled."

Rhonda patted Will's sleeve. "All set."

"Yes, Mom."

Rhonda stood. "I hope to see you again before we leave on Sunday, Tiffany."

"I'd like that," Tiffany said.

Rhonda stopped and spoke to their server before she disappeared through the oak doors.

"We don't have to do this. Mom has observed my friends, her friends, my relationships, and had a few of her own to give her stories authenticity." He placed his phone between them.

Tiffany looked at the time. "Will, we already know that we enjoy each other's company. We've been in dangerous situations and we've shared a bed. I'd like to know more about you."

Will tapped the phone and read, "Thirty-six questions to fall in love. Ready?"

Tiffany felt her heart thud. "Yes. Go for it." She could still choose how far she wanted to go. She was in control.

With the phone between them, he asked the first question. "Given the choice of anyone in the world, whom would you want as a dinner guest?"

"That's easy. Michelangelo, the most famous fresco artist in the world."

"Now it's my turn. Frank Lloyd Wright, the American architect. He did it all, from outsides to interiors. He wrote about his work and taught. Yes, definitely him."

Will turned the phone. Tiffany's turn to ask the question now. "Would you like to be famous? In what way?"

"Yes, for my progressive neighborhoods." She noticed his lips drop from a smile for a second and then he took a deep breath. "You?"

"I know I'd like fame as an artist, but I also want to be famous to my future children. I want to be their hero."

Some of the questions were random. "What would constitute a *perfect* day for you?" Tiffany wondered if Will would answer about a day when he could run, but he didn't. It was a day when he could ride for hours on his hand pedal tricycle.

"My turn," Will said. "When did you last sing to yourself? To someone else?"

"That's easy, today, to myself while I worked and probably anyone else who was walking past." Tiffany smiled. "You?"

"Singing is very over rated. Now humming or whistling, that I can do until I run out of breath." Will whistled a tune with trills and added beats.

"Wow. That's some tongue work going on in there." Tiffany checked around the restaurant and realized they were the only two customers sitting at a table. The staff were removing the condiments, changing table clothes, and vacuuming in another corner. "I think we should go somewhere else and allow these people to go home."

Will placed his credit card in the leather folder. "A coffee shop?"

"I was going to suggest that we talk while I drive, but you're staying here." Tiffany felt the loneliness settling in the pit of her stomach. "How many more questions?"

"We could go up to my hotel room, order up some coffee and a liqueur." He stood and waited for her to collect her purse.

Tiffany glanced at her watch. "Owen isn't coming to help with the sculptures until noon tomorrow and I haven't had fun in a very long time. But can we order herbal tea?"

"We can order special spring water from the highest mountain, if you like." Will's smile was huge. "Walk with me."

Will and Tiffany apologized to the hostess for holding

up the staff. "No problem. We're happy if you are enjoying yourself and you both seemed to be doing that."

"It had to have been your whistling." Tiffany squeezed his forearm.

"Perhaps it was your belly laugh when I told you my life story in four minutes?" Will added.

The elevator doors opened and Will pressed the floor number. She saw the fatigue around his eyes. "You've had a long day."

"But it is better now. I've missed you. I missed you at the Apex meeting."

"I had to leave. There wasn't any use in staying around. Whatever is going on with my parents and Aunt Pat, has to fix itself. I can't do it. Owen was trying to have the mural delayed or have me do some work from Apex, but this way it all turned out for the best." Tiffany tucked herself close to his side with her arm around his waist.

"Were you right? Is your neighborhood going to go ahead?"

"It will go forward, I'm hopeful it will be with my company's involvement. If I have to find some private backers, I will. I may even have to ask the residents to invest." The elevator doors opened. "But that's for Monday. Tonight, I'm convincing you to love me."

They entered the room. The drapes were open showing the Winnipeg skyline twinkling with lights.

Tiffany stopped in front of the windows and said, "I'm not sure why artists try to recreate beauty. Here it is, moving and shimmering before my eyes."

Will called room service and ordered herbal tea. He put his arm around her. "It is beautiful. I heard Mom describing your process. It sounds intriguing. I'm sure one of the questions is to tell me about it." He fumbled with his phone. "Yes, here it is, how do you produce a fresco and why?"

Tiffany reached for the phone. "It does not ask about my art."

"You could tell me anyway."

"I know but like your mom said, we're putting on layers in our relationship. How many more questions?"

"Twenty. But at the end of it all, we're instructed to look into each other's eyes for four minutes."

There was a knock on the door. "Room service."

Will stood and centered himself. "Coming."

The staff person pushed a cart into the center of the room. Will palmed the young man a tip. "Thank you."

"Thank you, sir." The young man backed out of the room.

"I have a feeling you were more than generous, by the surprised look on the server's face."

"It's expensive to get an education these days." Will slid a chair away from a table. "Miss George, your tea."

They sipped and asked each other the questions. Tiffany became more and more amazed at this man in her presence, with his answers. She was anxious to be at the point in the experiment where they would stare into each other's eyes.

Will tapped the phone for the next question. "This is the last question. It's intense. Do you want to continue?"

"Let me read it, please?" Will turned the phone in order for her to read it. "Share a personal problem and ask your partner's advice on how he or she might handle it."

Tiffany yawned. "To be honest, I don't want to talk about that tonight. It's been such a good evening. Can we just skip to staring into each other's eyes for four minutes?"

Will reached for her hands. "I agree." He stretched. "We'll tackle that one next time we're together."

"Or not, for a while."

Will's gaze drifted past her toward the comfort of a king-sized bed. "We could stretch out and stare in comfort."

They had shared a bed once before but Tiffany had fallen asleep immediately. He was taking a large jump in faith that her feelings were as intense his. This was more than lust, more than infatuation, he'd experienced them all. This was the real big love for him.

"Tiffany, I know you are my perfect match." Will pushed on the table, stood tall, and reached for her hand. "We'll set the timer on the phone. That way an alarm will go off and we won't fall asleep."

Tiffany slugged his shoulder. "This is supposed to be intense, not boring."

"I know, but we've both had long days." Will kicked off his loafers and sat on the bed.

Tiffany scurried around the other side and crawled over beside him. They thumped the pillows, positioned themselves on their sides, with a clear view of each other's eyes. Will pressed the start button on the timer.

Will turned on his side and tucked his arm under his head. Tiffany mirrored him. He looked into her eyes. She stared back at him. He raised his eyebrows and swallowed deeply. She smiled. He nodded and smiled back. They could do this.

Soon the rest of her face was out of focus and her blue eyes were his only focus. Her pupils extended and her lids fluttered open. The lines around her eyes fanned upward. All thoughts slipped away the longer he stared and accepted the unspoken intimacy they were sharing. They'd discussed thirty-five questions that gave each of them more insight into the other but this was something he had not tried in all his thirty-six years. A tear pooled in the corner of her eye. He wanted to reach out and touch it. To be part of her, as he had not been one with another. For a moment, he hoped he wasn't the cause of her tear. Was she finding him lacking?

His mind raced until he saw her lids slip and cover half of her blue, blue iris. Bedroom eyes.

The alarm rang. Tiffany licked her lips. He reached out and stroked her hair. He wanted to stay like this forever. Tiffany's hand searched for his. They linked fingers. "That was so powerful. I've never experienced anything like it before."

"Me either," Will said. His Adam's apple dipped with a deep swallow.

She ran her finger along his jaw. "Will."

"Tiffany." Will stretched his arm and she snuggled in close. He breathed in Tiffany's skin. She leaned back and exposed her neck to him. He grazed her neck and chin. Then moved to her mouth. She kissed him. They kissed each other for several seconds. She parted her lips from his but kept them almost to the point of kissing again. She touched his face and rasped her knuckles across his whiskers. Her hands floated to his face and shoulders.

He closed his eyes and enjoyed the sensation. He opened his eyes and touched her shoulders. Then he kissed her ears, chin, and the skin around her lips. She reached up bringing his head toward her and she kissed him hard with her moist lips.

When their lips parted, he wrapped his arm around her and whispered in her ear, "Tiffany, you have to go home. You have to work tomorrow."

"Yes." Her voice was husky.

He ran his hand across the top of her head. "No spikes."

"Not for you." Her eyes remained closed.

He moved his leg, which had been clamped between her knees. "I'd really like you to stay, but you have a commitment."

"I know." She reached and tugged down the skirt of her dress. "I'm so comfy and warm."

"I know." He shifted his hips away from her warm body. "I want you to want me in the morning, but if you stay now, you'll probably regret not being home to pack up your sculptures. They're important to you."

She slid to the other side of the bed and stood. "Right now, I don't give a hoot for the copper fish, but you're right, I want to give the mural my full attention."

Will reached for his crutches. "I'll walk you to your car."

She leaned against him. "I'd like that."

Will slipped into his loafers while Tiffany slid into her sandals and found her purse. "Ready when you are."

Right now all he wanted to do was drop his walking aids and wrap his arms around her and carry her back to bed, but he wanted her to want him again the next day, not just tonight. He knew all about waiting for a reward. As a child, he'd waited for casts to come off his legs and his reward was a stronger gait. And tonight Tiffany was more important than anything else he ever waited for. Tiffany wrapped her hand around his bicep and they walked side by side to the elevator. After the elevator doors closed, he leaned down and kissed her smooth hair.

They strolled across the lobby and out the front doors. The night air was warm. Moths fluttered against the parking area lights. She pressed the button on her key and her car doors unlocked. She took a deep breath. "Thank you, Will. I have to go to my shop tomorrow and then Owen and Scott will help me move the sculptures. I'm not sure how long it will take. Can I text you?"

"Please do, but only if it doesn't interfere with what you need to do. Remember this is important to you and because of that it is important to me." She wrapped her arms around his waist and pressed the whole of her tiny body against him. "I'm glad I affect you in this way."

"Me, too." He gripped the handles of his crutches. "Drive carefully."

She stepped away from him and slid into the driver's seat. "Goodnight, Will."

"Night." Will closed the door and walked back to the sidewalk.

Tiffany turned on her lights and reversed. She stopped, lowered the window, and called him over by crooking her finger. "Just one more for the road." She put her fingers to her lips.

He bent and leaned in for a slow, moist kiss. He broke the kiss. "Good night, Sprite."

"Good night, dog whisperer, dream maker."

Will watched her signal out of the hotel parking lot and onto the main thoroughfare. He may as well look over the reports he brought with him, he wasn't going to be falling asleep anytime soon.

Chapter 31

Tiffany drove home through streets that seemed to have halos around each street lamp. After parking in the garage, she opened her apartment door. Her one thought was to climb into bed, not wash away Will's scent, or the feel of his lips on her ears, neck and lips. She relented and brushed her teeth and washed her face but held the cloth away from her neck and ears.

Crawling between her sheets she put one hand under her ear and one hand on the side of her neck and fell into a deep sleep.

She woke to a vibrating buzzing on her bedside table. Reaching over she shut off her alarm, but it kept buzzing. Rubbing her eyes, she opened them and saw her phone jumping on the bedside table.

"Hello."

"Tiffany, are you still asleep?"

"Yes."

"I'm meeting you at the shop in thirty minutes," Owen said.

She sat straight up in bed. "Okay."

"You sound like you can use an hour."

Tiffany swung her legs over the edge of the mattress. Memories flooded back of a few short hours ago when she did the same thing only she had been making out with Will. She shook the memories free but she couldn't keep the smile out of her voice. "I'll be there in thirty," peeling off her pajamas, as she ran down the hallway, and skidded to the shower.

Half an hour later, at the shop, Tiffany unlocked the door and swung it wide, letting in all the sunshine. The dust motes floated up to the ceiling. The odor of burnt solder and ground metal clashed with the fresh air. Tiffany stretched between the tables and then fingered a fin here and a tail there. "Today's the day, my lovelies. You are going to your new home. You're leaving this dark shop with the odor of varnish hanging in the air. Now you will bring happiness to millions."

"Millions?" Owen called from the door.

"Didn't you tell me they were going to televise the unveiling?"

"And podcasts for their advertising. I hope your dance calendar is free for the next while. I have a feeling you'll be getting lots of inquiries." Owen handed her a cup of coffee.

"You're a friend, indeed." Tiffany blew across the surface of the takeaway cup.

"How would you like to organize this adventure today?"

"I've laid them out by size, each with a letter corresponding to the design. If we put the largest sculptures on the bottom of the crates and then add the Styrofoam popcorn between layers, we'll be able to carry them out to the van."

Tiffany put her coffee on the desk.

Together, she and Owen packed crates. "I'll text Scott. He said he'd meet us at the mall and help unload." She glanced at the time on her phone. "Could we hang some today, just to get a feel for the piece?" She was as excited as a kid before a school concert.

"Sure, why not, since Scott will be there to help with the heavy work." Owen reached for her last creation. "You've changed the design."

"I did." Tiffany ran her fingers over the bent tail and misshaped fins. "I wanted this fellow to be in the crowd, not separate, or on the fringes."

"We'll see," Owen said.

Tiffany placed the underwater sculpture in a crate of its own. She was taking this one in the car with her.

When the last crate was loaded, Tiffany locked the door on a shop that looked desolate without the sea sculptures.

Will returned to his papers after he'd ordered room service. When he heard a knock at the door, he mumbled something about remotes for door openers. Scrambling to the door, holding on to furniture, he opened the door to his mother. "Good morning, Will."

"Mom."

"You forgot I was here, didn't you?" She pushed past him and strode into the room. "You've been up all night?"

"No, not all night. I've found a significant error in the calculations for the Apex project." He felt his heart skip a beat. "Here, have a look, tell me what you think?" Will pushed papers toward his mother.

His mother sat at the table scattered with papers and a calculator. She ran her finger down the list of numbers and then down the calculator list. Raising her eyebrows, she said, "I think you might be right."

Will dropped down on the sofa beside her. "This may mean the difference between going forward or delaying."

Another knock at the door. "Room service."

"I'll get it. You stay there."

Will reached into his dressing gown pocket and dropped a bill into her hand. "Give this to the server."

Rhonda brought in a tray with coffee, toast, jam, scrambled eggs, and pancakes.

"I'll have coffee while you eat and you can tell me how my little experiment went."

Will sipped his coffee. "Generally, they are great questions that move toward closeness, but Tiffany and I have already experienced situations where we had to depend on each other. Those questions filled in some blanks and were fun, but beyond that you won't be getting any specifics." Will began eating.

"This is research for me, but I can see that you care for Tiffany a great deal." Rhonda swallowed. "She won't break your heart, will she?"

"She's just into a new career that could take off in so many directions. I don't want her to feel as if she is sacrificing anything for this relationship, or for me"

"You're earning a Master's degree in love because kindness is the key to a stable and healthy relationship." His mother set down her coffee cup into the saucer and wiped the corners of her mouth with her serviette. "I'm going shopping and then on a scheduled walking tour of the downtown."

"I'm going to work and wait. If Tiffany and I connect again today it will be wonderful, but if we can't then we will in the future. I'm that sure."

Rhonda leaned down and patted his shoulder. "You're one of the good ones."

"Thanks, Mom." Will piled the dishes from the table onto the tray. "Enjoy yourself. We'll plan dinner later."

Rhonda waved from the doorway with her sunglasses in her hand.

Will took a photo of his opened reports, his stacks of papers, and his open tablet, and sent it into cyberspace toward Tiffany. Now he knew that she probably wouldn't answer, but when she turned on her phone, he wanted his message to be there for her.

Scott met Tiffany and Owen at the back door with a trolley. The worked in unison until all the crates were in the secure area.

"Was there a reason we have to wait until tomorrow to place them?" Scott said excitedly. "I know you've seen these, but I haven't."

"I'll check the plaster." Tiffany climbed the scaffold. "If we're careful, we should be okay. We're not touching the surface, only the anchors."

Owen glanced at his watch. "I have a couple of hours before I have to be home. Tiffany?"

"What about the coffee-shop clientele and the mall patrons?" Tiffany called from her place above them.

"I'll ask security to lock this access door for today only and direct them to the other door." Owen dialed the security office, spoke briefly, and pumped his fist in the air.

"I'll ask the coffee shop owners if they'll draw the blinds for today only." Scott sauntered off to the counter in the coffee shop.

Tiffany watched him charm the servers, order three coffees, and point to the windows. The young woman nodded. With a wide smile, Scott began rolling down the blinds.

Tiffany stopped bouncing on her toes long enough to pump her fist in the air. "Yes, let's do this."

Tiffany climbed down the scaffold and helped wheel the crates out to the mural. Curious coffee shop patrons peeked around the closed blinds and a few people tugged on the locked doors before they read the sign redirecting them to another door.

"Scott the crates are numbered and the sculptures lettered for their section. I'll go up and Owen will hand you the piece and then you'll bring it up, and you can hold it until I attach it to the anchor. Owen, you can check the light reflection."

Owen laughed. "Give an artist a mural and suddenly she's boss."

Scott brought up a copper fish attached to plant leaves.

Tiffany threaded the wire and called down to Owen who suggested subtle changes in the angles.

"Tiffany, I have to go," Owen said. "You're almost done. How do you want to handle this?"

"Scott, can you stay?"

He nodded enthusiastically. "I'm not going anywhere until Tiffany leaves."

"Then we'll continue. When we meet tomorrow, can we fine-tune?" Tiffany asked Owen.

"I can. The family knows I'll be busy tomorrow. We'll have to cover this before we leave tomorrow." Owen moved slowly past the mural toward the mall. "I don't want to go, but I promised I'd look after the children this afternoon."

"I've got the hardware and material to put up a temporary drape," Scott said.

"Tiffany, I know you're too close to see the whole effect, but it is stunning." Owen continued staring at the mural and sculptures. "Even better than I anticipated."

"I'll come down when all of the sculptures are in their new home." Tiffany reached for her wire cutters. "Until tomorrow."

Scott climbed the scaffold with sculptures in hand. He held the sea creatures in position while Tiffany secured them. "So many visitors are going to receive so much pleasure from this throughout the whole year. But in the winter when the snow is banked along the streets, they'll be able to look at the sun reflecting off the fresco and the sculptures and they will feel warm."

"Thank you, Scott." She rubbed her back. "Almost done. Just the special feature for this anchor." She tapped in the middle of a school of fish. "It's in a box on my paint cupboard."

"Be right back."

Scott cradled Tiffany's sculpted large fish with a hinged tail and fin. "Would a creature with disabilities survive in the ocean?"

"I don't know but this is art, and anything is possible." Tiffany kissed the fish's nose and anchored it to a place in the middle. She ran her fingers over its too-small gills and misshaped tail. "Now I can come down and see the whole."

Tiffany moved from corner to corner, stopping and staring at the cycle of creativity. "Scott, it's beautiful." She checked the time on her phone. "Almost time for dinner."

She dialed. "Will."

"Yes."

"Can you come to the mall?" She wanted to share this with him before anyone else."

"Yes. I'll call a cab."

"Have the cabdriver drop you at the back door. Text when you arrive. I'll let you in." She slipped the phone into her pocket. "Scott, I need to show this to someone special. He won't be here for the unveiling. I'll help you with the drape frame until he arrives."

"Let's just enjoy this. The mall is closed. We can drape it tomorrow."

"Let me buy you a soda from the machine. We'll toast." Tiffany retrieved coins from her purse and plugged the machine then passed Scott a cold drink and they clinked cans.

"This will be my best fresco ever," Tiffany said. "I may perfect my techniques, I may work in different communities, I may receive awards, but this will be my best ever."

Will hung the *Do Not Disturb* sign on the door. He couldn't have anyone clean his room while his papers were scattered on the desk. He had backed up his plan for Nosh, Nosh, and Crane before he hurried out of his room. He was going to meet Tiffany, his friend, his *pièce de résistance*, the most important person in his life, his sprite. In the elevator, he corrected himself. Not *his* sprite, but Sprite Tiffany. She was her own person who chose to spend time with him.

The concierge hailed a taxi and held the door open while Will slid into the back seat. Will leaned forward, watching the houses change to a freeway on his way to Tiffany. He reached for his phone. He'd forgotten it in the hotel. His heart pounded. He couldn't text Tiffany that he was on his way. Will slowed his thoughts, allowing reason to take control.

"Sir, may I borrow your cell phone to place a call?" Will asked the driver.

"Sorry. Can't do. Against the company policy," the driver with a graying ponytail answered.

The taxi was behind a long line of traffic at a train crossing.

"Would you place the call for me and put it on 'speaker?'" Will's mind raced for a solution, rather than being frustrated at his own carelessness.

"No. Against the rules to talk on a cell phone while driving." The faded blue eyes met Will's in the rearview mirror.

"Can you help me out here? I need to make an important call." Will controlled his voice.

The train stopped on the crossing and began reversing.

I can find a solution.

"I could sell you my phone."

"Name your price."

The train stopped again. The signals clanged and flashed.

"Fifty bucks, and it's yours until we reach your destination, then I buy it back from you."

Will reached for his wallet. He didn't have any cash. "Unless you can sell it to me through your debit or credit card machine, I can't buy it."

"Sorry, man. All the transactions go through the taxi company." He shrugged. "Guess you'll have to hope that the recipient of your important call is there when you arrive."

A driver in the car next to them stood on the road and lit a cigarette.

"How long do these trains usually hold up traffic?" Will asked the driver.

"There's a city bylaw that says they can't for more than twenty minutes, but sometimes it's longer, a lot longer." He stroked his ponytail.

Will needed to believe that Tiffany would wait for him. He closed his eyes and thought about how he used to think that love was something that happened to him, but his mother's little experiment showed him that love was an action. He and Tiffany had created trust and intimacy, the two feelings necessary for love to thrive.

The taxi inched forward.

Will swallowed then sat up determined. If she had left the mall, he would go to her home. He'd find her.

Tiffany clutched her phone while she walked back and forth on the scaffold.

Scott moved equipment. He brought plastic pipe and yards of black material for a temporary drape.

It shouldn't take Will this long to get here. Maybe something happened. She called and got voicemail, again.

Tiffany snapped photos of individual sea creatures, from starfish to turtles, to the plant life.

"Tiffany," Scott called. "Someone is pounding on the back door."

Tiffany climbed down as fast as she could, ran down the hall, through the storage room, and pushed open the door. Will had his fist ready to pound again, when she opened the door. She raised her arms protecting her face. He steadied himself on the open door, his crutches abandoned on the ground.

"Tiffany, I'm so sorry. I forgot my phone in my hotel room." His face was red.

She reached for his hands and held them in hers. "I'm glad you're here now. Come." She led him to a dusty chair. "Wait here." When she put a block of wood to hold the door open, its alarm buzzing while she quickly retrieved his crutches and brought them inside. The racket stopped as soon as the door closed behind her.

Tiffany studied this man with his blue-black hair, and brown eyes that she'd stared into last night. She moved forward, and laid her fingers on his lips, lips that had been kissed by her and kissed her back. She held out her hands. "Got a hug for me?"

He braced one hand on the back of the chair and reached for her hand, stood, and wrapped his arms around her. She swallowed hard. She was whole. He put his head against her head and breathed in deeply.

"Thank you," he said.

She stepped away from him. "Come. I want you to be one of the first to see this." She put her hand on his forearm and together they found a way to maneuver around the bags of sand and lime, the hoes, and shovels.

They arrived in the wide-open space where the sun was pouring through the two-story glass wall. She led him to the chair she had sat in many times securitizing her work.

He chose to stand, move a few steps, and gazed at each sculpture as if he was having a conversation with it. He turned around and proceeded to repeat his movements until on his way back he stopped in the middle of the space, gazing at the center of the mural. Tiffany had watched the play of emotions cross his face, smiling at one moment, eyes wide open the next, thoughtful while leaning forward, and then when he stopped, his Adam's apple rose and slipped in his throat. With a deep jagged breath, he opened his arms to her.

"You." He squeezed her harder, joining her to him.

Tiffany clung to him. Her pent-up emotions slipped

past her guard. She wiped her nose and damp cheeks against her sleeve.

Scott cleared his throat. "Tissues, anyone?"

Tiffany reached for one. She felt Will loosen his hold, and snagged a tissue, too. "I don't know what to say. This is beautiful. Thank you."

"I hope it doesn't bring people to tears." She bit her lip.

"If they have any bit of feeling in their souls, it will." He leaned his head against her forehead. "Can we stay and be in its presence for a little while longer?"

"Why don't you have a seat while Scott and I finish assembling the framework for a temporary drape?" Tiffany looked around for Scott. "There's going to be an official opening on Wednesday. The company wants the completed piece draped until then."

"Don't hurry on my account." Before he opened his arms, Will bent and kissed her on the lips, then moved his lips away slowly, grazing his lips on her chin, and neck. He breathed in deeply against her skin before skimming her lips, again.

Tiffany's breasts were heavy, her core hot and tight. She pushed against his chest. "Will, I've got to help Scott."

Will loosened his hold and brought the crutches to his side. She reached up and brought his lips to hers, for just one more hot, wet meeting of their mouths. She shook her head. "Whew. You do know how to distract this woman from her responsibilities." Then she stepped away.

Together, Scott and Tiffany assembled the freestanding frame, then threaded the drapery onto the hooks on the rod, pulled the cord, making certain the drape opened and closed easily. Each time the drape opened, Will applauded.

Finally, when the streetlights came on, they were ready to go home, prepared to come back for fine-tuning the sculptures then disassembling the scaffold.

"I'll contact the crew that helped put this thing up," Scott said. "I'm sure a couple of them will be available."

"You will have my undying appreciation, if you can master that plan," Tiffany said, her arm around Scott. "Owen and I will be here at ten. You're welcome to be here too, for the fine-tuning."

"I'll be here." Scott beamed. "Good night, Tiffany, Mr. Cleaver."

Tiffany turned back toward Will.

He checked his watch. "Tiffany, can I borrow your phone? I should call Mom."

"Of course. I didn't ask. Do you have plans?" Tiffany's voice wobbled.

"Tentative. But she's an adult. And to repeat what a very close friend once told me, if I needed to be there, I would be." He held her hand for a moment and kissed her fingertips when she handed over her phone. "I'm right where I choose to be."

Tiffany sat on the white plastic patio chair. She had a sudden urge to take it home with her. She'd spent a great deal of time contemplating in it.

Will hung up the phone. "Why so thoughtful?"

Tiffany giggled. "Truth?"

"Of course."

"I'm trying to decide if I can take one of these chairs home. I feel like they belong to me. I've spent a lot of time being watched or sitting in one of them contemplating my next step."

"Your wish is my command." Will stood and pushed his chair toward the door. "Quick, we can make a chair heist and get away."

"Will." She jumped out of her chair and sat in the chair he was pushing forward. He couldn't move it with his crutches.

"Now that I have you where I want you, my dear." He let his crutches fall to the floor, gripped the arm rests on her chair, and got down on his knees. "Tiffany George, I choose to love you, and I would like to be with you for the rest of my life." His fingers laced through hers. "Will you marry me?"

She'd read the love in his actions as they spent time together, her dog whisperer, her soul whisperer, and her dream maker. "Will Cleaver, I choose to love you, and I want to spend the rest of my life with you." She smiled. "I will marry you."

He knelt firmly on the tiled floor, reached up, and cradled her face in his hands as he drew her mouth toward his.

Tiffany slid out of the chair and knelt in front of him. She snaked her hand into his hair, closed her fist, and watched his eyes close. When her fingers gripped his shirtfront, he moved closer, and she reached up and opened his mouth against hers, their lips sliding against each other, their tongues meeting.

Whistling from down the hall caught Tiffany's attention. She pushed against Will's chest. "Someone's coming."

Will kept his hand on her cheek and sat back against the floor. Tiffany joined him.

The security guard with the tattooed sleeve, called, "Everything okay, folks?"

"Perfect," Tiffany answered.

"I think you guys should take this somewhere else. You do know there are security cameras all around this area, don't you?" He chuckled and turned back down the hall.

"Tiffany George, we may have ruined your reputation," Will said.

"Artists are known for their strange ways." She stood and pushed the chair toward him. "Now you, Mr. Hotshot Architect, you, on the other hand, are supposed to be upstanding."

"I'll get to that." He moved toward the chair. "If you sit again, it will give it enough weight so I can stand." Using his body strength and one crutch, he stood.

"Are you ready to go back to the hotel and tell my mother her experiment worked?" Will asked.

"I don't think so. I'm hungry," Tiffany said, wiggling her eyebrows up and down.

"Now that you mention it. So am I."

"Order in at my place?" Tiffany placed her hand on his arm and they moved toward the back of the building.

"Sounds wonderful." He closed the door behind him.

"What time is your flight tomorrow?"

He held the driver's door open for her. "Noon." His voice resigned. "Back to a long distance loving?"

Tiffany watched the man she loved positioning his crutches with his head held high and manoeuver around the front of her car and open the passenger door. A man who found the positive in life. "With you, I'll take all the loving I can get, near or far."

Tiffany drove down familiar streets, not knowing what her artistic future would hold, but whatever it would be she'd have Will to share it with. They respected each other, understood their individual viewpoints, and listened to each other. Their love was real.

Also from **Soul Mate Publishing** and **Annette Bower**:

WOMAN OF SUBSTANCE

"You will never understand what it means to be fat." With those words, grad student Robbie Smith begins the Fat-Like-Me project. In order to support her thesis, she puts on a fat suit to measure people's reactions to the new her.

Accused of embezzling funds, Professor Jake Proctor returns home to spend quality time with the only father he has ever known. There, he meets an intriguing overweight woman who reminds him of his late grandmother. She's witty, charming, and cares deeply for those around her, including his dying grandfather.

When Robbie meets Jake while she's in disguise, she deceives him for all the right reasons. But how long can she maintain the deception before Jake discovers that she is not who he believes her to be?

Available now on Amazon: http://tinyurl.com/jotxzru

MOVING ON

Anna is a mysterious young widow who just moved to Regina Beach. The residents of the small town know everyone's business and they are very keen on discovering Anna's secrets. She meets Nick, a Sergeant in the Canadian Army, until a horrific accident sent him home to recover from his injuries sustained in an IED explosion. He helps Anna feel safe and comfortable in her new environment, just as he has always done for his men in strange, dangerous places. Meanwhile, he focuses on preparing for his future physical endurance test to prove that he is capable of returning to active duty. Because Anna doesn't talk about her past and Nick doesn't talk about his future, she is shocked to discover that his greatest wish is to return to active duty. Afraid of getting hurt, she won't love a man who may die on the job again. Intellectually, she knows that all life cycles end, but emotionally, she doesn't know if she has the strength to support Nick.

Available now on Amazon: http://tinyurl.com/jg9s8kf

CPSIA information can be obtained
at www.ICGtesting.com
Printed in the USA
LVOW01s1602251016
510213LV00012B/595/P